WHEN
GOD BROKE
GRANDMA'S
HEART

A NOVEL

Other Books in the Grandma Series

Non-fiction Books

Coming Soon

WHEN
GOD BROKE
GRANDMA'S
HEART

A NOVEL

HELEN GUMIENNY GLOWACKI

Library of Congress Control Number: 2007905982
ISBN: Soft cover   978-1-9847-2110-8

This book was printed in the United States of America.

To order additional copies of this book:

Visit the author's website at:
www.helenglowacki.com

For wholesale or multiple copy information:

Send inquiry to helen@helenglowacki.com

Contents

Dedication

The books of the Grandma series are dedicated to some of the people whose own lives helped shape mine. The values by which they lived, how they practiced their faith, how they carried their immense burdens, and how they dealt with their mistakes contributed richly to my life. Their passing taught me that love is so powerful it can even bridge the chasm of death. Through all these experiences, I learned how much God loves us, and how to love Him back.

For

Bobby, Granny, Robert, Paul, Mom, and Dad

Acknowledgments

To my loving husband, Wally, who lost me to computer, Bible, and concordance for long periods, made my computer behave, and painstakingly read and edited the manuscript, I send my love and give my humble thanks. To my children, Juliana and Joe, who provided me with the special gift of themselves and the very precious gifts of David, Michelle, Scott, and Samantha, I give my heartfelt thanks for their love and encouragement. I also owe a great debt of thanks to the many friends who encouraged me to write and prayed for my success; Dina and Ferdie, Anna Mae and Fred, Fred and Lillian, and Sue, Becky, Herold and Lisa. I am grateful to my sister-in-law Barbara for reading and critiquing the manuscript. To Richard Levinson whose kindnesses can never be repaid. To the ministers of the New Apostolic Church who pray for me. To Lynnel, Kathrina, Kevin J., Cheryl, Donald, Kevin D., and the many others who contributed to the production of this book. And most of all, to my heavenly Father, who guides my life, gives so much, loves so much, and allowed me to use His gift.

THANK YOU

Note to the Reader

The King James Version (KJV) of the Bible, which is public domain in the United States, is used throughout the books of The Grandma Series. However, for further study by the reader, the author recommends the New King James Version (NKJV) of the Bible for easier reading and less old world language while remaining true to the original text.

The books in The Grandmother Series are works of fiction. References to real people, events, organizations, or locales are intended only to provide a sense of authenticity and are used fictitiously. All other characters and all incidents and dialogues are drawn from the author's imagination and are not to be construed as real. Any resemblance to actual persons, living or dead is entirely coincidental. No part of the books may be used or reproduced in any manner whatsoever without written permission, except in the case of brief quotations embodied in critical articles and reviews.

This book contains a scriptural index. Instead of assembling it according to the Chicago Manual of Style, I have placed it in a format I believe might be more useful to the reader. I have chosen key words that may highlight the reader's specific concern or interest and under those words I have listed the scriptures which address those concerns.

Message from the Author

The desire to weave ordinary words into the beautiful fabric of a poignant message can be a daunting challenge. Combining the treasure of learning with the joy of entertainment can be an even greater challenge, but becomes a joy when the author's words can somehow move the heart, give respite from our complicated world, comfort the spirit, or miraculously touch the soul.

The right words can be of utmost importance to those whose heartache strikes over and over again, taking away happiness, and leaving debilitating exhaustion and a longing to understand why they must live through such pain. When questions go unanswered and we can't gain closure, when we suffer through sleepless nights and hate our pain, we are finally ready, finally open, to risk a different path.

To our dismay, that path may be uneven and strewn with rocks, making progress slow and painful. It may be a path which curves back on itself, causing us to travel in circles, making no progress. Others are so steep we are exhausted by our effort to move ahead, and even those paths which appear level and easy to travel may be deceptive in where they lead. Yet, each of us search, each travel a different path, each has encountered heartache.

Today's world burdens us with the anxiety caused by our incredibly hectic schedules and highly competitive environment. These challenges impede our ability to deal with our heartache. Our time constraints, problems, and solutions are different from those of our parents and grandparents and while the heartaches of past generations caused just as much pain as the heartaches we now face, we are a different people. Though laboring under the same weakness of our human nature which encourages the cruelties we perpetrate on one another, because our problems are unique to a more modern world, we've no one to teach us how to deal with them.

Sadly, we've lost our role models: the parents, grandparents, aunts and uncles, and neighbors who had the time, wisdom, and desire to teach us. We've lost the values of honor and integrity and allowed the line of acceptable behavior slip further away. We are losing our will to stand up for the morality demanded in the past and we are allowing our entertainment venues to become our teachers.

We've chosen to invest our free time in sporting events, video games, books, television, and movies which condition us to accept anger, revenge, and violence as ways to solve our problems. When we watch soap operas and sitcoms, we often laugh at infidelity and promiscuity, cheer revenge, and accept vulgarity and even profanity as natural. Rarely do we see acts of kindness, forgiveness, and empathy. Rarely are we taught to conduct our lives and choose our responses along a higher plane, with nobility of soul. How can we teach our children or grandchildren what we don't know ourselves?

Sadly, we know too little about our major source of grief; we don't understand the role Satan plays in our lives, what he does and why, what his goal is, or why he harms one and not the other. Nor do we fully understand how to obtain God's protection against him.

Without this knowledge, we cannot find the proper answers to our problems nor find the path we should take or the closure we require to end our heartache. Even more importantly, we cannot recognize when we are in spiritual danger. But when we suffer and our soul cries for help, asking God why, and finally asking for His help, we are finally ready, finally willing, to open our hearts and learn.

The Bible provides incredible insight into the personal problems we face. When we apply this insight to our circumstances of life, we learn how to cope with heartache, respond to cruelty, develop a peaceful heart, and become pleasing to God. These efforts have an enormous impact on our lives and bring us the incomparable treasures of God's blessings and promises.

We all benefit from a treasure which provides the hope we need and the answers we seek, which gives us genuine guarantees and long lasting fixes for our problems. A treasure which touches the soul and helps those struggling to find a way through tragedy and learn what God will do for us can be created when the tools we use are God's words. How wonderful would it be if this treasure was easily available to us and easily understood?

This is why I have endeavored to write novels grounded in Christian values. Scripture can provide miraculous treasures for solving life's tragic moments and when a Christian novel addresses life's tragedies by using God's words it can be compelling and uplifting to read. Scripture is the path to closure and peace, to eternal life, and to the gift of God's protection. Here is a gift from God, a treasure he wants us to have.

The heroes and heroines of The Grandmother Series struggle with differing circumstances and often suffer at the hands of others. They too seek to understand why they must endure their trials. Yet they triumph over these difficult moments and find God in the midst of their heartache, discovering the path which brings them the answers to their questions, and helps them find the peace they seek.

When God Broke Grandma's Heart is the first book of The Grandmother Series and the story of a special relationship between a grandmother and granddaughter who, through their faith in God, overcome what Satan brings them. Despite the failures, betrayals, and cruelties of those Grandma loved and trusted, those who should have been her role models, she retains her faith and moves from the captivity of Satan to the freedom God offers her. The first chapter begins as the granddaughter, through her grandmother's narrative meets the lovely and talented little girl who her grandmother had been and who, through a series of parental mishaps enters the world of anxiety and fear. The ever-threatening "Mrs. Meany," the mysterious death of her infant brother, the venomous jealousy of her sister, and a lack of understanding by her innocently narcissistic parents feed her fears.

Appearing to overcome her difficult childhood, she grows into a mature and accomplished young woman. All too soon after she marries, her life moves into the horrible realm of physical abuse and betrayal. The fear she had fought so hard to escape returns with a vengeance, bringing immobilizing pain. She feels that God has let her down, has broken her heart.

But God does hear her cries for help. When she thinks she can endure no more, He helps her take one more step. However, not immediately recognizing that God has helped, she continues to struggle to escape her pain. That one extra step, however, brings her to a crossroad where her heart opens to God, and she finally sees the good which can be wrestled from tragedy. As she seeks to understand what God asks of her, she gains incredible riches from the blessings God provides.

When her life finally turns around and she thinks she is free of these spirits, she is thrust into an even greater heartache. But this time, armed with a new direction, she ultimately wins the greatest riches of all: pleasing God, gaining a peaceful heart, and a truly incredible experience of faith.

Thus, despite visiting many of life's tragic situations, *When God Broke Grandma's Heart* is a heartwarming story of triumph. It is the journey of a woman who would not give up, who was willing to walk a path of integrity and forgiveness, learning along the way why bad things happen to good people and that God can change every circumstance. It teaches us how we can touch the heart of God and gain His greatest blessings. It is hoped that this story touches not only the heart and mind of the reader, but the soul as well.

As the reader begins their journey through the books of The Grandmother Series, they will not only be absorbed by the story, but also amazed by the inspiring verses from scripture which act as a guide for the characters. The reader will meet an incredible family who, through their struggles, learn that God is the ultimate comforter and counselor, that He loves them very much, and that He provides amazing direction and guarantees. They begin to understand how scripture can provide them with an answer to their problems, show them why they must endure heartache and also teach them how to obtain God's protection. And, best of all, they learn of the promises God gives for their future as well as their life on earth.

One of God's beautiful promises can be found in Deuteronomy 11:13-15:

If ye shall hearken diligently unto my commandments . . .
to love the LORD your God,
and to serve him with all your heart
and with all your soul,
That I will give you the rain of your land
in his due season, the first rain and the latter rain,

that thou mayest gather in thy corn,
and thy wine, and thine oil.
And I will send grass in thy fields for thy cattle,
that thou mayest eat and be full.

Here is found the true and ultimate quick fix for the fear and pain which can overwhelm us. Here can be found God's love and providence. May you find this verse a treasure, and may God bless you and keep you always.

Helen Glowacki

Prologue

ONE LAST JOURNEY

She rarely thought of herself as Victoria, not even as Vicky or Tory by which she had also been known. She was Grandma. Though the changes to her life came before she was a grandmother, it was as if Victoria had disappeared during that period of time when her life was so painful and her understanding so limited. She hadn't known that the young woman so full of innocent aspirations and so willing to give her all was in danger. What had occurred had been so unexpected and unwelcome that her mind would not allow her believe that it was real. Yet, from the ashes of her sorrow and without her knowing, as Victoria diminished, a new and better person began to emerge. The Adam-like nature with which she had been born had been slowly overshadowed by the Christ-like nature which grew from her stubborn refusal to give up.

It began when she asked God why He had given her a life that was so unfair and people around her who were so evil . . . and why He would not help her. She'd believed in God, but despite her belief, everything she'd loved and trusted had become a horror of betrayal. She lost hope and finally stopped demanding that life be fair and that there be reward for doing what was right. But then she would find the courage to continue the fight for the kind of family life she believed was so important and which, during her time of heartache, feared she would never have. Sadly, she'd fought too hard and for too long and believed so strongly during her time of tragedy that she had closed her heart to that little voice which kept telling her to leave, to run, to flee. She hadn't listened. Yet in retrospect, what she had learned and become was worth all the pain. It was the best thing that had ever happened to her and she vowed never to ignore that little voice again. Now, after so many years . . . that little voice had come back. It was telling her that she had yet another job to do, another journey to take and that this time she had to listen and to do what it asked of her.

Seated in her favorite chair, contemplating what lay before her, she gazed out the window and tried to understand what she was to do. Her chair faced a large floor-to-ceiling, wall-to-wall window, and was positioned so she could gaze at the ever-changing view before her. She could see across the narrower channel of the Intracoastal Waterway where the currents constantly changed and manatee persistently traveled. She could look across the narrow channel to where a wider area of water formed a lake dotted with lonely little islands full of lush green foliage and edged in sand. She could also see the ocean which lay across the barrier island on the opposite side of the waterway. The ocean's immense strength pushed its way into the narrow inlet which beckoned ships to the ports where they both gave and received their precious cargo. She could also watch the magnificent yachts leisurely entering or leaving the inlet and wondered what their destination could be.

Her chair boasted a walnut-stained hand-carved frame and had recently been re-covered in a rich striped fabric of deep burgundy, emerald green and golden beige edged in a multi-color fringe. A footstool with its matching wood and upholstery had been shaped into a curve which embraced the chair's edge and clearly defined its French style and designer influence. It was practical in design for all its beauty, and provided her tired body with the special comfort she sought. It was here in the quiet that she listened for the voice which she hoped would prompt her thoughts and explain how to accomplish the goal which it seemed so insistent she reach. Instead, her lazy musings brought her to thoughts of the people who were aboard the vessels she saw in the distance, and from where each vessel originated. *Where were they going and what had their lives brought them?*

She enjoyed her foray into these microscopic glimpses of other lives which were likely quite different than her own. For years she had been allowing her fantasies to carry her into their interests and their travels because she no longer ventured out as much as she once had. This exercise of her imagination allowed her to be transported from her confined life for a little while. It had also helped her ignore that little voice which had been following her wherever she went and whatever she was doing. But now she knew that she could no longer ignore its message and would have to take action.

She was still a pretty woman despite her many years and the slowed gait which advertised her age. Her quick, spontaneous smile was still her best asset. It was the warmth of her smile which drew people to her and made them want to linger. It was sensing that she was sincerely interested in them and that she not only knew *how* to listen, but also *wanted* to listen. She had that special quality which made others sense that she understood and empathized with their concerns and that she had the genuine desire to help them find a solution. She had a loving nature. She always had, even as a child.

She tired easily now and cherished her quiet time. She'd "listen" to the quiet around her and allow the peace which God had shown her years ago to completely envelop her as she gazed out the window. She would allow her eyes to fill her heart with the beauty of God's creation while her mind drifted to the memories she cherished. She was glad that she was not required to participate in today's world of rushing and hurrying, of deadlines and daily goals, of instant food and instant gratification, of seeking a peace which was illusive. She knew that nowadays, life seemed so stressful because it was filled with constant activity . . . though the sedentary kind . . . the kind which became a drudgery of exhaustion with no means of escape. She felt grateful that she did not have to live in that world and could bask in the precious peace which she now understood was so necessary to the soul.

As she sat, her eyes would grow accustomed to the wonders of the colors and the movement of the water and the clouds in the sky, and her thoughts would again wander to the past. She would turn her head a bit and look toward her living and dining rooms, at the furnishings she had gathered over the years with which to make her house her Bethany. Her eyes would appear to caress those possessions because they felt familiar and warm, and held such precious memories of fellowship and family. And she would smile as she acknowledged that their exact placement gave her a sense of order and that this had come from her discovery of the Divine Proportion which God used in His creation.

When she was still a young girl and living at home with her parents, she'd already felt a need to create a nest . . . her own space as they say today. She thought of it as a signature of sorts and understood on some deeper level that this was her way of creating a place where she would feel safe and comforted, where her pounding heart and racing mind could slow, where she could leave the fear behind, forget the horrors and find peace, even if only for a little while. Here, today, she felt content . . . she felt somehow embraced by her home and the warmth of her furnishings . . . she felt safe . . . and for this, she was grateful.

She loved the gleaming crystal of the chandelier, the lustrous sheen of dark wood furnishings, the elegant frames which embraced richly colored still life paintings, and the opulence of the thick burgundy Oriental rugs over- riding the intricate pattern of the porcelain tiles on the floor. She especially loved the room at night when the lights of the tall slender buildings on the barrier island reminded her, on a smaller scale, of the New York skyline. She loved the ambient recessed lighting emanating from behind the carved crown moldings and the soft warmth this lighting created for her furnishings. Many of her favorite pieces of furniture were antiques and her very favorite was her huge desk with its rich luster and clever secret compartment.

The awesome power of the elements, the sheer variety within the creation, and the incredible beauty always brought a stirring to her heart. She marveled at what she saw and found contentment in it. From the comforting haven of her home, she could turn, day or night, to the breathtaking view from the window and be reminded of what was really important and what her ultimate goal was. She'd once wondered why so many people lived through difficult times. She'd searched for answers about why some suffered and others didn't and she was grateful that she had been given answers which had satisfied her. She knew that those who desired to learn of God and develop their life of faith were often those who suffered most. She believed with all her heart that those who endured great troubles also built for themselves a loving, empathetic, and forgiving heart and were those who ultimately gained the greatest reward.

Sometimes when it was very early in the morning and she gazed across the water to the barrier island, and beyond the island to the ocean and horizon, she could feel her heart bursting with a sense of awe and thankfulness for what God had created. The ever-changing colors of the sunrise and how the sun affected the colors of the clouds moving across the sky touched her heart. She was enthralled by it! The clouds changed too, and sometimes she imagined the figures of animals or people in these puffy white shapes. Sometimes they reminded her of someone or some event, and she'd be off again into her world of memories. All in all, despite what she had gone through, she knew that she had been greatly blessed and she knew that what she had learned was the most precious gift she had ever been given.

When mornings brought a stormy day of pelting rain, where the bright colors were overcome by a somber dark gray and navy blue sky and the waters roiled and pounded, lightning lit the sky, and thunder reverberated in sudden explosion overhead, she'd watch the small boats rushing from the ocean to the inlet. They hurried to gain the safety of their docks and homes before the worst of the weather overtook them. She'd be reminded of the awesome power of nature and the incredible talent and goodness of God. She'd think, *If only everyone in the world could see and feel what I do now, they would surely know God, and they would understand all the beauty and perfection of what He offered us. They would understand why heartache exists and how a blessing can come from it.*

Yet even on these dark days, watching the changing scenes from her window, and thinking of the triumphs and failures of her life and the joys and pain of the past she knew that she'd learned the greatest lesson of all. She had learned to forgive. She had endured and triumphed. But now that little voice was asking her if she'd shared her knowledge; asked if she'd taught those she loved how to be victorious over the pain of betrayal, failure, and hopelessness which good people always seemed to pass through. She began to worry about whether or not those she loved would even understand what they needed to learn from their own experiences, or if they would simply ignore the lessons, never finding what they should, never developing a noble soul . . . never truly knowing God . . . never understanding why heartache existed.

A sudden reflection off the water brought her wandering mind back to the present and she once again appreciated the view, and resumed her assessment of the beauty before her—marveling at the great billows of clouds, the unique beauty and grace of the water birds, the incredible mix of color between sky and water, and she was comforted . . . she knew in her heart that despite her worries, all would be well. She understood that if she would listen carefully in the silence and through her eyes, if she would truly "listen" to what God wanted to tell her through His Creation and through the silence of the beauty before her, she would better understand God's plan for her and what He was now asking her to do. Deep in her heart she understood that she was to teach her family what *she* had learned.

She hoped that she could describe what the years taught her, wanting to impart the essence of her hard-earned philosophy. She truly believed in the importance of developing a character pleasing to God and owning it, proving it, as gold is tried in the fire. She wanted to share this realization and how she came to understand it and come away from that exchange knowing that those to whom she spoke would understand. If God looked after every sparrow, He surely would look after everyone she loved. Yet she knew that He wanted her to do this one last thing; make one last effort to tell her story and through it, teach her family the lessons she'd learned.

She thought of the days, long before, when she had felt such confidence in her talents and abilities. She remembered the trust she'd had in all people and circumstances and how this had been transformed into the energy and courage she needed to face adversity. That was when she'd felt that she need not fear to trust. Now she knew that trust was a precious commodity, best when earned. Now she felt that only someone yet untouched by life's hardships offers such a quick and open and innocent trust. She'd been that way herself.

She understood the ways one can lose trust . . . either gradually over time or suddenly and unexpectedly. She thought the sudden loss was easier to bear and the gradual type hurt the most and took longer to overcome. She guessed that one's heart doesn't want to accept that such betrayal could exist and rejects the truth, creating for the mind the excuses it requires to continue to believe in someone. In her experience, she'd been blindsided and held hostage by it for too long. Her heart was a compassionate heart, so it had been difficult for her to understand such blatant betrayal. She'd believed that there were barriers to how far a person would go and she'd never even imagined that those she loved could behave like the characters in soap operas. She didn't watch those programs because it was painful to her to witness such a lack of character and then see it rewarded. She'd thought remorse lived in everyone's heart when they did a wrongful deed. She'd thought remorse would be too great to bear, act as a preventive, or direct that person toward making restitution. She'd thought that life was fair, that hurtful people paid a price for their deceptions and their misdeeds.

She had been wrong, painfully and surprisingly wrong, and too slow to accept and act on this knowledge. Yet it was through this that she had learned so much and had been so blessed. Perhaps everyone experiences betrayal, but for her, the intensity and longevity of the pain had surprised her. The experience left her stunned and, for a longtime, questioning God, asking why. It crushed her confidence, shook the morality she'd attributed to people, especially those she loved and trusted. It took years to understand, years of willing herself to find the answers to her questions and gain the closure she needed. It was a difficult lesson, painful, but ultimately it provided the answers she sought. In the process, she learned that the heart which forgives is the heart God loves best.

It was such a waste not to have mastered those lessons when she was young and could have passed this wisdom to her children while they were in their formative years. For her, it wasn't that she *could* not have learned sooner, but that she *would* not because she insisted on believing in the goodness of people. She hadn't yet understood that Satan works through people. Now, when she finally understood, those who she wanted to reach so they too would understand were no longer children who she could mold and direct. She'd need a more convincing argument now. Was it still possible to teach them how to avoid the mistakes she'd made? Could she explain these complexities, be eloquent and convincing, demonstrate the rewards to be gained? Was there still time to do more? Were these crazy thoughts just a sign of old age? Or was God *really* telling her that she still had more to do? Why did she think about the past and about those she loved with such urgency? Why did she feel fear for her children and grandchildren in regard to the life struggles they would experience? Why this fervency? Was it simply that *she* wanted them to bypass the pain? Yet, she knew better than that.. she knew that pain was the teacher; the most efficient teacher.

She thought of the paths she could have taken . . . as opposed to the one which had brought her the knowledge she'd needed to become a child of God. She thought of the emotional crutches she'd sought to help ease her pain and allow her to deal with life when things had become impossible to live with. She remembered her forays into outlandish promises of quick fixes to life's problems. None of them had worked. She remembered reading about astrology, tarot, feng shui, fortune-telling, losing weight, and even a new hairstyle, which promised instant happiness. How foolish she had been to constantly search for an easy way to grab life and make it work the way she thought it should and find a quick and easy way to escape the horror of what was happening. What a journey her life had been and what amazing grace she had been given to have finally understood what really brought peace and joy.

Life wasn't about being the perfect wife and mother, or having the prettiest and cleanest house on the block, or the newest car, or the best education or job. It was about developing the prettiest, cleanest, and most loving heart! It was learning to harness one's will and putting that energy into *choosing* to love, understand, and forgive. It was about knowing that bad thoughts and urges would come, just as birds inevitably fly overhead. It was learning that letting those birds of thought land and roost was not good for us. It was the knowledge that shooing them and making them fly away was within our power. *With our will, we can make the thoughts which are not kind and compassionate, understanding and forgiving, leave our minds.*

Sometimes it had been unbearably difficult. For her, the birds had continually flown overhead, and she wouldn't be immediately aware that they had landed. She'd had to yell "no" to get them to move off again once she finally realized they'd landed. But the bottom line was it worked. At first, she'd had to yell *no* quite often; but now, to stop an unkind or painful thought, she could quietly say it to herself. And in this world of peace she'd finally created through God's help, the birds didn't even bother to land . . . certainly not like they once had!

Her mind raced through those earlier years and, when returning to the present, brought a flicker of fear to her heart for her family. Her fear was for what they had *yet* to experience, fear about the parts of their hearts which were closed to the important things they thought unimportant. She worried over experiences yet to befall them and hurt them which she could not prevent. She worried about their relationship with God and how seriously they approached their faith. She forced these thoughts away; they were too painful and made her feel once again the emotions and memory of her former acceptance of a terrible life where her faith had been mocked and scorned.

She was older and wiser now. Yet she wondered if her story would help her family in their journey through life. She'd wasted years fighting reality, holding onto the illusion of perfection which she believed would come if she worked hard enough. She hadn't known that some people are simply not worth such an effort and that God approved our leaving those situations. She hadn't understood that when someone is evil, a child of God should flee. Instead, she'd created an orderly environment which was so lovely that the horrors of reality could be kept at bay. She'd created this image to push away the pain, to prevent her from giving up, and to help her keep the fear at bay. By working so hard on and in her home, she could escape the reality of her life. Yet wasn't that what so many others did to escape also? Something had happened to her which made her stick her head in the sand and not face what had *really* been occurring. She had been hiding from the fact that she was *choosing* to remain in a terrible environment even though she felt that she had no other choice. She knew she was being harmed and that what was happening was detrimental to her soul.

She thought about the everlasting question, "Why?" Why did bad things happen to good people and good things happen to bad people? She knew the answer to this age-old question now; it was simple. The fact was that *every* experience, tragedy, and triumph had brought her closer to the answer. She survived her traumas of life and had grown in the process, hadn't she? Wouldn't that mean that there was hope for the next generation and the next and the next? Wouldn't there be something in the end which made it all worthwhile? Was there any way she could have learned sooner? Could she help her family so that they could learn sooner, could she teach them and save them from some of the pain? Was this the one last journey which God wanted her to take?

Deep in her heart and in the pit of her stomach, she felt the need to hurry, to finish what God seemed to want her to begin, to make everything right, fix all the ills, teach all that could be taught, and help where she could. But who listened anymore? Few listened, especially to their elders. When she was young, she herself hadn't listened, so why did she think *she* could make a difference now? Years ago she would never have appreciated or recognized what was precious in life had she not labored under the real teachers in life—the one's she paid attention to because they were so harsh and so painful.

Were life's difficulties the key and the path to an open heart, one ready to accept what God wanted us to know? She wished she could tell her story, tell it honestly, include the mistakes she'd made and tell it in such a way that it would make an impact. If she could tell it well, she was sure it would answer the question "Why does God allow this?" and be a story of happiness.. after sadness, betrayals, cruelties, and jealousy. Hers would be a story which would end in the triumph of understanding, and forgiveness and love. It would be a story which had a happy ending, led a seeking and troubled soul to God, and opened the door to joy and peace.

She decided to listen to the voice which was insisting she take this one last journey, and that she risk sharing her experiences and opening her heart by telling her story; show why there can be despair in love and evil in the human heart. Her story could prove the craftiness of Satan and his cohorts, and show how to overcome and triumph through the enduring, protecting, perfect love of God. She could do this. She would, and she must . . . for the sake of her family . . . it was time to let the skeleton out of the closet!

And Sarah was the one to whom God wanted her to speak. Sarah was her precious granddaughter and perhaps would be the one to internalize, understand, and then carry forth her legacy of faith. Sarah was to whom she was to bring her message. God would surely guide her, help her put her story into perspective and also touch Sarah's heart with understanding.

Chapter One

SARAH, THE GRANDDAUGHTER

"Grandma, I am so delighted that we can spend some time together! I have been so swamped with work, but now with summer here and classes ended I can finally take a breather! I do love working with the children though! And Grandma, Matt and I have decided to begin work on our doctorate degrees and will try to come up with the subject for our thesis this summer. But here I am chatting away when you, despite your sweet and perfect life have decided to begin some 'big project' of your own. What is your big project Grandma and why would you want to start a big project . . . whatever it is . . . won't it be too much work for you? Ohh, you set the table so elegantly . . . mmm . . . everything looks so good!"

"I made all your favorites Sarah and I too am so pleased that we can spend the day together. I'm delighted that you love your work . . . you always loved to help others and have a beautiful empathic heart for the work you do. Do you have an idea as yet for the subject of your thesis?"

"No . . . but I would like to do something which would serve to help others accept, understand and support children with special needs. Most parents want as much information as they can find, while others feel so overwhelmed that they simply don't know what to do and even deny that a problem exists. Oh Grandma, I love working with these children and I really want to find new ways to educate those who are close to these children so we could all work together to help them reach their fullest potential. It's sad though, because there is just not enough basic training for these parents and it impedes their effectiveness."

"Acknowledging a problem and learning what options and methods are there for solving them is incredibly important . . . and you are right . . . few know where to find or even that they can find this information. I am so glad that you have found your niche in life Honey, and I know that with your loving heart, you will always be a great asset to everyone you encounter."

"Thanks Grandma, I hope so. But what is your big news . . . what project are you talking about . . . why are you taking on a "big" project right now?"

"You make me smile Sarah, because I believe that you are envisioning me on ladder nailing shingles into the roof. But trust me, my project is not like that Sweetheart. It's something less physical at least. Let me try to explain . . . you and I have always been very close and I've felt so privileged that you have always opened your heart to me about many things which you felt that you couldn't share with others, but now *I* need to talk with *you* about something which *I* have never shared with anyone. I am feeling somewhat impelled to explain something to you but only to glean the lessons learned from it. It is difficult to explain because ultimately it is not the story which is important . . . it is what God did with it . . . with me . . . that I want to describe . . . and I'm not sure I will be able to do that justice."

"Just try Grandma, we have always understood one another, so I don't think that will be a problem. Please go on."

"Well, when you reached the age of fifteen and entered the world of cell phones, best girlfriends and college life, everything in your world went onto the fast track, and we haven't really had the time . . . or made the time . . . to sit and talk in depth. Therefore, much of what I'd always meant to share with you when you got older has not been said. But recently, I have felt an urgency to . . . to . . . well . . . teach you how to avoid some of the problems which life may bring you in the future. I keep thinking that it is through my *own* experiences, my *own* learning process that you might learn too. Yet, I'm not quite sure how to separate my story from its lessons and that is really what I want to do."

"Grandma, I think I know what you are referring to . . . it's like when a *good* emotion or feeling . . . somehow comes from something that *wasn't* so good?

"Yes Sarah, exactly."

"Is this about that time in your life which my mom always wanted kept under wraps for some reason?"

"Yes Sarah, that's a big part of it. Honey, do you remember when I'd visit with you and your mom and brothers for a few weeks and we'd lie down on my bed late in the afternoon so I could rest before dinner? I remember those times and can even remember you telling me that you were salivating from the aroma of what I'd placed in the oven and on the stove for our dinner as it wafted up to us . . . but then we'd spend the hour talking while dinner was cooking. Your lives were so busy that you usually didn't have the time to make or sit down to a regular dinner, so I always wanted to do that for all of you when I visited. I was the mashed potato and gravy specialist . . . remember?"

"I do remember Grandma . . . I *still* love your mashed potatoes and gravy . . . and everything else! But yeah, I remember those times too. We'd talk about every subject under the sun, and I wasn't afraid to ask you things which I thought might upset someone else. And I loved listening to your stories of how our great-great-grandparents came to this country, and I loved your version of old fairy tales, and also your stories from the Bible. I can remember that I'd arrive home from school about four o'clock, so there was time for us to be alone before the ruckus of family life would start again for the evening when Caleb and Josh and Mom would arrive home. They were very special times for me"

"I loved those times with you too, Sarah. They were the times when we would just talk and talk. It was a treat for me to listen to you because I could see into your heart and learn what a gentle loving person you are . . . and I loved telling those stories too!"

"Grandma, do you remember that I was always considered a tomboy in those days . . . and I probably still am . . . because I liked sports and didn't like to dress up. I didn't wear makeup because truthfully, I didn't know how to apply it properly and felt uncomfortable wearing makeup. I never liked drawing attention to myself. You used to bug me about wearing my hair so straight and flat instead of allowing it to be fuller and curl as it naturally wanted to. You were right but I never saw it back then and just kinda "yessed" you and did what I wanted anyway! I was the loose sweatshirt, ponytail, oversized jeans, and sneakers type . . . maybe it was having two brothers around that made me like that."

"Did I really bug you Honey? I'm sorry, but you did have . . . and still do have . . . such beautiful thick hair and you always tried to straighten and flatten it instead of showing it off and allowing it to swing full and lovely. You were a good student too and had so many great friends; but always . . . just like me, you enjoyed being at home in your own little nest, just chilling out. I always understood how you felt because I too had always had my own room . . . my "nest" . . . and could either be found in my room reading, thinking, studying, or listening to the radio . . . we didn't even have TV in my early days."

"I am smiling Grandma, with the memory of how you used to create what you called a "nest" for us on the couch when we were sick. You'd use pillows and comforters to make it warm and cozy, and we'd snuggle down to drink the hot soup or tea you'd make for us. When we were little, you would tell us stories which we could listen to for hours . . . I remember the ones which were similar to the fairy tales everyone heard, but you'd always change them so you could present us with some kind of a moral which you would weave into the story. You had Little Red Riding Hood discovering why the Big Bad Wolf was so mean, teaching that he was unjustly judged and really had a good heart. You would tell us that Little Red Riding Hood decided to take the wolf home to her papa when she realized how sad he was. And the Papa, when hearing the plight of the wolf, gave him a job. And the whole town came to know and love the wolf, and . . . finally finding happiness, the wolf was never bad again. The townspeople learned that they should never judge others unfairly, never make decisions without having all the facts, and never judge someone because he or she looked different . . . like the wolf—because he had a long nose, pointed ears, and sharp teeth. You were teaching us a lot in that story. In fact Grandma, I still have the video of you telling that story! And . . . and . . . do you remember that in the midst of the story, you'd stop and make us show you how long the wolf's nose was, how pointed his ears were, and how sharp his teeth were. We would respond by touching our own noses and ears and teeth. Sometimes you'd use animal puppets for the story, and we'd watch the puppets instead of you!"

"Do you really still have that video, Sarah?"

"Yeah Grandma I do, in fact I put it away thinking that when Caleb, Josh or I have children, we would pull it out for them! I even remember that we'd be scared when you'd describe the big ears and sharp teeth of the wolf. I can remember how the little puppet who was representing Little Red Riding Hood would show her fear by cowering into your chest, with her head down, when first accosted by the wolf; and we'd feel the little puppet's fear! You could have been an actress, Grandma, because you performed those stories and puppet shows so well. I remember when you set that camera up and made the video for us so we could watch it when you were not with us. I can remember that your voice would rise and fall, sometimes taking on raspy tones, or become loud or very soft and sweet, depending on the character which was speaking through you. Sometimes we'd jump with fear because we weren't expecting you to speak so loudly all of a sudden like when the wolf jumped from the closet in the grandmother's cottage when he first accosted Little Red Riding Hood. You always caught our attention with your stories and you kept us mesmerized. Every story you told had a special lesson in it which you wanted us to learn, and though we never knew it, your stories were really teaching tools for us. They were always about how love can change people, how people have to try to understand one another, and how differences don't make someone unacceptable."

"Sarah, I am so pleased and so amazed that you have remembered all these things. I always wanted to create wonderful memories for you . . . and I . . ."

"Grandma", Sarah interrupted, "Do you remember the story which taught how important it was to have good manners? None of us were as open to those lessons, although we did realize later in life that those stories had also made an important impact on our life."

"Well, I tried didn't I?" Grandma laughed.

"Yes Grandma, you sure did! And you would try to teach us how important it was to keep God first in our lives and would tell us stories about the characters in the Bible and about the angels' protection, teaching us to ask God to send His angels to protect us. Before mom died, I remember you teaching us how precious and hardworking our mom was by creating a story which described a mother who'd been hurt in an accident and a housekeeper named Hildegard who was hired to run the household while the mother recovered. The housekeeper was very strict and made the children help out, causing the children to be angry and plot to run away from home. We thought that Hildegard was formidable at the onset of the story; her German accent sounding heavy and guttural and her strict rules frightening. Ha-ha, I mean *your* accent when you pretended to be Hildegard . . .but as the story unfolded, the love which Hildegard had for the children and her concern for their mom became clear, and the children began to understand Hildegard. Even Hildegard's voice became gentler (ha-ha your voice Grandma) as the story developed. The story kept our interest. We were afraid of Hildegard in the beginning of the story, but later, we realized that she was doing what was best; and by the end of the story, we liked Hildegard. I think we learned how difficult it is for a mother to run a house without any help. And . . . your moral in *that* story was that you hoped we'd start to help our mom more around the house or at least keep our own rooms neat."

"I am amazed that you remember those stories so well, Sarah. I always worried about your mom and what she had to endure in life. She was such a strong woman and she fought for all of you and denied herself so you could have all you needed. I was always so proud of her."

"Yeah Grandma, she was strong, and I really miss her."

Sarah, worried that her grandmother was feeling sad about the loss of her daughter, quickly changed the subject. "Grandma, do you remember the story about a teenage boy who meets a girl he really likes, but the girl has another boyfriend who is the star of the football team? You would change from a girl's voice to a boy's voice and by the end of the story the hero wins the girl's heart because she was impressed with his good manners, kindness, and his attitude toward others."

"I'd forgotten that story, Sarah."

"Yeah well . . . you told us that one when Caleb met Ann and could not get her to date him . . . at least not right away! That story gave him the courage to keep asking her out! It's sad that the stories ended as soon as we became teenagers and knew we were being, ugh, taught something! We began to grow up and didn't want to be reminded about how we were to act; we felt that we already had the answers to life. Our lives entered into a busy time where we didn't spend much time with the adults. I never even thought that you might miss the closeness we shared when we'd sit together to talk, now that I'm older I can understand it. But you know Grandma, we still liked to listen to you at the dinner table . . . you would tell us stories about different experiences of faith and how God always fixed things. You'd make us sit together at the table and talk about our day because usually we were on the run when it came time to grab something to eat. You found ways to *make* us tell you what happened at school, even though we hadn't wanted to, and certainly not in front of everyone else at the table. But Grandma, a lot of my best memories were of these times."

"Mine too, Sarah. And as you were speaking I was reminded when Caleb had his first experience of faith. Do you remember that? It was when you came to visit me for a few weeks. Just before you left home for the airport, Caleb had been cleaning his hamster's cage and adding fresh food and water, when the hamster disappeared. You had to leave for the airport before finding the hamster so you would not miss the plane. But your dad, who was working at home that day, promised to keep looking for him. When Grandpa and I picked you up at the airport, I noticed how sad Caleb was and asked him what was wrong. He told me about the missing hamster and began to cry because he was afraid that the hamster would die. I asked him if he had prayed and asked God for help and he said no. So when we got to the house, I asked all of us to sit together so we could pray aloud that the hamster would be found, and that Caleb would not have to worry for the rest of the visit. Each of us prayed and we had just said 'amen' together when the phone rang, and it was your dad, telling us that the hamster was found and was safe in his cage. Caleb's eyes widened in awe, and he looked as if a miracle had occurred . . . and it had!!!! God had heard and answered our prayer! Caleb never forgot that experience."

"I do remember that Grandma . . . I was very young then but Caleb often told that story so I do remember it. That hamster was so important to him so he was incredibly moved by that experience and from it he learned the power of prayer and learned to pray not only regularly, but also whenever something happened."

As Sarah sat with Grandma, she suddenly noticed that Grandma was aging. Her knees and hands had become riddled with arthritis, and she seemed to require extra effort to sit in or rise from her chair. Her walk had slowed, she'd climb the stairs slowly, and she'd rub the bony protrusions on her fingers as if trying to ease their pain. But her sparkling eyes, her quick mind, and her love were just as vivid as ever, therefore Sarah tried not to think about her age or about her dying or getting sick, and she suddenly realized how insensitive children can be to the pain of others and to the process of aging. She should have been more attentive.

Grandma was almost 90 now. Her long wavy hair had turned white, and where little tendrils broke loose from the confinement of her bun, tiny curls framed her still pretty face. Usually, she would pull her hair into a bun atop or to the back of her head. This was an easy style for her to keep and one which kept her looking neat and tidy. She dressed well with her colors well coordinated. When she wanted to dress up, she wore a braided chignon pinned over the bun she formed by rolling up her ponytail and this gave her coiffure a more elegant look.

In fact, Grandma always looked elegant, especially when she added lipstick, cheek color, and a little eyeliner. She'd never worn foundation, so never looked made-up, just natural. Her favorite outfit was a pair of black slacks, a black tank top under a richly colored blouse open in the front, and often a well-tailored thigh-length black jacket. She'd wear a large and colorful brooch on her jacket which would pick up the colors of her blouse. Her earrings would be small, usually gold, and she'd wear a gold necklace. And she always wore rings . . . her wedding and engagement ring on her left hand and a ring on her right hand which coordinated with her outfit.

If the family didn't know what to buy Grandma for Christmas, they knew that a new brooch or the perfume she'd worn most of her life would always be welcome. They associated a particular fragrance with Grandma and when they were little had made up a song and dance celebrating her look, her walk and talk, and because they loved her perfume . . . their little song always made reference to her perfume usually by including its name in their poem. They would perform their little routine for her and it always made her smile.

As Grandma spoke about the past, Sarah began to see her in a different light, recognizing her advancing age, how the years were showing on her, and how much effort it took for her to perform simple tasks. And she saw that Grandma was tired. But Sarah could also sense the urgency in her grandmother's words, and felt a sudden fear that Grandma wanted to do this one 'project' . . . whatever that was . . . before she died. *But Grandma can't die!* Sarah was frightened and realized how strong her love was for her grandmother. But then as her fear peaked, and she was about to mention it, her grandmother began to speak again and Sarah's thoughts turned to what her grandmother was saying

"Sarah, you are probably wondering why I asked you here today because I did tell you on the phone that I had a favor to ask of you regarding a project that I would like to complete. I mentioned something about 'telling my story' in a way that the lessons learned from it, could be shared. But how I want to accomplish this is to ask you to help me write a journal. I haven't the foggiest idea how to make my project a success. But when you graduated from college with a master's degree in psychology and both began to work with special needs children and then think about beginning your doctorate work, I began to wonder if the material for this journal could possibly become a subject for your thesis or used in conjunction with your work. You have been working in the field of special education since graduating with your master's. You've told me that you love your job and have chosen a field which you believe will make you happy. You always said that doing something with your life where you can help others is something you need to do. This is how I feel about my journal . . . I want it to help others. And Sarah, I feel as if it is something that God wants me to do. As I said, it is not so much a story which I want to tell . . . but a lesson about how God wants us to view our heartaches and what we can learn from them. I want to try to explain how God can turn every difficult circumstance into a blessing for us . . . even the tough times we live through! I believe that you can help me accomplish this goal. Will you help me, Sarah?"

Sarah was concerned by her grandmother's request because she felt inadequate as a writer, and had never tried to create stories which could be used as teaching tools. Yet, Grandma could always do that . . . she had that talent. Sarah wondered why Grandma needed her for this project and how she could possibly help create what Grandma wanted . . . yet how could she say no? She thought about Matt, her "unofficial" fiancé, and their plans to marry but not until they developed their careers and completed their doctorate degrees. They'd thought it best to wait a few years before taking on the big wedding they wanted and the chore of finding and refurbishing the home they hoped to purchase. They wanted to buy a house, furnish it, and have it move-in ready by the time they were married. Then they could settle right in and get back to their careers. They hoped to do this within the next two years. As all these facts ran through Sarah's mind, she searched for how she could provide the time and expertise required for Grandma's project. She realized that now was a good time because she had no formal classes. In terms of her writing ability . . . well . . . she would just have to do her best.

"Grandma, right now, other than my job and working on my thesis, I am somewhat unencumbered. So, I *can* make the time for your request, but I feel inadequate for such a project. *You* are the writer in the family and *you* are the one who always sees the glass half full . . . and *you* are the one who is closest to God, so how can I possibly help you?" But deep in her heart Sarah knew that she would help her grandmother.

"Sarah, you have a background in psychology and know what happens to children who are traumatized . . . well . . . I have a story about how God can heal a child or prevent that trauma from harming her . . . so together . . . together . . . we could prove God's miracles . . . prove how He brings a blessing from heartache. Writing a thesis requires having an original idea, determining its interest and importance, presenting your facts, and then proving your conclusion. But it also requires some writing skills . . . you know, using the correct grammar, gathering meaningful information, setting forth your premise, creating a logical sequence of events, building a case, and finally coaxing the reader toward agreeing with your conclusion. I believe that God wants us to gather, set forth, build and conclude why we have heartache and why it can be beneficial to us . . . and . . . somehow demonstrate the miracle of what God does as opposed to what psychiatry says should occur. Questions such as: Why does heartache exist? Who brings us our heartache? What good does it do? If God loves us and is all powerful, why does He allow us to suffer? And . . . why is there no long term consequence to a demonstrated trauma which science tells us *should* have long term consequences? I don't know if I can accomplish this goal either . . . but it's similar to what you wish to teach the parents of the children you help . . . and adds to that teaching by offering a different approach to a solution . . . so maybe this project could benefit both of us."

"Gee Grandma, I never even imagined that anyone could obtain an answer to those questions. Many of the parents I see wish that they could understand why their child has to struggle and why their lives require such patience. Some people fall away from God because of the heartache they see in the ravages of war or illness or poverty and ask where God is in all of that. Living the ravages of the mental and physical health concerns of one's children really hits home . . . and some lose their faith over it and others turn to God because of it. It would incredible if I could see how your story could "prove" that God can heal these traumas. I'd assumed that these types of questions could not be answered."

"I can understand these feelings of despair Sarah . . . and I am not sure how I can prove this either . . . I just know that for me . . . those questions *were* answered and the permanent damage that should have occurred . . . didn't. I really don't know if we can do this Sarah . . . but for some time now . . . something inside of me has been prompting me to contemplate these questions and kept telling me that if they were answered for me individually maybe they can be answered for others. Every horrible circumstance in my life turned into such an incredible blessing that I am thankful for those heartbreaking experiences . . . and that's what I am trying to explain . . . why that happened."

"Well, Grandma, I spoke with Matt and also with Caleb before coming here today and they were so pleased that we'd be spending this time together. And we all spoke about trying to make more time over the summer months for all of us to be together. So, for my part, I can help, and maybe we can even discuss our ideas and our findings with Josh and Caleb and Matt . . . and Ann too. Who knows, perhaps writing your story will enhance my journalistic skills for when I have to tackle my thesis. But I can't imagine what skills it would take to portray emotions and heartbreak, and even faith in God . . . and get it right on paper. I encounter emotion and heartache every day helping families who struggle with the mental or physical health concerns of the children they love. Documenting their problems and the search for solutions is exhausting and sometimes makes me feel sad for days. In fact, I've sometimes labored for a long time to find the words to describe the emotions they experience. But maybe you are right, Grandma . . . if I could learn to do this, I would develop better skills for communicating on every level with the children and their parents and in the required documentation I must file. And . . . if we can demonstrate how or even that God healed what should have been a long term effect of trauma . . . that would be another miracle! Maybe . . . along this journey, I will, as you suggest even find the subject for my thesis."

"You are such a sweetheart Sarah. I've learned never to say no to God and never to doubt that through Him we can accomplish great things. So, let's pray about it, let's pray every time we meet and every time we think about this project asking God to bless us and open our hearts to what He wants to provide through our work. Then we can't go wrong."

Sarah still wanted to tell Grandma no because as she thought of the enormity of what Grandma wanted to accomplish . . . well . . . it just seemed impossible. Everyone would like the answers to those questions . . . so Sarah was afraid to try to write such a story. Despite her few college classes in journalism, she felt that she did not have the skills to tell Grandma's story, to do it justice. But now to "prove" a miracle of healing . . . well . . . that would be even more difficult. Perhaps there wasn't even a story there. After all, despite Grandma's creativity, she was just a person living a normal life. How could there be any really interesting story or lesson in that? How could she even begin to answer such complex questions through only her own experiences? Could there even be something which would interest anyone outside of the family or even teach someone anything new?

Yet when Grandma voiced her feelings and her deep desire to touch just one heart, help just one person by telling her story; Sarah felt a stir in her own heart, recognizing what it felt like to want to help others. After all, her career choices were based on that same desire, those same feelings, and it had been impelling for her. She knew how rewarding it was to make even one breakthrough. She also marveled at Grandma's faith and wanted to know where it came from.

Finally, Sarah agreed in her own mind that it would be a challenge to write Grandma's story and interesting to learn about the skeletons in the closet which her mother had worked so hard to hide. She was old enough and wise enough now to deal with whatever they were and it might even be fun to psychoanalyze some of the emotions involved in what happened and why her grandmother had been so affected and her mother so diligent in her avoidance of any discussion about them. Learning what they were might even broaden her horizons in her profession, if indeed these things were there. *After all, didn't all the psyche books tell us we should face our fears and our disappointments so we could lay them to rest?* Hadn't Sarah been taught that one needs to understand to resolve?

So Sarah replied to her grandmother's words by saying: "Okay Grandma . . . you've always told us that the power of prayer is incalculable so we will surely be testing that statement! But okay, we'll tackle your big project and see what we can come up with!"

"Thanks, honey, I will also be enjoying the time we will spend together."

Sarah thought about how lucky she was to be pretty "normal"—no big hang-ups, no traumas that she hadn't been able to sort out. Her immediate family, like most families, had gone through their failures and heartaches; but despite these, she and her brothers grew up pretty well grounded and goal oriented. Yes, sometimes they'd heard crying and yelling and arguments and stuff and had hated it. But who hadn't? Sometimes she had cried herself, but hadn't most people at one time or another? And . . . in the end, she was okay and so was everyone else in the family, so she wasn't afraid to learn about Grandma's troubles. One aspect of her job was to uncover the inner feelings of the family members who interacted with a special needs child and Sarah had learned that once people understood themselves and their reactions, they understood others.

Sarah loved helping people. At the end of a tough day at work, she could see how insignificant her own concerns were next to the problems her students and their parents faced. As all these thoughts ran through her mind, Sarah began to think that it would be a challenge to tell Grandma's story correctly. Her main concern hovered over the bit about faith and God and how God created these blessings which Grandma mentioned . . . this worried her. Grandma had always spoken to them about God and explained that He knew everything and was ultimately in charge of every circumstance anyone ever lived through. The family was not as religious as Grandma was, didn't quite grasp that same degree of faith, and at the moment, probably could not even describe such strong unwavering beliefs. They all believed, though not like Grandma, and Sarah wasn't sure why and suddenly wondered what made Grandma different? They did all believe. But how could someone actually write about something which was intangible? That had Sarah worried.

When Grandma asked Sarah when they could begin their project and how often they could meet, Sarah voiced her concern about not knowing how to start or how to write about something not seen, not tangible. Grandma suggested that perhaps she could begin by telling Sarah what she had experienced and that Sarah could just take notes . . . asking questions whenever needed. Grandma suggested that she begin by simply narrating as best she could . . . but then warned Sarah that the story would contain areas of gross human cruelty and incredible irresponsibility. Grandma's voice faltered as she told Sarah that perhaps she would think her weak to have stayed in such a bad situation. She said that while Sarah viewed her as strong and capable, she had many moments of concern, weakness and failure. She went on to say that despite these experiences, her faith had bloomed because of what she'd endured. Sarah's immediate thought was that if this was so, then perhaps by relating Grandma's faith to her response to an act of cruelty, she could discover where Grandma's faith came from. Such a story could be rich with the triumph of the human spirit if indeed it was laden with examples of cruelty, irresponsibility, and the spirit of survival. Sarah had always marveled at the strength of the human spirit as she watched the parents of her special needs children continue day after day in love and patience.

Sarah responded to her grandmother's concerns by telling her that she'd probably see her as courageous rather than weak; and if those experiences had built her faith, Sarah wanted to know how! That made Grandma feel better, and Sarah was curious now to learn what had occurred. Sarah also wanted to allay Grandma's fears about uprooting the skeletons in her closet and said:

"Grandma, I knew a little more than anyone gave me credit for, though I didn't know it all because mom preferred to stick her head in the sand rather than face confrontation. Mom was adamant that we never be affected by what others experienced. Dr. Spock's influence, I guess! Personally, I like to know up front what people are thinking and I feel strongly that open and honest communication is the key to any kind of a decent relationship . . . and it helps us if we can learn from someone else's mistakes, right? When mom and dad divorced, some of the problems between them had to come out so we could accept the fact that they were divorcing and mom hated that. So though it was very difficult, I learned that sometimes you had to face the truth about someone you love to understand what happened. In fact, knowing that there were serious problems allowed *us* to "allow" the divorce! It never meant that we loved any less . . . it just meant that we acknowledged what was wrong. My dad sure hadn't learned his lessons, and while I did not want to alienate him, sometimes I had to face some hard facts about him and sometimes even stay away from him even though I loved him. I think that we learn from the mistakes of others."

"Sarah, yes . . . exactly! That's true . . . you *have* lived through some tough times too so let's see if we can make sense of them and make them work *for* us instead of against us, and let's make it our goal to pass that wisdom on to others. Deal?"

"Deal!"

Sarah, with her curiosity piqued, with part of her not wanting to tackle this project, part of her wanting to know what made Grandma tick, part of her not wanting to disappoint Grandma, and part of her incredibly intrigued by the idea of finding the answers to why God allowed heartache, suddenly decided to just to jump in. Over time, if she didn't make any progress, or she didn't find the value they sought in the project, they could always re-evaluate and decide if it was worth continuing.

Grandma became excited by the prospect of starting the project and the potential that it had to provide help to others dealing with problems similar to hers. She wanted to demonstrate the good which could come out of the bad, how God turns ugly into beautiful. She wanted to provide an answer to why bad things happen to good people. She wanted to demonstrate that we need not fear because God will not only see us through our heartache but can . . . if we learn . . . bring a wonderful healing and blessing from it!

It was difficult to understand this concept let alone write about it . . . but with God's help and a lot of prayer, they would do it! Grandma's enthusiasm made Sarah wonder again if Grandma's story could apply to a doctoral thesis. After all, if the story were indeed about behaviors and reactions and emotions, it would help solve some of the problems her special needs kids and their families faced. If this idea could work, it would be a great way to kill two birds with one stone. *Wow, that would be a good deal for me! The thesis thing has been hanging over my head for a while now.*

So Sarah took pen in hand literally and decided to tell this story of the life of an old woman who was once a little girl born without any trauma in her heart. Grandma said that it was to be a story however, of many traumas: a child's death, sibling rivalry, raging envy, a cruel marriage, a good marriage, and, ultimately, the struggle to forgive. It was to be a story about the heart of a loving child who became the woman who would not give up and who, through her anguish, learned how to touch the heart of God.

Chapter Two

THE BEGINNING

Sarah had been thinking about how she'd write Grandma's story and had finally made the decision to develop an outline where the first step was to learn more about Grandma and what her life was like as a child. When she explained her plan to Grandma, Grandma gave her some old photographs and home movies and even some letters written by Grandma's godmother from which Sarah gleaned a great deal of information.

Sarah had covered her dining and cocktail tables with these treasures and put them in chronological order. But she was mesmerized by a series of six beautiful pictures of Grandma when she was five years old which had been taken by a professional photographer. She used these as a basis for describing Grandma as a child.

The pictures were of a little girl with silky light brown hair with auburn highlights sporting the big sausage curls so popular in her day. She had a pretty oval face with deep dimples dancing in her chubby cheeks. Her face beamed with her quick and effortless smile and her eyes were lit with intelligence and wit. She had a dainty slightly turned-up nose and a little bow mouth with nicely shaped pearly white teeth which were slightly rounded at the edges.

In the home movies which Sarah viewed, she saw a child with a delicate but sturdy little body moving with speed and grace and never holding back an embrace with her chubby little arms for anyone who sought a hug. Yet with all her exuberance and her fast pace, she never appeared to spill food on her clothing or allow chocolate to dribble on her chin even when she held a melting ice cream cone. In one part of the movie, Sarah watched her washing her hands in the water fountain at the park, frowning at hands that were sticky. Looking directly at the camera, the little girl held up her hands, made a face, and laughing, ran to the water fountain to wash them, knowing the camera was catching it all! When she was finished, she turned back to the camera, held up her hands, and smiling, wiped her wet but now clean hands on her jacket and ran off, turning back to look at the camera every few steps still laughing with the exuberance of her youth!

It was easy to understand why she was the delight of everyone in the family. She was the first girl child preceded by two male cousins ten years her senior who were attending military school. Thus the family doted on her. She loved to sing and dance and would do so whenever asked and for anyone holding a camera, therefore the home movies also caught her dancing. She wasn't shy at all but smiled and laughed and seemed to gain so much joy from what she did that whoever looked at her had to smile themselves. Her sweet little face reminded Sarah of an old movie she'd seen of a young curly-haired tap-dancing Shirley Temple with arms bent at the elbows and hands in the air moving to the beat of the music. Even the oldest and most stodgy and particular of the relatives seemed to adore her. Sarah could see their faces in the movies, not waving to the camera when the camera panned them, but focused on watching this exuberant, adorable dancing little nymph who could coax a smile from them when others couldn't.

Grandma told Sarah that every few weeks her maternal grandmother came to spend a few days with the family and that these were special times for her and times when she felt that their house exploded with love. She said that she'd sit on her grandmother's lap and listen to stories of life in the "old country" and wonderful narrations about the characters in the Bible. Grandma said that she just loved to hear these stories and Sarah thought that perhaps these memories of her grandmother had inspired Grandma to tell Sarah and her brothers' stories.

Grandma also told Sarah that on Saturday mornings when her maternal grandmother wasn't visiting the house her dad would take her for a walk across the park to where his parents' and brother lived, and a few doors away, his sister and her husband. On occasion, her cousin would be home from the academy he attended, so they would visit with him too. They were a close-knit family, sharing holiday meals and festivities in a large family gathering which included the siblings of the in-laws and their children as well.

Grandma said that she loved these visits especially when she was bounced on her grandfather's ankle as if she were riding a pony. During the warm summer months, they would sit on the open front porch and talk, and either her grandfather or her uncle would play with her. She absolutely adored her uncle. He'd had to leave school when he was in the sixth grade. His teachers told the family that he could not "keep up," and as a result, he was labeled "retarded." Grandma felt that he might have simply been dyslexic, but that since in those days they did not understand dyslexia or any other physical or mental challenges, these children had to leave school. *How sad!* Sarah thought.

But Grandma said that she'd always thought of her uncle as was one of the smartest people she'd ever known, and surely the happiest person she'd ever known. Her uncle performed most of the domestic chores in his home since he'd had to leave school and did not have the training to seek a job outside the home. Yet he never complained and loved having family members visit. His life revolved around the family and his hobby of building immense erector sets. He also helped create the huge train sets and villages which the family put together for Christmas every year.

Sarah could see from the home movies that Grandma's uncle had straight fine brown hair over a high forehead and lively sparkling brown eyes. He was tall and slim, like his two brothers, and was always smiling. He wore solid-colored slacks of beige or brown, always with a belt and sometimes with suspenders too. In almost every camera pan he was seen tugging at his waistband to keep his trousers pulled up high and seemed to be wearing them too high on his waist. Yet, he seemed more comfortable that way.

But everyone would remind him not to hike his trousers so high, and he'd shake his head as if to let them know he'd heard them, but that it was something he'd heard over and over again. But he'd smile and temporarily lower them to his proper waistline. A few minutes later, he'd hike them up again! Grandma said, *Believe it or not, Sarah, it was endearing to see him wrestling with his belt or suspenders because of the adorable and sheepish look he'd have on his face when he'd be told to lower the waistband closer to his hips. At these times, he'd wink at me and I'd squeal in delight at the conspiracy we shared. He was always cheerful and made me laugh and he never took offense at being scolded . . . never!*

Grandma told Sarah that he always wore crisply ironed shirts which he ironed himself . . . in fact he ironed all his mother and father's clothes too since they worked and he stayed at home. Every movie and photo of him demonstrated that his shirts were always fashioned either from a plaid or a striped fabric and that he would wear a solid-color cardigan sweater atop when it was cool. His feet were encased in brown lace-up shoes. He walked with his feet splayed out a bit and with the long stride of those with very long legs. He was slender, tall, wiry, and strong. Family members always reminded him to stand up straight as he was inclined to lean forward when walking; and here too he'd straighten, wink at Grandma, and, if no one was looking, he'd slump over again to make his point to Grandma!

His erector sets were a marvel of complex working parts and sometimes occupied the entire guest room. He loved demonstrating what they could do and would work for hours developing all their moving parts. The home movies caught the huge Ferris wheels, parachute jumps, tractors, bridges and all sorts of complicated items he'd built, all with moving parts and some five feet tall!

When the family gathered for holidays they gathered in the huge walkout basement room which extended the length and breadth of the house and had its own kitchen. The room was so large that it accommodated not only room for a sitting area, but also a huge dining area and plenty of space for the incredible train set and village which they always constructed for Christmas.

Grandma's uncle would help create elaborate miniature villages with mountain backdrops for the train layouts which the family would work on from Thanksgiving to Christmas. Sometimes the trains would run around the room, travel into every nook and corner and come back, entering a complex tunnel system fashioned from cardboard and plaster, to emerge into a miniature town with houses and roads and cars, trees and people. All the tracks and each set of trains would eventually pass the train station where activities associated with loading docks and transport trucks and baggage and people awaited the incoming trains.

There were freight trains and passenger trains of all kinds and all colors. Some of the locomotives could emit a puff of smoke, and most could sound their whistles. Grandma told Sarah that it was wonderful to watch them and see such a perfect miniature version of life. She remembered that she'd squeal with fear thinking one train would hit another as they careened around a corner toward one another, but suddenly veered onto another set of tracks neatly bypassing each other with inches to spare.

The men in the family would begin work on this huge enterprise on Thanksgiving Day by unpacking everything which had been carefully packed away the previous year and contemplating how to add the new additions created for the upcoming Christmas gathering. One or more of the men was there each day working on the electrical hook-ups and backdrops and then on the placement of the tracks and villages until Christmas Day arrived and it would finally be completed. Everyone would marvel at what they had created. It was like walking into a land of fairy tales to a small child, and Grandma loved it. Even the Christmas tree was elaborate and always so tall that they had to cut the top branch down to accommodate the angel which sat on top. Grandma said that she was always asking one of the men to make the trains whistle and to make the winch lift logs from the truck and swing them onto the side-railed flatbed train. Then the trains would run, fully loaded with cargo, and make their way around the tracks. When the trains again approached the station, the winch would remove the logs from the train and place them again onto the truck, and the process would begin all over again.

One of the home movies caught Grandma lying on the floor on her stomach, watching the gates go up and down at the railroad crossings whenever the trains went by, their lights blinking and bells ringing their warning to the miniature automobiles waiting to cross the tracks. Lumberyards were filled with workers loading rock or brick, lumber or roofing materials onto pickup trucks. Mercantile stores had outdoor platforms filled with bales of hay, which could also be lifted by winches into the waiting trucks.

Miniature people walked the streets and crossed the roads, stood at the train station and in front of the tracks, and sat in the train station. Cows were in the fields at the outskirts of the village, and milk trucks and mail trucks and postmen and farmers in pickup trucks filled the tiny roads.

Now Sarah understood why Grandma had carried the tradition of trains and a village under the Christmas tree into her own family, though on a smaller scale. Grandma said that the memories of these family times and of being together as a family lived in her heart forever and were an example of how a family can work together to bring joy and excitement to a special day and create incredible memories in the hearts of the children. She said that as she looked back, she remembered the laughter and did not recall any sorrows or arguments which she now knew they must have had . . . as everyone has . . . but seemed never to hold onto.

Grandma's uncle loved to laugh and to play tricks on everyone. Grandma told Sarah that if her dad took his shoes off to relax or to get down on the floor as he was fixing the trains or working the winch, one shoe would invariably be "missing" when it came time to leave. With a lot of fanfare, a search ensued until the shoe was finally "found" by her gleeful uncle. Grandma's dad always played the straight man to his brother's teasing and would make a big fuss about the missing shoe and pretend to look for it under his chair. He knew his brother had taken it and hidden it, but he'd never let on and would always go along with the game. Grandma said that it was such fun and that she now realized what a big heart her dad had to play along!

Though Sarah had never known most of these people, she loved this family through the photos and home movies and the stories which Grandma told her and thought, *"I can see the love and kindness they had toward their special needs child and the patience and love they showed to Grandma . . . and I can now see that this became the legacy for "family" which Grandma is trying to show me."*

Grandma went on to tell Sarah that when everyone gathered at her grandparents and uncle's house, her uncle would ask everyone what beverage they wanted to drink. If they requested lemonade, they might receive a glass of orange juice and, of course, Grandma would hear him giggle and see him wink at her so they could share the joke. After a period of time for feigning unawareness of the error, he would eventually produce the already poured glass of lemonade and remove the orange juice, which he'd planned all along to drink himself. He'd be so proud of himself for making everyone laugh, and his own laugh would be so contagious that everyone in the room would be compelled to join in.

"One year", Grandma said, "I was sick with bronchitis. In those days, the treatment for bronchitis was to stay in bed with a plastic tent hooked over the bed and a vaporizer with medicated moist air blowing into the tented area to help ease my labored breathing. I was allowed to get up only to go to the bathroom and sometimes had to stay in bed for weeks on end. On this particular occasion of which I speak, I had been confined to bed and was sad to learn that I would have to remain in bed through my birthday."

"But when my birthday came, my uncle telephoned my mom and told her to have me watch for him from my second-floor bedroom window. He planned to walk across the park to our house, carrying my birthday present with him and he wanted to be sure that I knew he was on his way. My window faced the street, and I would be able to see him from almost a block away as he emerged from the park to walk to our house.

"I watched and watched for him, thinking that he would never arrive. I can still remember . . . even today . . . the incredible excitement and the tickling sensation of butterflies fluttering through my stomach that only an impatient child can experience. Finally, after what seemed a lifetime of waiting, I saw him. Actually, it probably was not too long by an adult's concept of time, but an eternity to me as a child waiting for a gift!

"Finally, there he was, unmistakable because of those long legs, splayed feet, and forward stance! I remember watching him with such fondness and an incredible excitement mounting in my stomach, and I saw that he appeared to stagger under the weight of a box larger than half his height and more than twice his slender width. His legs seemed to buckle more and more as he approached my window and under it to the front porch and entry door. Now I know that he did that because he knew that I was watching!"

"I remember being worried that the weight of the box would hurt him, but I forgot that worry quickly when he arrived because all I could think about was him getting up to my room with his unexpected surprise. I wondered what could be in so large a box and I was so excited because it suddenly became such a special birthday!

"Straining to hear what was being said downstairs, I heard my uncle greet my mother; then after what seemed such a long time, I heard him grunting and puffing up the stairs with his burden. He struggled from the stairway through the hall to my bedroom door. He seemed unable to get the box through the doorway, bumping into the door molding with the box, having to withdraw the box from the door opening to try again and again. Now I realize that he did that on purpose!

"I can actually still remember aching with anticipation as I watched him, wanting to leap from the bed to help him, but not allowed out of my breathing tent. Finally, with great effort, he came bursting through the door to lay the box on the floor, grab the chair beside my bed, sit down, and gasp for breath!

"Can I open it? Can I open it?" I asked. "Please, please?"

And he replied, "Wait until I catch my breath."

"Hurry, hurry, come, get under the tent with me" I'd said. "We can close the tent and it will help you get your breath,"

But he just laughed and said, "No, I'm okay, I've caught my breath, I'll put the box on the bed so you can open it."

"But it's too big," I'd cried. Remembering how heavy it had seemed when he carried it, I said: "Put it on the floor, and I can open the tent flap and if I sit on the edge of the bed, I can reach it."

And so he finally agreed and placed the box near the edge of the bed. I remember now that I never noticed that the box was lighter than it should have been for its size or the fact that my uncle had appeared to stagger under its weight while walking toward my house and now lifted it so easily."

Grandma laughed remembering this and so did Sarah!

"I excitedly opened the huge box and found another box inside, almost as big as the first box, and it too had been wrapped with fancy paper. My uncle disengaged the smaller box from the first box and pushed it toward me, and I opened the next box to find another, and then yet another box. Each was wrapped in fancy paper. And I remember my uncle laughing and laughing at my excitement and the joke of it all, and soon I was laughing because he was laughing and simply because he was enjoying himself so much.

"Eight boxes later, each individually wrapped, I uncovered a tiny little box embraced in a pretty paper and a ribbon with a dainty bow, and somehow I knew immediately that this was *the* box. And sure enough, there was my treasure! Inside the box were crisp green bills which I knew I could spend to buy myself whatever I wanted from the five-and-dime store! The bills were curled to fit into a pretty little ring which my uncle had saved from a Cracker Jack box. I was thrilled! I could wear the ring every day and could go shopping to spend my money when I got well enough to go out again! I even remember telling him that I would accept the Vicks VapoRub on my chest and nose and swallow the horrid cod liver oil and spoonful of dried iron with a drop or two of water without complaining because I really wanted to get well quickly so I could go shopping! I was so excited by this thought and proudly put the little ring on my finger and kissed my uncle to thank him for my wonderful gift. He beamed. He really loved me and it was such a great feeling to know that I was loved so much and could see so clearly what a loving heart he had.

"I never forgot that experience. Times like that made memories for me which filled my heart with love and which taught me how to share those memories, those actions, and that love with others. Memories like these were something we could keep in our hearts forever and which could sustain us in times of sadness. These were memories which taught me about the meaning of love."

Grandma leaned back in her chair and stopped her narration and Sarah got up to make them both another cup of tea. As she puttered in the kitchen and Grandma rested for a moment, Sarah remembered that they'd talked about this "trick" of the empty boxes many times because Grandma had created these boxes inside boxes for each of them too. Sarah marveled at the time and effort Grandma's uncle had spent on this project and the love and planning and thought that went into it. Sarah knew that this was a wonderful experience which Grandma had had and understood why she had shared the same experience with her family by imitating it for them. She suddenly understood that this exchange had now taught her to appreciate the thought and love it took to prepare such a gift. She thought about the many times Grandma played that trick on them. She felt blessed to be given this insight into what love is and to know what a joyful and loving uncle Grandma had. She also felt blessed to learn through Grandma that a so-called infirmity could not take away the love which shines from the heart. And Sarah suddenly wondered if this story about Grandma's uncle had, perhaps subconsciously, influenced her choice of vocation—helping children with special needs. She would never cease to be amazed by the beautiful hearts and cheerful attitudes of these children.

Sarah suddenly thought that perhaps she could introduce into her thesis the idea of how, when, or why adults develop prejudices toward someone who is different. *Children are born without prejudices, with a heart filled with love and trust. At what age is that lost?* she wondered. *Do parents cause that loss by voicing their own prejudices, or does a child sense how others react to differences and adjust their thinking to that?* Her mind was going a mile a minute and she realized that she was getting more and more interested in Grandma's story and thinking more seriously of somehow using this material for her thesis.

When they finished their tea Grandma resumed her story by telling Sarah about an experience which emanated from her mother's love of decorating, describing how, as a teenager, she would be lying in bed at night and suddenly awaken . . . then wonder what had awakened her. As she lay there, she could hear noises coming from downstairs and would concentrate on listening to the strange sounds and would hear a gentle tapping. Tap. Tap, tap. Tap, tap, tap.

As she listened, she would realize that she'd heard those sounds many times before . . . and could relax because, as she came fully awake, she knew exactly what these strange sounds were. It was the sound of a hammer gently coaxing a nail into the wall with the least amount of sound possible. It was usually 2:00 or 3:00 a.m. and it was her mother wielding a hammer to rearrange the pictures in the living room.

"My mom, I realized, must have had another decorating inspiration while trying to fall asleep and could not wait until morning to execute her new plan. So there she was . . . a ghost in the night, impulsive, impatient, intent upon nailing the pictures into their new position without waking up the rest of the household. Patience wasn't a virtue in my household!

"I remember somehow knowing that the pictures my mother was rearranging were a set of four European landscapes. I don't know how I knew this, but I did. In fact I could always guess what project my mother was working on when I was awakened in the middle of the night by my mom's decorating excursions. Recognizing what the sound was, I'd just turn over and easily fall asleep once again, not to be awakened again even if the hammer worked its magic all night long."

Sarah now had an idea about who little Victoria was and how she had begun her life. She was like most young children and hadn't yet faced any traumas, any heartache, or any fear. Sarah was amazed that Grandma could still remember so many details and tell her stories with so much animation and love.

Watching the home movies, looking through the photos and letters which Grandma had given her and now having this chat with Grandma had given Sarah the background she'd wanted so she could begin to understand the little girl with the big name . . . Victoria. As Sarah glanced down at her watch she realized that quite a bit of time had passed. She was surprised to see that it was dark, and that it was way past the time she'd wanted to leave. Yet she was already anticipating when she would come again to listen to the many wonderful and joyful memories Grandma had to share with her.

Grandma had warned her that not all the stories would be happy, that there were difficult times to describe, and an understanding heart would be required. Sarah knew that their next subject would be about a time when Grandma was just three and a half years old and blamed herself so terribly and so needlessly for a family tragedy and Sarah wondered what it could be.

Chapter Three

DEATH AND THE NIGHTMARES

Sarah learned that Grandma's brother was born when Grandma was a little over two and a half years old, and that the family was ecstatic to have a boy. All the relatives told them that they were the perfect family now, two such nice-looking parents with a home of their own at a young age, and two children, a son and a daughter!

The baby was a chubby, fair-skinned, blond-haired, blue-eyed baby and, like his sister, had a smile which captivated everyone who saw him. He had deep dimples, which he inherited from his dad. Their father had a great job, and their mom could stay at home to care for the children. Everything seemed perfect.

"But Sarah", Grandma had interjected, "life isn't that easy; it is in fact quite cruel at times, not staying problem free for very long. And my parents had their share of terrible grief. They also had to carry a huge burden because they made mistakes . . . which later haunted them. Don't forget, Sarah, in those days there was no Internet from which to seek information, there were few how-to books, there was a stigma attached to seeking help for depression or emotional pain and people had to pay cash for everything so had to be careful about their finances and did not spend unnecessarily. But let me try to tell you what happened. I learned most of this later in life but let me try to piece this together for you."

"The baby seemed unable to keep his milk down, and the doctor told my parents that he required testing at the hospital. The tests indicated that he had a problem pertaining to his intestines. I never learned what it was. But he would require two surgeries—one right away and one when he was a year old to fully correct the problem. The first surgery was performed, and within ten days, the baby came home from the hospital; and with all well again. Life went back to celebrating his birth and celebrating this wonderful little family unit.

"The baby grew and seemed to thrive. He had a sunny disposition and always wanted to be in whatever room the family gathered. I loved listening to his cooing when he was in his playpen in the living room. As he grew and learned to hold a toy, we played together by me running to pick up the toy he would throw out of the playpen onto the living-room floor and giving it to him to do over and over again.

"My grandmother would visit often, and the house would fill with the aroma of the wonderful potato pancakes which she made so well and the family loved. I remember the smell of furniture polish too and the sound of classical music which often came from my father's Victrola. I remember listening to "Peter and the Wolf" from their record player and how the crescendo of the music made the story it was portraying exciting and I remember that my dad thought it important that children be exposed to classical music to gain an appreciation for it.

"I loved sitting on my grandmother's warm and comfortable lap and listening to wonderful stories about people in the Bible and about the angels who helped them. I loved these stories and would often imagine sequels to them when I was trying to fall asleep for my daytime nap or even at night when I was put to bed. Whenever the baby was crying and my mother would take the baby upstairs, I would ask my grandmother if I could sit with her, knowing that I would be hugged, and experience the love and softness in my grandmother's heart as I listened to her wonderful tales of honor and love and courage and help.

"One evening, the family gathered in our big old-fashioned kitchen to prepare dinner. We'd eat at a large round metal table with a red Formica top edged in silver metal which was placed in the middle of the room and which had wooden chairs arranged around the table which had been painted red. The kitchen was warm and cheerfully decorated with bright red and white gingham curtains at the window which looked out over the backyard. There were six prints of fruits and vegetables on the soft yellow walls, each set into a thick wood frame which was painted red; and there was a large red metal breadbox on the counter.

"A heavy wood high chair with a rounded tray table sat in the corner, angled toward the main area of the kitchen and easily pulled to the table once everyone sat down. This was where the baby would sit to watch the family prepare the meal. He loved being with everyone and would contentedly munch on a Zwieback biscuit while his little feet rested on the wooden footrest attached to the seat of the high chair, and he'd laugh and gurgle to get attention. He was a beautiful child, sweet tempered, and loving.

"He had been crying a lot that day. Everyone thought he was teething. A cold pacifier, extra diaper changes, naps, cookies, and bottles hadn't cheered him; neither had the rocking or the hugs and kisses which everyone offered him whenever he fussed. As dinnertime approached and he was placed in his high chair to watch what everyone was doing, he began to cry even harder. Everyone was baffled. I was about three and one half years old then and remember trying to distract him by explaining how to set the table—where the knives were to be placed, the forks, the spoons, and the napkins. The baby usually loved it when I explained what I was doing to him and would look as if he understood every word I would say to him. But on this evening, nothing worked to quiet him despite the entire family taking turns to cheer him.

"The constant crying began to prey on everyone's nerves, and nothing anyone could do would help. Soon the crying became intermittent screaming, and everyone began snapping at one another because no one knew what to do. All the usual tricks to quiet him brought no relief from his cries. I'd give him a toy, but when he took it, he angrily threw the toy to the floor time and time again, until finally, I, who was still so small that I could barely reach the high-chair tray with my hand stretched high over my head, also became frustrated.

"The cries continued; and finally, I reached up to the high chair footrest and slapped the baby's bare foot which was banging in agitation against the hard wood where his feet rested, telling him that he was being very bad. He was astonished for the moment and stopped crying. But then he resumed crying even louder than before, angry at such an insult.

"After I slapped the baby's foot, my grandmother came to me and took me by the hand, drawing me firmly away from the high chair. She seemed very angry with me and sternly told me that I should never ever hit a baby because since they are so little, even a little slap could hurt him, maybe even kill him. I was of course duly chastised and felt terrible, for my grandmother had never scolded me before and had never had occasion to be disappointed in me. I said that I was sorry for what I had done, and remember that I even apologized to the baby, but with the baby still crying, not much else was said; and dinner got underway as quickly as possible. I felt very bad because I'd never hit anyone before.

"Right after dinner, no one was inclined to sit around the table and talk because of the baby's incessant crying. I was tucked into bed by my father and told to be good and be quiet so my mother could get the baby to sleep. It was a little earlier than usual for my bedtime, but I knew it was because the baby was still crying, and they all had to see to him and the kitchen cleanup. My mother attended to the baby, trying to get him to eat, and, giving up, changed his diaper and put him in his crib. My grandmother washed the dishes and tidied up the kitchen.

"No one came to read me a story as they usually did, and no one came in to kiss me goodnight. The baby continued to cry; I could hear him even though his bedroom door and mine were both closed. I worried that maybe I had hurt him and worried that perhaps everyone was still angry with me for hitting him and feeling alone, soon cried myself to sleep, hoping that everything would be okay again in the morning.

"I had always been so pleased that at such a young age, I was allowed to sleep in a "sort-of-grown-up" bed since the baby needed the crib which had once been mine. I loved my "sort-of-grown-up" bed, which was actually called a youth bed and just the right size for a toddler. It had a wooden frame shaped like a racing car and was painted in bright colors and just like a real car it had big headlights painted on the front footboard and tires painted on the side. It had been my cousins' bed and was on loan to me, so when I grew out of it, it would go back to my aunt's house, and I would get a "real" grown-up bed.

"The next morning when I awakened, I went downstairs in my pajamas and found my grandmother busy in the kitchen. No one else seemed up and about, just my grandmother who served me my favorite breakfast. I remember having an uneasy feeling in my heart because no one else seemed to be home, my brother wasn't in the high chair, and my grandmother wasn't as talkative as she usually was. There were no hugs and no stories. I remember thinking that I'd better be very, very good that day and maybe then my grandmother would be happy again and would love me and hug me as she usually did.

"Once the kitchen was in order, my bed made, and I was dressed, my grandmother told me that we would be going to my aunt's house for a visit. So we packed a suitcase with my clothing and my coloring books and crayons. I hadn't seen my parents all morning, nor the baby, and felt bad that I was leaving and wouldn't be able to say good-bye to them. I wondered where they'd gone, but for some reason I held back from asking any questions. I don't know why.

"We took the bus and then a train, and in about an hour, we arrived at my aunt's house. She greeted us with a big hug and then sent me to the living room to play while she and my grandmother went into the kitchen. They spoke softly with one another for a long while. I played quietly until my grandmother got up to leave, telling me that I would be staying with my aunt. My aunt was also my godmother, and we'd often spent time together, always had fun and shared lots of love, so I looked forward to staying for a while and did not think it unusual.

"My aunt was tall and slim; her hair was pure white, and her eyes sky blue. She and I had a very close relationship, and I sensed that something was wrong because she didn't want to play with me, tell me a story, or take me for a walk they way she always had in the past. I'd always enjoyed staying at my aunt's house in the past and had spent many weekends there but this time was different and again I felt that flicker of fear which was so foreign to me. I wondered if my aunt knew I'd slapped the baby's foot and was angry with me. I felt frightened although I imagine that I didn't understand what I was feeling, and what is so strange is that I can remember this so clearly.

"I stayed with my aunt for several weeks and began to worry whether or not I was ever going back home. I had never been away for so long, and though I loved my aunt and loved being with her, I missed my mother and father and brother. I didn't complain, just quietly asked each day when I would be going home, and my aunt would say, "Soon, dear, soon." We slipped into a routine, and most of the time, I felt that it was fun to be there and be together.

"Finally, the day came when I was to go home. My aunt told me that we would travel by train and then bus as we usually did. It was a treat for me because the train would pass an amusement park, and I could see the roller coasters from the window of the train. One was the huge roller coaster so high in the sky that my neck hurt to look to the top. The other roller coaster was a smaller version, and I wasn't sure I'd even have the courage to ride the little one. My aunt really loved roller coasters however, and she liked the parachute jump ride too. I could also smell the damp air from the water and see the water birds from the train.

"Before we left my aunt's house, she sat both us down at the kitchen table and she told me not to speak about the baby when I got home . . . ever . . . because it would make my mother and father cry. I wanted to ask why, but was afraid to ask any questions. I looked forward to seeing my mom and dad again, and vowed that I would be a good girl, and would be a good sister to the baby too. I was excited by the thought of being home again, in my own room with my "sort-of-grown-up" bed, and playing with the baby. I guess that I hadn't really understood the significance of my aunt's words.

"When we arrived, after walking the two blocks from the bus stop, I was sent to my room while my aunt spoke in hushed tones to my mother in the kitchen for what seemed, to me, a long time. I was sure that they were deciding whether or not I would be allowed to stay with the family because I had slapped my brother's foot.

"I felt afraid again and felt that they must still be angry with me and was suddenly afraid that they may even call Mrs. Meany who my mother telephoned whenever I misbehaved. My aunt and my mother had explained that Mrs. Meany took disobedient children out of their homes to an orphanage until they learned to be good, and even though I had never seen Mrs. Meany, I was terribly afraid of her."

"Grandma, that's terrible . . . do you mean that you were threatened with . . . with . . . with . . . abandonment . . . if you did anything wrong? Grandma . . . that's . . . that's . . . child abuse!"

"Wait now Sarah before you judge. You must remember that in those days there were no TV shows or self-help books and no child psychiatrists to explain the dangers of this. All parents spanked their children and all believed that discipline was important. I do too, although certainly not that kind. But you have to realize that they did not understand what they were doing. They would never have done it if they had known. They meant well. They were simply trying to raise a child who would be obedient and respectful. And while I was afraid, I somehow did not doubt their love."

"Well, maybe you're right, but Grandma, that kind of threat to a child can be incredibly traumatizing."

"I know that *now* Sarah, but I also know . . . and knew then . . . that my parents were good people who loved their children and did the best they could. Now I can look back in retrospect and see that they made some pretty serious mistakes but made them while *unaware* of the danger in them. We all make mistakes one way or the other and most of us look back on our life finally recognizing those mistakes . . . and we feel badly about them. But . . . the reason I am even telling you this is because I believe that if we sweep our errors under the rug, we can't learn from them nor can others learn. Our goal with this project is not to judge but to learn and then from what we've learned . . . teach. I am not bitter nor was I harmed in the long run. In fact, God brought an incredible blessing to me from my experiences and for that I am grateful. So let us try to address all that I am about to tell you with the attitude that we want to learn about and understand the psychological ramifications of our actions, but more importantly how God brings a blessing from our heartache. Satan nudges us to make errors, and he especially loves it when we do not recognize our actions as errors . . . yet God sees all and He turns all that Satan does into something good. You will see this as the story goes on."

"Well Grandma, I guess you are right. I guess that because *I do know* what damage can be done to a child's psyche from this, I feel angry. I can understand though . . . now anyway . . . that maybe we do these things without even knowing what we are doing. So maybe you're right and maybe by trying to understand this it can become a learning experience for me too. Obviously it has for you. But please go on with the story . . . I can clearly see the emotional battle you must have had though . . . now I want to see how you overcame it."

"I only tell this story Sarah so we can incorporate into our journal the concept that parents *must* examine their words and deeds to see if they are frightening their child . . . or even bribing them . . . to be better behaved. It isn't to point a finger but to explain how a child might interpret what we do and say or even be damaged by it. In fact *now*, you might be better equipped to inquire how the parents of the children under your care cajole *their* children into good behavior . . . because they may not understand what they are doing as my parents didn't."

"That's a good point Grandma . . . maybe this happens more often than I know and in different ways, so for me to be aware of it may be a very good thing. Please go on,"

"Well, whenever I misbehaved, my mother would telephone Mrs. Meany . . . I thought anyway . . . and she would describe what I'd done and ask whether or not Mrs. Meany thought it was time for me to be picked up and taken to her house for punishment. I would pull on my mother's skirt begging her to hang up the phone and promising to be good. I remember my mother telling me about the tall building where Mrs. Meany lived with all the bad children and that at Mrs. Meany's house all the doors were locked so the children could not leave. She also described the wagon Mrs. Meany used to pick up bad children explaining that it had nails in it which would hurt if a child tried to climb out of the wagon. I was terrified of Mrs. Meany and would do anything to make my mother forgive me and not phone Mrs. Meany to come and get me.

"One time, when shopping with my mother, I asked where Mrs. Meany lived; and my mother pointed to a tall brick apartment building, and I stared at the building, trying to see the children encased behind the walls. I felt sorry for those children and vowed never to get into any trouble whereby I would be sent to Mrs. Meany's but I also wondered if I could somehow free the children that were there. I imagined them throwing rolled pieces of papers out the windows asking passersby to help free them . . . that saddens me now. It makes me realize that even little children can feel a deep empathy for others.

"Anyway, when I arrived home with my aunt and no one said anything about calling Mrs. Meany, I assumed that everything would be all right so I played quietly in my room and waited for my mother and aunt to call me downstairs. When that finally happened and I said good-bye to my aunt, she gave me a big hug before she left. My mother was very quiet and seemed sad. Sometimes it looked as if she wiped a tear from her eye, and I'd ask her if she was sad. She'd hug me, then tell me she was just fine, and that I should play in my room until dinner.

"After I'd been in my room for a while, and when I knew that my mother was in the kitchen, I sneaked down the hall to the baby's room, opened the door to look in, and found the room completely empty. There wasn't any furniture in the baby's room. I walked into the room and opened the closet door and found the closet empty too. I didn't know what to make of this, but suddenly, I felt so frightened that I ran to my room and shut the door.

"I was sure that they had sent the baby to Mrs. Meany and that Mrs. Meany had taken him away because he was crying. I hoped they would keep me and not call Mrs. Meany to take me away too. I started to cry, asking myself over and over again, *"Where's the baby? Has Mrs. Meany taken him?"* This thought made me feel sick inside, and I was determined to do everything that was asked of me and never give anyone a reason to be angry with me. I wondered if there was anything I could do to help my brother, rescue him from Mrs. Meany. *Maybe I could steal him from Mrs. Meany, bring him back home, and hide him in my room.*

"That night, the nightmares came. I woke in fear during the darkest hours of the night and saw the forms of monsters on my walls and ceilings, and I knew they were looking for me. I'd recite the prayer that my grandmother taught me. *"Now I lay me down to sleep, I pray the Lord my soul to keep. If I should die before I wake, I pray thee Lord my soul to take."* I repeated it in both English and German, in case one language worked better than the other with God. I hoped this prayer would keep the monsters away from me. But the monsters were still there, even after I finished praying . . . they were on the walls and ceiling and under the bed. They were black and gray, and they were larger than life-sized people, and they looked very mean, and I knew they wanted to take me, and I was afraid.

"My father didn't come home that night. But the next day, he was home but would sit in his chair, and he would cry. I dared not go to him. I wanted to ask what made him cry, but was afraid to ask and afraid that it was what I had done that had made him so unhappy. *Or maybe he was upset that Mrs. Meany had taken the baby! Or that Mrs. Meany would be coming for me.* I was terrified, but there was no one to help me.

"The nightmares were with me every night and seemed so forceful and frightening that what I saw slammed into my chest with a force I had never known before, leaving my chest heaving with fear and my breathing raspy and uneven. Sometimes I'd have to gasp for breath. My hands and feet would be damp and my mouth dry. Sometimes my nightgown would be wet from the perspiration of fear. I was afraid to tell my parents what was happening to me because I was afraid of being sent to Mrs. Meany's.

"Sometimes I'd find the courage to crawl on the floor from my bed to my parents' room and try to get onto the bottom of their bed without them knowing. Sometimes they would let me stay with them, and I could sleep, but sometimes, they would become angry and send me back to bed where the monsters were waiting for me. The terror was almost unbearable, and my body suffered from the stress of all I was enduring. I began to bite my nails so much that they would bleed, and my parents put a horrible-tasting lotion on my nails hoping to prevent me from biting them. But I bit them anyway, and soon began to suck my thumb as well. My thumb became sore from the pressure of my teeth, and my parents would wrap my thumb with bandages so I couldn't put my thumb in my mouth. This made me feel even worse because I could no longer use these mechanisms as a source of comfort and it made my fear worsen.

"Since I'd needed to suck my thumb or bite my nails for comfort, my body suffered because I had no outlet for my fear and this brought about a deterioration of my health. I began to have severe bouts of bronchitis and spend weeks in bed. But the monsters were afraid of the tent which medicated the air around me, so I felt safe there. I could sleep better when under the tent but knew that the monsters lurked outside, ready to grab me. All this occurred because I could not tell anyone what was wrong . . . either I did not know how to articulate what was happening, or was afraid to do so.

"This is why I worked so hard to communicate with you as you grew up, Sarah. I know now that if I could have explained all this to my parents they would have been horrified and done what they could to remove these fears. They did love me . . . very much, but just had no idea about what I was imagining, feeling and fearing which was affecting my psyche.

"The nightmares continued and I was always afraid at night. Whenever I closed my eyes even for just a moment, I'd feel the flutter of the monsters clothing on my face . . . I knew that if my eyes were closed, they'd come down from the ceiling and hover over me and wanted to take me. But if I kept my eyes open, they would stay on the walls and on the ceiling and not come too close to me. The fear was incredible, and the lack of sleep and the fear of falling asleep were taking a terrible toll.

"In time, my mother and father returned to their normal routine, and I once again began to feel safe. With the special resilience of a child, I began to feel better and came down with bronchitis less often. I was very careful, however, to be good and never ask where the baby was. I still had questions about whether or not he had been sent away because he had misbehaved and whether or not Mrs. Meany had him. Sometimes I'd wonder if I could have hurt my brother by slapping him just as my grandmother had said. Either way, I knew that this was why the monsters came every night.

"It was difficult to be perfect all the time. I worked hard at school and at dancing lessons and piano lessons and at helping my mom around the house. I hated to dust the tiny opening between the intricate carvings of the dining room chairs and often rebelled when given that assignment. I also hated to weed the garden. When I did rebel, my mother told me to get the flat-backed hairbrush and to lie across her lap and take the punishment I knew I deserved. I did what she said because Mrs. Meany was the alternative. And when this happened and I realized that I'd misbehaved, I became more terrified than ever because I knew in my heart that I deserved the monsters. And when I felt the fear, I was jolted back to thoughts of the baby. Even when I'd think that I'd finally forgotten, certain situations would trigger the memories, and I'd be transported back into the terrible fear . . . and to a vivid picture of the empty baby's room . . . the empty room would fill my mind.

"But as I listened to my grandmother read from the Bible and learned that there were angels who would protect me, I began to ask the angels for their help every night, and they did help me. My grandmother told me that the strongest angel was named Michael and I began to plead with Michael to come and protect me. I began to trust that the help I asked for would come; in fact, it was God and the angels I trusted the most as my life picked up a semblance of normality again.

"When I was four and a half years old, my mother told me that a new baby would be coming to the family. My parents and relatives were excited by this news, but I was frightened and wondered where my brother was and if he would be coming back. I thought that my brother would have liked to have another baby to play with. But I also wondered if this new baby would also have to go to Mrs. Meany if it cried.

"Then the new baby came, a girl this time, and I began to accept the fact that my brother would never come home. My parents seemed happy once again, and their lives went back to a normal routine, except for me . . . the monsters still came every night. Yet this period of my life changed me Sarah, and good came from it because through this ordeal, trusting God and his angels had been implanted into my heart.

"It wasn't until I became a teenager that I learned that my brother had died in the ambulance on the way to the hospital. He had been born with a defect in his intestines, and this is why he needed surgery shortly after he was born. I also learned that my parents had blamed themselves for his death, believing that if they had taken him to the doctor or hospital earlier that day or even earlier in the evening, rather than let him cry, he may have not died. He could have had the second surgery, which the doctor planned to do when he was one year old. The baby died on the way to the hospital in the wee hours of the next morning . . . my parents had decided that they would not risk angering the doctor by phoning him in the middle of the night, but would phone him when the sun came up.

"It was then that I realized what a burden my parents carried because of the choice they had made. I could understand my parents' terrible grief at the loss of their child and their self-blame for not bringing the baby to the hospital sooner. I also realized that their grief kept them from recognizing the needs and fears of their little girl. They thought that I would not understand death and therefore elected not to tell me what had occurred in an effort to protect me. They did not realize that I would miss my little brother . . . they thought I was too young.

"I also learned that Mrs. Meany was a fictional character which my aunt had made up, and that it was my aunt who my mother phoned, not Mrs. Meany. They used Mrs. Meany as a way to keep their children in line, not realizing that any harm would come from what they were telling their children.

"Let's stop now Sarah and have a cup of tea. In fact, this is probably enough for one day anyway and my throat is dry from so much talking! I am not sad, but feel emotionally drained and think it best that we absorb what we've gone over and leave the rest for another day. Would that be okay with you?"

"Okay Grandma . . . you are right . . . it's a lot to absorb . . . but it is fascinating . . . mainly because I am beginning to understand how parents can assume that they are doing exactly the right thing and it not be right at all. I think that I am beginning to recognize the underlying message here that parents . . . in fact all of us . . . must be very careful in how and what we do . . . and do not . . . communicate . . . to children or adults. And that we need to understand that children are far smarter than we give them credit for. I think that there may be many parents in the world who do harm without knowing it and sure would like to know how to change that."

Sarah felt terribly sorry for Grandma because she had lived through so much pain. She did feel a surge of anger toward Grandma's family for causing her such mental and physical anguish. Sarah knew that it had changed that little child forever and set the course for Grandma's future acceptance of anguish and abuse throughout her life. Her parents though, had not known.

But Sarah had studied psychology, and she knew. She wondered if God had protected Grandma from the damage which could have been done to her psyche and affected her entire life . . . permanently. She thought about what Grandma had said about God turning heartache into a blessing and began to think about what Grandma told her about that.

*Grandma could have been harmed for life, yet she thinks back on this time as a family tragedy **through which God worked His miracles** and through which He opened the door for her incredible faith. She believes that her faith eventually blossomed from these events to sustain her and eventually bring her profound peace and joy. Grandma also said that her parents had done the best they knew how to do at the time, that they may have reacted incorrectly, but understands that they did not know another way.*

In that statement, said silently inside her head, Sarah recognized the beautiful act of forgiveness which came from the loving heart of Grandma. Sarah marveled, because she thought that she might have held a grudge and was curious now to know what had happened that could make Grandma say that these experiences developed her faith and was therefore worth the suffering, thus the suffering had not been in vain. Sarah felt angry with Grandma's family and knew she'd have to work on that. But she did develop a personal goal to work toward the development of mandatory parenting classes in every high school in the country to help future parents raise well-adjusted children and never harm a child the way Grandma had been harmed.

Grandma told Sarah that in later years, she'd looked through her concordance to locate the scriptures which spoke about the angels who helped people, and to find some of the biblical stories where God himself brought the required help. When she found these passages in the Bible and remembered her grandmother reading them, she refreshed her mind with them. Sarah too remembered that when she was little, Grandma used to tell *them* about the angels and God's help, especially when they needed assurance to cope with their own fears.

"Grandma, do you still have that list of verses you once told us about which spoke of the angels who helped God's children?"

"Yes, Dear, I believe that I do!"

Grandma rummaged through a little chest on her desk and found those verses and handed them to Sarah to read and use for the journal should she desire to do so. "I wish that everyone who has ever felt afraid could read these passages", Grandma added.

And they brought Daniel, and cast him into the den of lions . . . .
The king . . . passed the night . . . arose very early in the morning . . .
and when he came to the den . . . said to Daniel . . .
is thy God . . . able to deliver thee from the lions? . . .
and said Daniel . . . My God hath sent his angel,
and hath shut the lions' mouths, that they have not hurt me.
—Daniel 6:16

Shadrach, Meshach, and Abednego,
and to cast them into the burning fiery furnace . . . .
The fire had no power, nor was an hair of their head singed . . .
and Nebuchadnezzar spake, . . . Blessed be the God . . . who hath sent his angel, and
delivered his servants that trusted in him.
—Daniel 3:19-28

The LORD shall fight for you . . .
and the angel of God . . . went behind them . . .
and the pillar . . . of the cloud . . . stood behind them . . .
between the camp of the Egyptians and the camp of Israel . . .
and the children of Israel went into the midst of the sea upon the dry ground . . .
for the LORD fighteth for them against the Egyptians . . . .
And the waters returned, and covered the chariots . . . and all the host of Pharaoh that
came into the sea after them.
Thus the LORD saved Israel . . . and Israel saw the Egyptians dead.
—Exodus 14:14-31

Peter was . . . bound with two chains . . .
the angel of the Lord came upon him . . .
saying Arise up quickly. And his chains fell off . . .
And when Peter was come to himself, he said,
Now I know of a surety, that the LORD hath sent his angel,
and hath delivered me.

—Acts 12:6-11

And there was war in heaven:
Michael and his angels fought against the dragon;
and the dragon fought and his angels,
And prevailed not; neither was their place found anymore in heaven.
And the great dragon was cast out, that old serpent,
called the Devil, and Satan.

—Revelation 12:7-9

Michael, one of the chief princes, came to help me.

—Daniel 10:13

Fear not: . . . be strong . . . now will I return to fight . . .
there is none that holdeth with me in these things,
but Michael your prince.

—Daniel 10:19

And at that time shall Michael stand up,
the great prince which standeth for the children of thy people:
and there shall be a time of trouble,
such as never was since there was a nation even to that same time:
and at that time thy people shall be delivered.

—*Daniel 12*

Thou shalt not be afraid: . . .
Be not afraid of sudden fear . . .
For the LORD shall be thy confidence,
and shall keep thy foot from being taken.

—*Proverbs 3:23*

They took up Jonah, and cast him forth into the sea.
Then Jonah prayed unto the LORD.
And the LORD spake to the fish, and it vomited
out Jonah upon the dry land.

—*Jonah 1:15; 2:1, 10*

Chapter Four

FRANCESCA AND VICTORIA, SISTERS

The next time that Sarah and Grandma met to work on their joint project, Sarah had to shift gears because Grandma laughingly told her that she was going to become Victoria again. She wanted to introduce Sarah to Francesca who was the new baby born when Grandma was almost five years old. Grandma thought that if she narrated by name rather than use "me" and "I" in her narration, the memories would be less personal and hopefully less painful not only for her, but also for Sarah and allow Sarah to view what was occurring dispassionately. She wanted Sarah to see the two sisters simply as sisters and not as "Grandma and her sister". She wanted Sarah to see them as young and learning, as children with parents and struggles . . . not personally . . . but professionally. Sarah understood and marveled at how Grandma sought to protect her by calling on her professional viewpoint rather than her personal reaction. She had wondered how anything to come could be any worse for Grandma than what she had already revealed but now feared that she'd been wrong in that assumption.

Yet Grandma seemed happy. She had prepared some blackberry tea and some buttered scones and little tea sandwiches with their crusts removed. Everything was artfully arranged on beautiful Royal Doulton plates with matching tea cup and saucer. Sarah marveled at the elegant manner in which Grandma set a table and presented food. But most of all she marveled at Grandma's strength . . . and lack of anger and resentment. Sarah was still fighting her anger . . . but realized it was a general anger at the mistakes people make which brings harm to others, but she knew that she was feeling anger towards those who'd hurt Grandma.

As Grandma began her story, Sarah leaned back in her chair, tea cup to her lips, notebook and pen at her side and listened as Grandma began the story of her sister's arrival into the family circle.

"Francesca was born ten weeks before Victoria celebrated her fifth birthday. The whole family awaited the new baby with joy in their hearts knowing that her arrival would ease the pain of the tragic loss of Victoria's brother a little more than a year earlier. Anxieties ran high as the baby was due and relief soared when finally the baby arrived and all seemed well. Francesca's arrival brought relief from the sadness of the previous few years and everything that would make a new baby content was ready and waiting for her.

"She was sturdy and perfect. She was a good baby too, eating well and with great gusto, and soon sleeping through the night. The family slipped back into the life they had enjoyed a few years earlier, and everyone was happy again. A comfortable routine was established, and life seemed back to normal.

"Francesca had very dark brown hair and brown eyes which were more of a golden topaz color in the center and were ringed in black and a much darker brown. She had an olive complexion, which she must have inherited from her maternal grandfather because everyone else in the family had fair skin. The baby was a few inches longer than the other two children were at birth, indicating that she might grow tall. Her feet were bigger too, further supporting the thought that she would be tall. With many tall relatives in the family, this wasn't unusual. Her dad, his brothers, and both grandfathers were tall; and their aunt was tall.

"Victoria loved having the new baby in the house and loved seeing her parents happy. She started to sing and dance once again and rarely felt the fear that had once consumed her. Even the nightmares came with less frequency. She had started kindergarten three months before the baby arrived and she loved it. She was old enough to play outside with the neighborhood children after arriving home from school and with these new freedoms, she felt very grown-up.

"She loved her kindergarten teacher, Miss Feraco, with her long dark hair and warm smile and Miss Feraco loved Victoria too. Victoria worked hard at whatever she was asked to do so Miss Feraco would be pleased with her.

She wanted to be just like her teacher when she grew up. Victoria loved being with the other children too and easily made friends. Her best friend Rosalie taught her how to jump rope and during recess when they would play usually they played double Dutch.

"When spring came, Francesca's playpen was placed in the tiny vestibule near the front door where she could watch the children playing outside and also get some fresh air. Victoria enjoyed being greeted by Francesca with her sunny smile and gurgling noises when she came home and would give her a hug and pick up the toys she had thrown out of the playpen.

"Francesca watched Victoria when she was playing outside with the other children and squealed in delight when Victoria would occasionally run back to the playpen to pick up the toys the baby had thrown to the ground. Francesca would become angry if Victoria didn't come quickly and would sometimes cry until she did return. It was obvious that the two girls loved one another. They would laugh together and when Francesca first began to form words, she called Victoria "Shish-a" for sister, and it made Victoria feel special to have a nickname and one the baby could pronounce so sweetly.

"If the baby cried too much, Victoria would sometimes worry that she would disappear just like her brother, so she catered to the baby, wanting her to be happy. But her sister wasn't taken away; she stayed and grew into a robust, sassy, intelligent child; and Victoria adored her. Where Victoria was delicately boned and small, the new baby was stocky and larger boned, so Victoria could seldom hold her or keep her from touching the knickknacks that neither of the girls were allowed to touch. Francesca however, was intent on grabbing what she wasn't supposed to touch, and Victoria knew that her parents would be angry if anything was broken . . . and she worried when her parents were angry and thought of Mrs. Meany.

"Surprisingly, the new baby would rarely be punished when she broke something because her parents couldn't catch her or hold her long enough to mete out any punishment. Victoria was secretly pleased to have a little sister who was so strong-minded. She wished she could be more like her and would think, *"She's gutsy, that little one!"*

"The family was happy. Victoria became proficient in her tap dancing, ballet and piano lessons, and she would perform for family and friends whenever asked. She was an excellent student and applied herself to her homework every night. Her parents complimented her and were pleased with her. She loved to play school and pretend to be Miss Feraco, who had remained a role model to her. She also loved the role of teacher. Victoria would set up a classroom in her bedroom placing pillows on the floor in front of her blackboard on which her friends could sit as she taught. They'd play school for hours on end. Victoria always included her little sister who enjoyed the time they spent playing together. Sometimes, though, Francesca would get angry when she could not do what the older girls could and would walk off in a huff and wouldn't play with them any longer.

"Sadly, Francesca's impatience and easy anger impeded her and held her back from learning. But it was her jealousy of the girls who did learn that seemed to upset her the most. She would become so angry she would erase the lessons which Victoria had placed on her little blackboard or knock it over. Sometimes she'd kick Victoria's friends or pull their hair. Victoria would try to placate her sister, but when she could not, she'd complain to her parents. Her parents would tell Francesca that she should not expect to do what her big sister or the other older girls could do. This infuriated Francesca, and she would express her anger vehemently. Though Victoria secretly loved watching her sister stand up to others, and wished she could be so sure of herself, she wished that Francesca wouldn't be so cruel.

"As the girls grew and as Victoria applied herself diligently to her tasks, Francesca would expect to do whatever Victoria did and was angry when she could not. Her parents continued to tell her that she could not expect to do what her older sister and her friends did because they were older . . . never explaining that it was work and practice which helped them achieve what they did.

"One day Victoria noticed a frighteningly venomous look cross Francesca's face when her parents told her that she simply could not expect to accomplish what Victoria had accomplished. Victoria began to feel that her parents should not compare Francesca to her or her friends; she thought it discouraged her sister from doing as well as Victoria knew Francesca could do. She had seen how her parent's words hurt her little sister and it made her fearful. At first, Francesca would yell back, saying she could do everything anyone else could. Sometimes she'd cry. But over time, Francesca would glare at her parents, at Victoria and even at Victoria's friends and become incredibly destructive.

"When she was very young Victoria had developed an interest in paper dolls. The women's magazines which her mother purchased each week from the grocery store contained a page or two which was dedicated to a paper doll, properly named, with three or four outfits specifically created to fit the featured doll. Sometimes another issue of the magazine would contain additional outfits for a previously published paper doll. There were skirts, blouses and jackets, and perhaps a hat, a pair of boots, or a purse to match. Victoria painstakingly cut out the dolls, the clothes, and the accessories. In those days, paper dolls were not pre-punched and required very careful, time consuming cutting.

"Victoria had asked all of her relatives to give her all the shoeboxes they could and explained that she wanted to place one doll and all her accessories in each box. She painted the boxes and labeled the ends with the names of each doll. She used her best handwriting. One day her mother had even helped her add bits of wallpaper to them to create a collage of color making the boxes even more attractive. Victoria kept the boxes on the open shelf of the bookcase which had been placed in her room. She looked forward to coming home from school and playing with all her well organized paper dolls. Sometimes her friends would come and play with her. They always helped her put the dolls and clothes back in their assigned boxes because they knew how careful Victoria was with them and how much work went into developing her collection.

"There were no televisions in most homes during this era, so children were used to engaging in projects which they could create themselves and play with whenever they had free time. Most children took good care of their possessions because they had few of them and they often had to put a great deal of work into creating them. Their primary source of evening entertainment was to listen to the radio. At night, the family would gather around the radio to listen to their favorite program, which was *The Green Hornet*, and which kept them enthralled and on the edge of their seats. The program opened and closed with an eerie laugh which was most distinctive, very frightening, and exciting at the same time. The whole family loved to listen to this show.

"But most of the time, dancing and piano, paper dolls and playing school, coloring books and reading were the activities which occupied Victoria's time. She loved to read and devoured the Nancy Drew mysteries. Once in a while, she would read a comic book. She had two favorites: *Wonder Woman* and *Sheba, Queen of the Jungle*. She and her friends would pretend to be these characters and laugh and laugh together, and they created tents from blankets and sheets spread over a card table which her mother allowed to be set up in her room. They would pretend they were in the jungle, but when summer came, they played in the empty lot on the corner where weeds grew so tall they looked just like real a jungle to the little girls.

"Victoria's mother often needed to rest after running around all day caring for Francesca, so one of her chores was to care for her sister for an hour each day while her mother rested. Victoria longed to play paper dolls with her little sister, but Francesca was rough with the dolls and clothing, for they were only made from paper and would tear easily. Her sister would purposely rip the clothing if she thought that she didn't have the prettier doll. Eventually, Victoria stopped trying to play with the paper dolls when she was with her sister, put the dolls away and found something else to do with her.

"One day when Victoria arrived home from school, she saw that her sister had gone into her room, taken almost half the shoeboxes from her shelves and destroyed the clothing and dolls in those boxes. Victoria was devastated, knowing the hours of work to cut them out and the months it would take to replace them and she cried over the loss.

"Francesca had been waiting for her when she came home from school and followed her upstairs to her room, watching to see when Victoria would notice what she had done. She wasn't afraid or remorseful. When Victoria noticed the destruction and began to cry, Francesca laughed and ran to the bookshelf to throw the remaining boxes to the floor. Victoria scolded her sister, but she laughed only louder and tried to step on the boxes she had thrown to the floor hoping to crush them. Victoria called for her mother to come upstairs quickly and tried to protect the rest of her paper dolls. Her mother came to her room and when she surveyed the damage she wasn't even angry. Victoria was surprised and then terribly hurt as she heard her mother remind her that Francesca was still very young and didn't understand what she had done. Victoria was shocked when her mother simply told her that she could always get more dolls from the magazines another day. Francesca laughed listening to what her mother said and, satisfied with her day's work, left the room. Victoria felt another tremor of fear.

"One day when her mother was angry with Francesca and again told her that she could not expect to do all the things that Victoria did, instead of crying as she had in the past, Francesca was quiet and simply looked at her mother, and then she looked at her sister but with a look which made Victoria cringe and think that something was very wrong. Francesca had looked at her as if she wanted to kill her. When Victoria thought about this change she felt that Francesca had not been hurt this time by what her mother said but was instead filled with a rage which was so intense that Victoria was frightened.

"A few weeks later, some of the relatives were visiting and asked Victoria to dance for them and to play something on the piano. Her dance routine included a spinning step, which she repeated around the accessible perimeter of the room. As she passed Francesca, she purposely tripped her, and Victoria fell and hurt her knee quite severely. When she got up and looked at her sister, she felt chilled because she knew that her sister had tripped her on purpose.

"Another time, when Victoria was playing the piano for everyone, her sister turned on the radio so loudly that the piano piece had to be interrupted and restarted. One of the relatives rebuked Francesca and was shocked that her parents did not back up what she said and began to berate them for letting such cruelty continue. Victoria's father then told Francesca to go to her room. But then everything simply went back to the way it always was and Francesca did something almost every day to hurt Victoria. She seemed to look for ways to destroy something Victoria liked. On many occasions, Victoria went to her room and closed the door to avoid her sister and cried from the hurt she felt from Francesca's actions; unable to understand why she treated her so badly. She tried to be extra kind to her sister and tried to include her in everything when her friends came to play, hoping that her sister would stop being so cruel.

"But one day, Victoria arrived home from school to find all the remaining paper dolls and the clothing (which Victoria had scotch-taped together after the last attack on them), and each box she'd so painstakingly painted, systematically destroyed by her sister. Every one of her treasured comic books had also been destroyed. Her collection of Nancy Drew mystery novels were crayoned on every page and some pages had been ripped out of the books. Her blackboard was filled with deep scratches, the bed was stripped, and Victoria's closet door was open and her clothing had been pulled off the rod and was lying in a heap on the floor.

"Once again, her mother came to survey the destruction and reached to spank Francesca; but she squirmed away, taunting her that she could not catch her, and ran from the room. Thus, again Francesca was not punished for her cruelty and destruction. There wasn't anything anyone could do about the destroyed dolls, books, or blackboard. Victoria was devastated by her loss and angry and hurt that her mother told *her* to clean up the mess.

Victoria wondered why her sister would behave this way, especially after the first episode when she'd been told how much they meant to Victoria. They wanted to put a pad lock on Victoria's bedroom door but then realized that Francesca might try to lock it when Victoria was in the room.

"Her mother never punished her sister for the destruction, and whenever her sister got angry, she would find something else to destroy and was now attacking items in the garage such as Victoria's roller skates, bicycle, and hula hoop. Victoria again felt a flicker of the old fear, this time wishing that Mrs. Meany would come and get her sister, then feeling afraid because she even *had* such a bad thought. At this point, Victoria no longer believed in Mrs. Meany; she didn't really believe in Santa Claus either. But it had felt good for the moment to think of Mrs. Meany rescuing her from Francesca.

"Some of the relatives thought that perhaps her sister was jealous of Victoria because they too often witnessed her cruelty. They suggested that Francesca begin dance and piano lessons so she too could perform for everyone. She was enrolled in these classes but hated the dance class because she could not catch up to the other students quickly enough and dropped out of the class. Once again, Victoria's parents told Francesca that perhaps she should not try to dance but find something else that she wanted to do.

"Her sister did like the piano lessons and learned to play a few songs which she would perform for relatives when they were visiting. She'd been enrolled in a preschool program as well but would not behave in the classroom and would fight with the other children, hitting them and becoming jealous of those who could recite their lessons well. The teachers would contact her parents to tell them that Francesca needed more discipline at home. But her parents secretly admired her independence and did not want to quench that side of her nature. Francesca however, recognizing her parent's complacency, gained the power to become even more of a problem in school. Finally, in desperation, her parents asked to change teachers, and Francesca was happy for a while because she liked the new teacher. She began to learn her alphabet and numbers. She was very smart and learned quickly but consistently did poorly in deportment and in tests, nor would she apply herself to completing her homework . . . therefore she did not obtain good grades. Francesca was always in trouble for fighting with someone; and because she was tall, strong, and aggressive, she ruled the classroom. Her sense of humor rescued her from the punishments she deserved, causing her teachers to believe she would achieve great things in life if she could be taught to direct her will in a positive way and apply herself to her grades.

"Her parents continued to tell Francesca that she was not like Victoria, that the two girls were as different as day and night, and that she should not try to compete so intensely. Victoria on the other hand saw talent and ability in her sister and felt uneasy about her parents making comparisons between the two girls. Victoria wished she could stand up to people the way her sister did and that she could make people laugh as easily. Victoria loved to listen to Francesca, but she was afraid of her.

Grandma and Sarah decided to take a break and walk out to the waterway for a few minutes before coming back to resume the story. As the story of Grandma's early life and her experience with her sister unfolded, Sarah realized, because of her training, that the manner in which Francesca was addressed and enabled, could impact the psyche of *both* girls and create a jealousy which could cause a lifetime of enmity. Sarah was amazed that Victoria, at that young age, could sense that the way her parents handled Francesca was wrong. It confirmed what Sarah had always believed about the special insight of young children. *They are smarter than we give them credit for. I wish Grandma had had someone to talk to about her fears.* But parents, Sarah knew from her work with the special needs children, did not always realize the harm they did, and often acted in innocence. They did not understand that their method of discipline and certainly no discipline at all, was of no benefit to their children nor did they understand that it could cause terrible and long-lasting harm even without them intending to do so. After their little walk and a few minutes of fresh air Sarah and Grandma arrived back at her apartment and again sat down to resume their project. Grandma began her narration once again.

"As the girls grew, their parents began visiting their neighbors for a short one hour visit after dinner. When Victoria and her sister were in their nightgowns and ready for bed, their parents would leave. Victoria was to look after Francesca, wash and dry the dinner dishes, and was instructed to keep the house neat.

"Francesca knew what instructions her parents had given Victoria so while she was in the kitchen, Francesca would mess up the house by throwing pillows on the floor, by moving doilies from tables to floor, and by taking her father's shoes out of the closet and throwing them all over the living room floor. Victoria would scurry around, pick everything up and tidy the house before her parents came home. Francesca thought it a big joke and laughed at Victoria's frantic attempt to clean up the mess.

"When Victoria would complain to her parents, they would say, in front of Francesca, that more was expected of Victoria because she was the older one, or the smarter one, or the one they put in charge. Victoria knew that Francesca was just as smart, if not smarter. But her parents were consistent and Francesca reacted to what they said with hatred toward Victoria.

"In her heart, Victoria loved her sister and thought that she was just a little girl who would grow out of her mischievous stage. She loved that Francesca could make everyone laugh and would always use her wits and her sense of humor to get out of trouble. Victoria was fascinated by her sister's ability to think so quickly and respond with such clever answers. Victoria knew that despite her poor grades, her sister was smart and could do the required work if she would apply herself. Victoria often thought, *It's just that Francesca is big for her age, and doesn't want anyone telling her what to do. Perhaps being the youngest in the family is difficult for her.*

"Victoria longed for a close friendship with her sister. She'd seen the closeness between her friends and their sisters and wanted the same in her family. But it never happened no matter how hard Victoria tried.

"When the girls were a little older, the family moved to a larger home in a new area where the girls would enter new schools and make new friends. It was hoped that Francesca would make a new start and apply herself properly. New routines were established, and they began their new life with great hope. Their parents began to go to a movie every Thursday evening and required Victoria to "babysit". Though there was almost five years' difference in their ages, Victoria noted that Francesca was now as tall as she was, weighed more, and was much stronger and far more aggressive.

"When movie night arrived and Victoria tried to keep the house as perfect as her mother left it, again her sister would mess it up and laugh loudly at Victoria's attempts to tidy. As Victoria would pick up after her sister, Francesca followed behind her to mess it up again. Now that Francesca was older and Victoria no longer thought of her as a baby and also did not think about her baby brother as often, she would allow herself to become angry with her sister and chase her away. But when Francesca would turn on her and often hurt her and threaten her, Victoria became afraid to challenge her. Francesca began to tell Victoria that she hated her and would kill her someday.

"Victoria decided to tell her parents what was happening. Her parents realized for the first time that the "new baby" was bigger and stronger than Victoria. But her parents also suddenly realized that they could no longer control Francesca and buried their head in the sand, turning a blind eye to what was happening at home and at school. Victoria could do nothing but keep trying to tidy the house before her parents walked in the door and not aggravate her sister in the process. Her parents were no longer as harsh with Victoria when pillows or shoes were strewn around the house.

"However, one day her parents were angry with Victoria. They arrived home to discover that the intricately carved cherry frame of their beautiful Victorian loveseat was cracked. Francesca had pulled on the back of the love seat when running away from Victoria after being mischievous again. Victoria chased Francesca from the living room when she sat on the down cushions of the sofa, the chairs, and the love seat to flatten them after Victoria had fluffed them the way her mother instructed. When Francesca ran from the room and passed behind the loveseat she pulled on the back and it had tipped over and fallen on its back cracking the wood frame. Victoria righted the love seat and knew that this was going to upset her parents. But again, Francesca wasn't disciplined . . . instead, both girls were sent to their rooms. Another incident occurred when Francesca unrolled bathroom tissue over every surface of the living room and dining room just before their parents were to return from the movie they'd gone to see. The toilet paper was wound around every piece of furniture and around every lamp, insulting the otherwise perfectly decorated room. When her parents walked in and saw the mess, they were astounded. The entire room looked outrageous! Before they could stop themselves and before they felt anger and comprehended the time involved in undoing the mess, they burst out laughing. They laughed even louder when Francesca told them with a straight face that Victoria had spread the toilet tissue throughout the room. Francesca's expression when making that statement clearly said that she knew they would not believe her statement, and this only made them laugh more, so much in fact that they cried. Even Victoria started to laugh, thinking how spunky and quick and witty her sister was. It amazed Victoria that her sister could think of so many things to say, could make faces which made everyone laugh, and tell such blatant lies with a straight face . . . she had absolutely no fear! Victoria couldn't help but think of her sister as incredibly courageous.

Sarah however, with her training and insight saw that no one had realized that laughing at Francesca's bad behavior was rewarding the bad behavior.

It wasn't the correct way to teach her, and the end result would encourage her to continue her unacceptable behavior, and in fact, escalate it. Sarah felt a tremor of deep concern about what this story would reveal and what her grandmother had faced.

"As Francesca's grades and her poor choice of friends increased, Victoria was at home less and less. She began performing her dance routines at school events and made many friends through her school activities. She was becoming a beautiful young woman, sweet natured and polite. Through her dancing school, she was invited to join a troupe of dancers to sing and dance where the troupe performed. Her favorite routine was performed to the music of "I've Got Rhythm, I've Got Music." The pianist would perform the piece in the key of B, the perfect range for Victoria's voice, and everyone seemed to enjoy the performances.

"These were rewarding activities for Victoria and she loved the camaraderie she shared with the other performers. In addition to her dancing, her piano teacher asked her to perform at a special piano recital. Her picture was in the paper, and all the relatives attended the performance and were proud of her.

"With all these activities, Victoria was away from home often, and when she *was* home, she went to her room to complete her homework, or into the finished basement where she would practice her dance routines rarely having time to interact with her sister. On Saturdays, she and her mother cleaned the house in the morning; and on Sundays, they went to church, then either out to eat or to visit a relative; so there wasn't much time to be alone with Francesca.

"Victoria loved her sister, admired how tall she was, how straight she stood, how broad her shoulders were, how bright her smile was, and she loved her sister's sense of humor and her sassy, brassy manner. She also loved her sister's beautiful swarthy skin color and the square cut of her jaw which warned of how defiant she was. Victoria also loved that Francesca was a tomboy and physically and emotionally strong in everything she did and she often wished she could be more like Francesca instead of delicate, prissy, and self-controlled. But in her heart of heart, Victoria was afraid of Francesca because of the cruelty, even hatred which her sister seemed to direct toward her. She recognized her terrible jealousy and could do nothing about it; she was also sadly aware that Francesca could not be trusted. Yet she wished that she could stand up to people the way Francesca did because then she could stand up to her sister.

"Time passed; Victoria became a young lady, attended school proms, graduated from high school, and planned to go to college. She took a summer job and bought a ramshackle secondhand car against her father's wishes. She was proud of herself because she bought the car on her own and, for the first time, she had gone against her parent's wishes . . . and succeeded! When summer ended, she attended a nearby college. At five feet two and 110 lbs and with a sweet pretty face, Victoria looked younger than she was and was even stopped by the police on occasion and asked for her license to prove that she was eligible to drive.

"But when Francesca began attending junior high school, serious troubles began brewing. Coincidently, that year was the first year that both the junior and high schools were granted the funds to hire two psychologists to provide counseling to students. This had never been done before and was to be a pilot program, thus the new psychologists were anxious to find students who might be in need . . . and they needed to make the program demonstrate its worthiness.

"Because of Francesca's poor deportment, poor grades, and excessive truancies, she was one of the first students they sought to help. After obtaining permission from her parents, Francesca was required to meet regularly with the school psychologists to see if they could learn why she had these problems and how they could help her. At first, Francesca was more than willing to meet with the psychologists and seemed to enjoy the challenge of those sessions.

"Years later the family learned that Francesca had lied to the psychologists telling them terrible stories about her family to gain their sympathy and circumvent any potential disciplinary measures. She told them that her father was having an affair with another woman and that Francesca had seen them together, she also told them that her mother had had an abortion (unheard of in those days) because her father did not want another child, she told them that her parents often beat her, and an uncle had molested her along with his own daughter who had had to move away because of what had happened.

"Initially, the school psychologists were sympathetic to Francesca's plight, later they were alarmed. Eventually, however, the psychologists saw through the stories Francesca told, amazed that she lied with such incredible ease.

They recognized that she had presented no remorse for lying, nor about causing harm to others. They were soon to label her "a child with sociopath tendencies."

"After hearing all the allegations which Francesca made against her family, the psychologists examined what they knew about the entire family, and then they spoke at length with the parents in numerous interviews. They looked at Victoria's school record and achievements, and asked permission to speak with the family doctor to see if he had noted anything about Francesca. Assessing the glibness of Francesca's lies and her incredible lack of fear and remorse, they made their preliminary diagnosis and recommended concentrated psychiatric counseling outside of the school. But her parents refused and became highly indignant that anyone should even think such a thing about their child. They adamantly refused the advice they received and refused to meet with the psychologists again. The counselors could do no more.

Sarah realized that Grandma's parents had made another wrong decision, and that perhaps if Francesca had received the counseling she required, she might have become a better person. Sarah wondered if pride had prevented Grandma's parents from agreeing to counseling for themselves or their child. She wondered if they'd been offended that anyone would think them less than perfect.

They were probably embarrassed by the thought of "mental illness" and the stigma which existed around such a label. They had been indignant and simply swept the matter under the rug, closing the door to any further discussion. Obviously the psychologists could not continue without the parents' consent unless the child caused harm to herself or to others at school.

Sarah knew however that the psychologists could encourage Francesca's instructors to demand that attendance and homework standards be enforced and the parents informed of any infringement. Sarah surmised all this because she'd witnessed similar reactions in some of the parents of her students.

"When Francesca was almost fifteen years old, she dyed her long hair jet-black and began to dress in a bohemian style becoming to her five-feet-eleven inch frame. She was defiant, sassy, and self-assured. She was funny too and entertained with her wit. But she was also cunning, and without any family member aware of what she did, she dropped out of school. Her lies were beginning to catch up with her.

"Francesca took a job in an office in Town Hall, claiming that she was eighteen when she was, in reality, not quite fifteen. No one in the family knew she was not attending school and didn't learn of it for almost two years. She signed herself out of school, forging her parent's signature. Frankly, it was easily accepted because the school officials were glad to see her go because of the trouble she caused. Francesca loved earning a salary to spend on clothes and cigarettes, hamburgers and shakes, and anything else she wanted. She was proud of herself for not getting caught for dropping out of school and doing what she wanted every day. No one had even noticed! Later she was to tell her family that she could get away with anything if she set her mind to it.

"In time Victoria realized how fortunate she was to graduate from high school before her sister had her encounters with the school psychologists. With a difference in their ages of almost five years and the different schools for Junior High and regular High school, Victoria always attended a different school than did Francesca, so she did not have to live under the stigma of Francesca's bad behavior. She viewed this as a great blessing to her.

"A few years passed and their dad lost his job and future pension, and because of the drastic change in their finances, Victoria could no longer continue her college classes and accepted a job in the area, hoping to go back to college sometime in the future . . . which she eventually did. She married at the age of twenty, never hesitating to ask Francesca to be her maid of honor despite the heartache she'd endured at her hands. Thirteen months after her wedding, Victoria had her first child and asked Francesca to be the child's godmother. And a year after that, Victoria and her husband bought their first home.

"But previously, soon after her first child was born, Victoria asked her mother if she would look after the baby for a few hours while she and her husband met with an insurance agent to purchase a life insurance policy for the family. At the last minute, her mother was called elsewhere, and Victoria asked her sister, who lived at home, if she would watch the six-week-old baby. Two hours later, when Victoria left the insurance agency with her husband and crossed the street to their car, she saw Francesca at the top of the hill, riding tandem on a motorcycle. Victoria and her husband ran to their car and drove as fast as they could to her mother's house. They found their newborn alone in the house in an upstairs bedroom. Within minutes, Francesca, still riding tandem on the motorcycle pulled into the driveway behind their car and was sardonically amused by Victoria's anger.

"Victoria never left her child with her sister again and could hardly accept the fact that anyone, let alone her own sister, would be so irresponsible. When Victoria told her parents what had happened, Francesca was furious with Victoria and denied leaving the baby alone. She adamantly stated that she had been outside in the yard, and that Victoria was lying. Victoria was shocked by her sister's behavior and blatant lie and thankful that no harm had come to her baby. What was the most shocking was that her sister had no remorse whatsoever for what she had done, and Victoria finally saw in her sister what no one else was willing to see. She would never trust her sister again.

"Soon thereafter, Victoria's parents discovered that Francesca had quit school but there was nothing they could do to change the situation. It was too late. They had their hands full with her and chose, again, to bury their head in the sand. Getting away with quitting school made Francesca feel she could get away with anything. Her parents would come home in the evening to find Francesca openly smoking despite their rule that she not smoke in the house. The driveway would be filled with motorcycles, and the house filled with friends, mostly boys who were much older than Francesca. They would find beer bottles all over the house, sometimes in the master bedroom. They would yell and argue and lay down rules, but Francesca did what she wanted, and they had no control over her. The next year brought Francesca's wedding and her parents were relieved to have her out of the house and even changed the locks on their house the day after her wedding.

"Victoria invited Francesca to her home from time to time, hoping that marriage and children had brought her a modicum of maturity and responsibility. But Francesca would never accept any invitation Victoria extended. For each holiday, anniversary, and birthday, Victoria's mother, father, aunt and uncle and grandmother would gather at her home; but Francesca would not come. Neither did Francesca invite them to her home claiming that she hated the pristine perfection of her mother's and sister's houses, was more comfortable in her own home. She would adamantly state, *"I don't cook, I don't clean, I don't want people over."*

"Francesca worked part-time as a bartender. She also bought and sold contraband merchandise, never reporting this income to the IRS, yet making what she termed "loads of money." On the nights she didn't work; and since her husband worked the night shift, she'd hire a neighbor's child to babysit and go to a bar or a disco until the wee hours of the morning to dance.

"She once bragged to the family about making a fortune from purchasing contraband guns, ammunition, and knives and reselling them, moving them illegally from one state to another and over a bridge which banned explosives. Everyone in the family was upset by this, but again, they could do nothing. Some chose to think that she was exaggerating and looking for attention and did not actually engage in such activities.

"In time, Victoria had another child and, shortly thereafter, built a larger home a few miles further away. She remained close to her parents and aunts and uncles and grandparents and still shared visits and holidays with them. She was active in her church, providing her children with a religious background which she hoped would carry over to their adult life. She took a part-time job and joined a number of organizations to help raise money for charities. She worked hard as a homemaker, wife, and mother and learned how to refinish furniture, make draperies, and craft items. She learned how to garden and became an excellent cook. She encouraged her husband to go back to school, spending hours reading his assignments and highlighting what she thought he'd need to read and remember for his exams. She wrote his book reports and other papers.

"Life went on, and the sisters rarely saw one another nor spoke on the telephone; but one day, Francesca phoned and wanted to visit. Victoria was happy about her call and looked forward to their meeting. She longed for a sister who would be "normal," would be her friend and an integral part of the family.

"When her sister arrived, they had a pleasant visit; and when leaving, Francesca gave Victoria a necklace. It was a cross on a chain with engraving on the back of the cross itself. Francesca told her that she'd found the necklace and wanted Victoria to have it. Victoria had always given her sister a Christmas and birthday gift but had never received one in return, so this gift was unexpected and she was thrilled . . . and her heart was touched.

"Victoria, always the one who tried to "fix" the problems in the family, wanted to help her sister and hoped that they could establish a better relationship. Her sister's visit inspired her to find a way to improve her sister's life. She remembered a talented young man she knew who was about to open a new business. He was married, had two young children, and had built a prior business from the ground up, which he had recently sold. Within the month, he planned to launch his new project and hire people with varying levels of skill.

"The business would be located within commuting distance of her sister's house. Since her sister seemed so different when she visited a few weeks earlier, Victoria decided to ask him to give her sister a job, explaining that Francesca did not have a high school diploma but was smart, resourceful, and a hard worker. The young man agreed to give Francesca the job because of Victoria's fine character . . . believing that sisters would be similar in character.

"The family was thrilled with her sister's job opportunity. They hoped that she could work her way up in this new company and maybe go back to school for her high school diploma. But Francesca worked there for few years and then left, bragging about how she had plotted to destroy the reputation of Victoria's friend, the man who gave her the job despite her lack of a high school diploma. Victoria was appalled and later learned that he had left the company he'd built from scratch, selling out to his partner . . . because of the harm that Francesca had done to him . . . and the wedge she'd plotted to place between him and his partner. Victoria was devastated that he had been hurt.

"Victoria had trusted her sister to do the right thing, especially to someone willing to give her a chance, and felt so badly about what her friend had experienced. As usual, Francesca had no remorse for what she had done and was proud of her ability to plot and execute her long-term plan to destroy this man. Francesca bragged openly about what she'd done and claimed that she hated him because he had admired Victoria and because he was a "goody two-shoes" just like Victoria.

"Victoria was surprised by what her sister had done. She could not understand why a person would hurt anyone who provided so much help. But now there was no mistaking what Francesca was capable of doing and Victoria saw Francesca in a new light, realizing that she'd never outgrown her cruel and vengeful nature. She was sure that something was seriously wrong with the way her sister thought and remembered that Francesca's motto had always been, "Get before you are gotten," She'd once thought it was one of her sister's jokes, and now she realized this was how her sister really felt. It was not just one of her sister's jokes or smart replies, but a way of life for her.

"Finally Francesca decided to take a GED (general equivalency diploma) course to obtain her high school diploma so she could get another job. But after a few weeks, she dropped out of the program, saying it was too difficult. This was surprising because she was a whiz at Scrabble, Yahtzee, Skip-Bo, Canasta, and crossword puzzles. Sadly, her experience in the GED course caused Francesca to become even angrier and to be more distant with the family, always angry with one or the other and always telling everyone how much she hated them.

"To explain her estrangement from her family, Francesca began telling her children terrible stories about the family, using these stories to demand their distance from their relatives. Victoria later learned that Francesca told her children that her father (their grandfather) was a wimp and a womanizer, her mother (their grandmother) was a "nutcase", Victoria (their aunt) was an alcoholic. Francesca even made up the outlandish lie that Victoria's son (at age seven) sexually abused Francesca's daughter (who was four months old at this time). She also told her children that her uncle was a sex offender.

"Victoria, unable to think the worst of people never understood why, a few years later, slowly and inexorably her life became unbearable; and she didn't understand why things had changed so drastically for the worse. She hadn't realized until years later that the burning, raging jealousy which Francesca felt toward her caused Francesca's determination to destroy her. Victoria never expected that her interactive relationship with their parents and relatives, her lovely home, her standard of life and personal set of morals, her marriage, and her community recognition had infuriated her sister. She'd never suspected that Francesca as an adult was still capable of a rage or jealousy so dangerous that it could produce such intense hatred and need for revenge. Victoria had never hated anyone and couldn't understand a hate which could spawn such destruction, especially from a family member.

"Victoria was stunned to finally have to accept the depth of her sister's hatred, for she would always love her sister and forgive her for the incredible cruelties she brought into her life. She never knew that over the years, watching Victoria bloom and flourish and become beloved of so many, Francesca was busy plotting Victoria's destruction desiring to take away Victoria's home, husband, and job, and destroy Victoria's children in the process because of her jealousy. Francesca hated her and what Francesca termed her "Holy Roller" nature which Francesca also wanted to destroy. Francesca perfected a plan which took years to accomplish and would result in the total annihilation of much of what Victoria loved.

"Francesca had vowed to succeed . . . and her plan would succeed . . . but she had not counted on Victoria being a woman who, through the testing of those experiences, would truly touch the heart of God.

Chapter Five

DAMON, VICTORIA'S HUSBAND

After the next little break from Grandma's narration and another trip to the kitchen for the fruit which Grandma had sliced for them and the cool drink she prepared for them, Grandma explained that she wanted to move back a little bit in time so she could talk about her first husband and what he was like before they married and then follow-up with what that marriage brought into her life. When they settled back into their seats and Sarah began munching on a cool crisp slice of fresh pear, Grandma began again and spoke about how Victoria had met her husband.

"Victoria had to leave college to take a position in the accounting department of a large firm when her father lost his job and finances were tight. She loved her work and the people she worked with, but planned to go back to college the following year when finances permitted. It was at this job that she met her husband.

"Damon was twenty-one years old, had been raised in a small town about twenty miles from where they worked; a town where he had lived all his life. His parents were immigrants from Europe who had been raised with a strong work ethic and they wanted to instill the benefits of hard work into their children. But Damon thought his parents too strict, often rebelled against his father, and wanted to move from their home as soon as he could. Not having the money to do so was the only reason he stayed. He remained at odds with his father right up to the time he died and even thereafter, despite his father's earlier heart attack, and many efforts to begin anew with his son. Damon wasn't a good student in high school, but he had been on the football team and kept up his grades just enough to be sure to play. He was a football fan throughout his life.

"A few months after he graduated high school, he felt the need to leave home because of continued conflicts with his father and his venomous hatred of a brother who was mentally challenged and with whom he shared a bedroom. He had few options in his desire to leave home because without a college education or a specific skill, he could not obtain a job which paid enough money for him to afford his own home. So he joined the armed services. As he entered the rigors of boot camp, he found himself subjected to greater discipline than he had at home and was resentful of the discipline imposed on him. He hated every minute of his experience, made no friends, and decided to find a way to leave the military. His father's recent heart attack made him think of asking for a medical leave, and by faking some dates, his request was granted.

"While home, Damon enlisted the help of a friend with an uncle associated with someone in politics. With their help, the necessary letters requesting a discharge under a family hardship clause were sent to the proper authorities. Damon was discharged and returned to his hometown to look for a job. He was forced to live at home both in case his discharge was investigated and because he was financially dependent on them for his housing. This is when he found a job at the company which, a few months later, hired Victoria.

"He'd seen Victoria at work and asked her for a date. They'd occasionally go to a movie together and have a hamburger and root beer afterward. Victoria didn't want to date exclusively because she wasn't ready for a serious relationship, and she was planning to return to college the following year. Victoria told him that she had completed her first year of college and wanted to return because she felt that an education and the development of specific skills were important to those wishing to become successful and independent.

"Damon had been impressed by Victoria. Hearing her dreams for the future and her goals to finish college, he applied for a football scholarship to a small southern college. Within a few months, he was granted the scholarship he sought and left for school at the end of July to begin his football training before classes began. Victoria was delighted with his decision, promised to write, and wished him success.

"However, after five weeks, he left college and returned to his old job. When he saw Victoria again, he told her that he'd endured terrible hardships at school. He felt that they expected too much from him, explaining that the college was in the south, the temperature too warm for practicing football, and he'd been expected to practice for hours despite feeling faint in the heat. He told her he would probably not have been a starter on the team, and this had discouraged him. Classes were also difficult, and many assignments were given out which he could not find the time to complete if they expected him to spend time on the football field. He didn't think they had been fair to him.

"Victoria didn't . . . or wouldn't . . . see that he'd railed against the same discipline and productivity the college expected from all the students; that he left the school rather than accept their rules; just as he had with his military experience and while under his father's roof. What Damon told Victoria was an example of his true character, yet Victoria had not paid attention. Neither did she wonder about his hatred for his father and for his mentally challenged brother. She should have.

"Instead, Victoria felt sorry for him, believing him, thinking that what had been expected of him was, as he stated, unfair, and wished she could help him. There was something sad about Damon, something that touched her heart. She wanted to encourage him and see him go back to school and make something special of himself. They began dating again, and soon, they dated exclusively.

"Victoria's parents were concerned. They did not think that Damon was a proper match for her and were concerned for her future. But Victoria, despite their protests, married him the next year; and her parents nevertheless gave them a beautiful church wedding with two hundred people in attendance.

"They'd gone to Grand Bahamas Island for their honeymoon. During dinner on their first night on the island, Damon found fault with the waiter who served their dinner, behaved badly to the waiter and became vehemently angry when the Maitre de also intervened on the waiter's behalf. Back in their room, Victoria told him that he had been unkind to the waiter, and that what Damon had taken as an insult was simply the protocol of good manners. Damon became angry with her for "telling him what to do" and stormed out of the room. It was their wedding night yet he did not return until 4:00 a.m. and was very drunk. Victoria was worried about his safety and in tears until she fell asleep. She'd been stunned by his actions, and also by how he treated the waiter and responded to Victoria's observation. She did not yet internalize that Damon could not and would not be criticized in any way, even if the criticism was imagined or no criticism had been intended, or that his temper was irascible and uncontrolled.

"This incident and Victoria's acceptance of his actions were to set the course for their relationship over their entire marriage. His temper, his drinking, and his abusive nature were to increase over the years and become the biggest secret Victoria had ever kept from her family. She loved Damon and, with the innocence of youth, thought he would change, thought that with responsibilities, a nice home, and children to love him and need him, he would change. Victoria worked hard to please him; she was a good cook, kept a nice home, took pride in how she looked, and invited friends and family over as often as she could to keep him home at night. He'd stay home when his friends visited, but more often than not, he would not be there if her family visited. Slowly, Victoria realized she would not find in him the tender, stay-at-home family man she wished for. She was disillusioned, and she was disappointed in his lack of character, but still she loved him and hoped for change.

"At first, when he did not come home at night, she worried about him, concerned that he had been in an accident, knowing he would have too much to drink. At first, she'd pace the floor with worry as the hours passed, and he was nowhere to be found. But he'd be angry to find her waiting up and angry when she'd tell him she worried about him.

"Her pregnancy didn't change him either. One night, they argued when she told him that she didn't want her child to grow up in the environment in which they currently lived. He was so angry with her that he grabbed her by the arm and threw her out the front door into the snow in her bare feet and would not open the door. Hearing her pleas to be let back into the house, the landlord came downstairs to open her door and let her in, telling Victoria that she could overhear quite a bit and was very upset by the kind of man Damon was.

"Their first child arrived about thirteen months after they married, and Victoria was so in love with her child that she was happy despite Damon's out of control behavior. She'd found a house they could purchase with very little money down and she bought the house by borrowing money from a loan company as a down payment. They obtained a short-term interest only mortgage from the man who built the house, with the stipulation that they would refinance in two years when the increasing equity in the house gained them bank approval.

"Victoria worked hard to be frugal and paid off the loan company quickly. She made the house as beautiful as she could by painting and papering and by decorating with some new and some hand-me-down furniture. She took cuttings from her parents' garden to create her own lovely landscape projects. She bought wonderful accessories at garage sales, made her own curtains, and turned the house into a little paradise. She designed a set of shutters for the front exterior of the house, purchased the wood to create them and drew a pine tree design on the boards which she cut out with a saber saw. She painted the shutters and asked Damon to hang them on the two front windows.

"Damon was very proud of his house and impressed with Victoria's ability both to create and keep such a lovely environment. And he did use his salary to enable them to keep and improve their home. He was satisfied because, unknown to Victoria, his expense account at work which he misused for personal gain kept him in drinking money.

"Victoria had a wonderful relationship with Damon's father despite Damon's feelings toward him. She loved her father-in-law. He'd visit often and do things around the house for her. He built a wall hutch for her dishes and put much thought into what she would like and how it would match her décor. She was touched by his kindness and delighted with what he created. He was very good to them, but still her husband hated him, held his grudge, and would not relent in his attitude toward his father nor was he willing to have him stay for dinner.

"Damon's father died shortly thereafter, and there was no sadness in Damon's heart. He continued to stay out at night and drink, and when Victoria would question where he was, he would start a fight and in anger, purposely break those things which Victoria had made or particularly loved. Sometimes she'd phone his office to ask him what he'd like for dinner in the hope that he would come home if she prepared something he especially enjoyed, but he would still stay out. There were times when his friends would have to carry him home because he had passed out at the bar. There were times when he came home himself and passed out on the bathroom floor and when he awakened, had ridges along the side of his face from the design of the tiles on the floor.

"Despite his drinking, he performed well at his job, continued to earn the money necessary to keep the house running smoothly, and was even promoted. Victoria always saw the part of him which she believed was good and loving, and when he did stay home and hadn't been drinking, he'd tell her he loved her. She believed him and kept hoping for change, willing herself to believe that a change for the better would come in time. Damon continued to do well in his job and received yet another promotion and pay raise, and they decided to build a larger house on a larger lot to accommodate the new baby which would arrive in a few months.

"Victoria would try to reason with Damon about his behavior when he hadn't been drinking, but he would become incredibly angry, telling her he didn't want to be told what to do. He'd storm out of the house to drink even more. And sometimes he'd be missing for the entire weekend.

"When their second child arrived, Victoria kept busy with her new home, her children, and her love of gardening and decorating. She spent time with her parents, grandparents, and aunts and uncles. She developed good friendships which helped her loneliness, but nevertheless felt the loneliness when other families would walk together or sit together on their porch in the evenings and she was alone. If she read a book at night after she put the children to bed, and the story would be about a married couple, she'd wonder what had gone wrong in her marriage; and when she visited friends and would be the only wife in attendance without a husband, she'd wonder why he could not be like the other husbands she knew. She felt a deep loneliness during these times and would cry when no one was around. She began to wonder if she wanted to live every day of her life facing another night at home alone, knowing he was somewhere drinking.

"She worked hard around the house and with the children during the day, thinking that she wanted to be tired at night so she wouldn't think about Damon not being home. She'd want to read at night to take her mind off her loneliness. She wanted to be asleep when he came home so he wouldn't hit her in his drunken venom.

"One night, Damon came home after midnight, and Victoria was still awake. She was tired and angry and asked him where he had been, and he began to call her vile names, and an argument ensued. She told him that he needed to stop drinking and be home at night, not just for her, but because the children were growing up, and they didn't even know their father. She asked him if having a relationship with them was important to him. He was furious with her and hit her so hard that she was knocked off her feet and hit her head on the kitchen floor and passed out. He went to bed, leaving her there, unremorseful and angry.

"Thus began a pattern which psychologists termed, "the abused wife syndrome". If Victoria were up when he came home, she would be hit, spit on, kicked, and called foul names. He would pull her hair and twist her arm. Spittle would fly from his mouth as he ranted, and if Victoria cried, he'd only become angrier. If she did not respond and remained quiet through her ordeal, he'd storm out of the house unsatisfied.

"Damon's vengeful attitude soon became apparent to Victoria, for even when sober he was cruel. He began phoning her in the afternoon, asking her to make a specific meal for him, often her homemade chicken, mashed potatoes, and gravy. She'd run to the store if she didn't have the ingredients on hand so she could create the meal he wanted. She'd put makeup on before he was due home and change her clothing. But then, he wouldn't come home despite his demands that she cook something he wanted that evening.

"Whether she left the meal on the table or in the oven for him, or had wrapped it and placed it in the refrigerator he'd find the plate and throw it against the wall, angry no matter what she did. The food would slide down the wall and onto the floor over the shattered remains of the plate. Victoria slowly slipped into a deep depression. Yet because of her responsibilities to her children, she continued to be a good mother and homemaker. She just became more quiet than usual and felt a terrible and constant sadness in her heart. She'd work harder to forget and to cover up her pain. She was ashamed to tell anyone what was happening.

"One Sunday, after a particularly vicious attack by Damon on the previous Friday evening, Victoria hid her face when she went to church because of what her husband had done to her. Brushing one side of her shoulder-length hair toward the front she managed to cover the side of her face that had turned black and blue. She also hoped to hide her jaw and her one blackened eye with this hairstyle. When she went up to the altar for Holy Communion and tilted her head back to accept the wafer, her hair fell away from her face and the minister gasped aloud to see the damage to her face. The next day, he phoned and asked if she would be willing to talk with him and asked if they could pray together. She felt relief in her heart to know that now, finally, someone else knew what was happening and might be able to help. Knowing that Damon would not be at home, she told her minister that he could come to the house the next night.

"When he came, accompanied by one of the older deacons, she told the story of her misery, and they were horrified. Before they left, her minister prayed with her with fervency in his heart, and it brought her peace. It was a relief that someone else knew what she was going through, and someone would be praying for her. She believed that God would help her. She'd read the Bible and she believed that God would turn Damon's heart if she would set the right example. She trusted the words in the Bible and she felt that she was required of God to remain with Damon.

"Her minister had suggested she tell her parents what was happening. Having seen her face, he understood how brutally her husband had attacked her, and he was afraid for her. Victoria agreed to follow his suggestion and decided to tell her parents, but she also decided to ask them if she could stay with them for a while. She thought that if she left Damon and he believed it permanent, he might miss his family enough to change his behavior. But when she asked her parents if she could move back home with them, her father was willing, but her mother was not, saying she would be too nervous to have little children around again. Victoria was surprised by her mother's response and panicked to think that she had no one to help her and no safe haven to which she could run.

"Victoria tried to be the perfect wife so Damon would not find reason to attack her. She pretended to be asleep when he came home at night. She filled her time with friends and family, craft projects, charity work, and a part-time job. To circumvent any criticism she'd work around the house to keep everything in perfect order until she'd drop from exhaustion. She ironed his boxer shorts. Sometimes she would garner the courage to ask where he'd been when he was gone for days at a time, but he would just walk away from her sneering, telling her it was none of her business. His conduct worsened as if he were testing her and as if he knew that she had no place to go.

"Her ministers continued to pray for her day and night. They would visit her home every few weeks so they could all pray together. But, one evening, Damon came home unexpectedly while the ministers were there. They greeted him warmly and invited him to pray with them before they left, but Damon refused to join them, staying at the back of the house. When they did leave, Damon came into the living room where Victoria was tidying up and, furious, slapped her across the face, telling her that it was his house, and he didn't want them there . . . ever. He placed his hand over the top of the zipper area of his trousers, grabbed his body through them, and, moving his hand up and down, said to her, *"That's what I think of them and their praying and your whole church for that matter. If I ever see them in this house again I'll kill you and them too"* Victoria had to ask her ministers not to come to her home again. They offered to pray with her in the sacristy after church services. And Victoria wondered what God had thought of what Damon had said and done in reference to the ministers and the church. When she prayed, she asked God where He was and why He did not protect her. She asked why He did not change Damon's heart.

"Her children were now old enough to understand—one close to graduation from high school, the other two years younger. When Damon was especially violent with her and she screamed, her youngest child would awaken and come from the bedroom to try to stop Damon from hurting her. Occasionally, Damon would come home before the children went to bed, and they would witness his attack; and if they intervened, he'd hurt them too. After the attack, he'd leave and sometimes be gone for days, often over a weekend. It never occurred to Victoria that he must have kept extra clothing somewhere else.

"Victoria began to notice that she would see an unusual shine or gleam in Damon's eyes when he was about to launch a severe attack. When she saw his eyes light up in this fashion, she felt strongly that some evil had entered him, ruled him, and made him enjoy hurting her. Her heart would pound in fear. She learned to watch his eyes because it was a sure indicator of danger. She learned that when she saw this occur, it was best to run and hide.

"Sometimes she would lock herself in the bathroom to get away. But as often as not, he would break the door down or make so much noise that the children would awaken. He was furious if the children tried to protect her and would often lift his son off the floor and put his shoulder through the sheetrock wall. Victoria was not strong enough to protect herself or stop him from hurting her child; she could only warn her children to stay in their rooms. Damon weighed over 220 pounds, was stocky, and had powerful arms and shoulders and no compunction about harming his wife or children.

"On occasion, Victoria found the courage to fight back, hitting him back and yelling, asking him why he did these things; but this re-action only fueled his anger and somehow gave him the "right" to do more harm, cause greater injury to her. There were occasions when she just didn't care anymore and would let him know what she thought of his actions and what he was doing to their family. His pattern of hitting, cursing, yelling, laughing, calling her vile names, hitting some more, kicking, spitting, breaking something which Victoria loved, storming out of the house, and then staying away for days seemed endless to her. She knew that she was starting to give up and thought that he might even kill her.

"One day, Damon came home in the middle of the day, his car careening into the driveway. He ran up the stairs to the bedroom with Victoria following and thinking that something terrible must have happened. He went to her dresser and rummaged through her jewelry while she asked what was wrong. He located the necklace which Francesca had given her, slapped Victoria across the face, spit at her and ran down the stairs and out the door, and all Victoria heard was the squeal of the tires as he left.

"He did not come home that night. When he came home the following night, he was the most vicious she had ever seen him. He went into the bedroom and took a small three drawer end table which Victoria had just finished sanding, staining, and painted with a beautiful paisley design then varnished, and he threw it off the deck with all his strength where it hit the ground and smashed into many pieces. He walked over to her and viciously kicked her knees bringing her to the ground, then told her to stay out of his way, called her names, but would not otherwise speak to her. He threw the food from the table onto the floor then went into the bedroom and packed a suitcase, all the while screaming that he had thrown her "boyfriend's" necklace out the window of the car, and if she wanted it, she could crawl on her hands and knees along the highway to look for it. Victoria hadn't the foggiest idea what he was talking about, and when she tried to ask him, he beat her severely using his fists and left the house with his suitcase. He was gone for three days and when he came home would not talk about the incident.

"During the course of the next two years, Victoria began getting letters in the mail. They were not signed and were written as if someone wrote them with their left hand or as if the author was somewhat illiterate. The letters said that Damon was having an affair. They hinted that the husband of the woman with whom he was having the affair wrote the letters. They were addressed to Victoria, warning her to tell Damon to stay away from his wife. The letters came almost every week. Victoria brought the letters to the postal authorities, and they kept them, telling her that they would investigate to see if they could locate the person who was sending them. Since the letters threatened both Damon and Victoria's life, the post office had reason to take action.

"About a year after the letters began Victoria came home from the grocery store, pressed the garage door opener, and pulled her car into the garage. As she opened her car door, a man ran out of the door leading from the house to the garage. He ran through the garage toward the driveway, slamming the car door into the leg which Victoria had extended out of the car onto the garage floor. He ran through the open garage door and up the driveway to the road and turned toward the highway.

"The man Victoria saw was unfamiliar to her, but he was nicely dressed in a rust-colored leather jacket and matching shoes, had reddish hair cut just below his ears, and had either a thin beard or a goatee. He had fair skin which appeared flushed. Victoria called the police. The police inspected the house and determined that he had entered the house by forcing the basement door. However, nothing was missing and nothing seemed amiss, except that another letter had been left and was lying on the floor in the master bedroom next to the bed, on the side where Damon slept. The letter again accused Damon of having an affair with the wife of the writer and also, this time, of having affairs with at least half a dozen other women.

"After years of abuse, years of pain and desolation, years of trips to the hospital for her bruises, Victoria could take no more and decided that she must do something. She'd tried prayer, she'd tried to be faithful to God and to obey what she believed the Bible asked her to do, she'd tried to be a good wife, she'd tried making herself as attractive as possible, and nothing worked. Her ministers had believed that God would change Damon or bring a change of some kind to this suffering family. At this point, even they felt she should get a divorce rather than risk permanent injury or death. They advised Victoria that her children needed her, and that she was their only role model and their only link to the church.

"Victoria thought things over carefully. She decided that she would give the marriage one last chance by waiting one year. She asked God to help her be a truly perfect wife, never yelling back, never complaining, never asking where Damon had been, even if he was gone for days. She wanted to graciously accept whatever he brought . . . for one year. She wanted to do this to prove to *herself* that she had done all she could and to prove to God how hard she tried, and also so that Damon would also someday know how hard she had tried. She asked God to bring about that which He wanted for her by the end of this year, so she would know beyond a shadow of a doubt which path to take.

"Victoria looked at herself objectively to be sure in her own heart that she had done the best she could. She'd wanted to make her husband see what a treasure he had in his home, his children, his family, and even in her. She'd followed suggestions made by other people, even when she did not agree with their advice. She'd gone to counseling, to her ministers, she'd prayed, she'd tried to talk with her husband when he had not been drinking, she'd even tried to talk to his best friend. She'd even asked and followed Francesca's advice for a while. She'd done everything she could. She knew that she had made mistakes in the past; that she too had yelled, hit back, and had done many things wrong; but she also knew that she had done everything humanly possible to make the marriage work. She had mastered her willpower and did not respond in kind to his cruelty and she could now act rather than react to what he did.

"Toward the end of that year, Victoria saw a lawyer and started the proceedings for a divorce. She had no money. Over the past five years, Damon had systematically taken and cancelled her charge cards and checkbook, giving her only grocery money in cash. The lawyers required a retainer, without which they would not take her case. She borrowed the money for a retainer from her father who was now retired and who was to become her staunchest ally during the divorce.

"It was a bitter divorce. Damon told her that he had hired the best lawyer money could buy and would spend every penny he had to make sure that she would end up "in the gutter" and "totally alone". As with all abused wives, she still thought that she loved him; that he was a good person inside and just a sad and misguided person outside, and she did not believe that he meant what he said. Thus, Victoria was genuinely startled by his venomous attitude and actions throughout the divorce. She'd thought he would split everything evenly and allow her enough time to get a job, an apartment, and to make a life of her own. Instead, he would call and tell her that he hated her, had never loved her, wanted to be free, and planned to make the proceedings a fight to the death. He wanted everything. He said that he would not rest until he saw her ruined. He even said these things in front of the children who were also still afraid of him.

"His affidavits were full of lies. During the court proceedings, Victoria was shocked to learn that he had also lied about a home improvement loan they had taken for a rental property they had purchased. Whenever they had applied for a loan in the past, Damon told her to fill out the forms, and either he would sign his name or tell her to sign his name if he would not be coming home. The routine into which they'd fallen was that she would obtain the loan money, put it in the bank, order the materials they needed for the renovations, and begin the work. He was rarely home, so she did most of the work connected to their projects or hired people to do what she could not. It was the method they had always used because he recognized how hard she worked on these projects and how much he reaped the benefits of her labor and of her decorating skills . . . and *he* always kept the income he collected from these properties. In the past he would pay off the loan over time and because Victoria had no access to the checking account she'd assumed he'd done the same with this loan. But he had not.

"Damon had always said that because she worked so hard on the rental property that no matter what ever happened between them it would be hers. Victoria and her family, and often friends from her church had labored to improve the properties and therefore Victoria trusted in those words. But when the divorce proceedings started, there was an outstanding loan for sixteen thousand dollars which Victoria had used a year earlier to renovate the lower floor (and kitchen) of a beach property. Knowing that Victoria had signed Damon's name to the loan (via his instruction), he claimed that she took the loan and the money without his knowledge. He told this to his lawyer, to the judge, and to the bank. As a result, the bank wanted their loan paid back immediately, or they would file fraud charges against her. Victoria had no funds with which to repay the loan. Her lawyer told the bank what had happened and asked them to wait until the divorce was over as they would be paid from the top of all proceeds. Damon wanted to refuse the bank the money but his lawyer explained that Victoria's bookkeeping records, photos of the renovation, and her children's testimony would hurt Damon if he did not agree to pay the bank. His goal had been to ruin Victoria's reputation and future credit record. His lies and vindictiveness shocked her. Thoughts and plans of such venom had never been a part of her heart, and she did not understand them thus was never prepared for them.

"Every penny of the loan proceeds had gone to remodeling the rental unit they owned (per Damon's instruction), and as usual, Victoria and her family had done all the work attached to the project. Victoria's uncle had worked for weeks to help her install the kitchen, driving two hours each way, each day to get there and never accepting a penny for his work! The irony was that Victoria, knowing green to be Damon's favorite color, had completed this renovation using green as the predominant color scheme . . . just to please Damon. Victoria was stunned to learn that the judge and the bank were informed via an affidavit that Victoria had signed Damon's name to the loan without his consent and had kept the money, thus it appeared that Victoria was a liar and a thief and that her character was blemished.

"Victoria was truly shocked by Damon's behavior, by his ability to lie so easily, and his willingness to lie so vehemently about her. She had no defense except for the receipts for what had been purchased for the renovation and a set of photographs of the before and after pictures she took of the renovated area. The judge however, was not convinced that Damon had always previously and then again this time authorized Victoria to obtain loans and held this false accusation against Victoria. Victoria could not believe that Damon had gone this far.

"Further, Victoria's timing was off. Courts were swaying toward husband's rights rather than considering the plight of the stay-at-home mom's future financial status, and Damon told her that he didn't care how much the divorce cost; he would continue to fight and to drive up her attorney costs until she gave him what he wanted. With Damon determined to drag it out until she caved and the stress of worry and testimony and all the paperwork his lawyer kept demanding, Victoria, after two years of lawyers and courts, decided to give him what he wanted and just end it.

"Still, in her heart of hearts, she foolishly thought he would do the right thing rather than have on his conscience what he had done. But he did not. He took most of the assets she had built by her hard work and the hard work of her family, and what she had invested in their twenty-seven-year marriage was for nought. Victoria gave up and came away knowing that Damon was gloating over his win and hoped to see her broken. Despite her stay-at-home status and a marriage of twenty-seven years, he paid no alimony and gave her far less than half of what their properties were worth . . . and he kept one and she had nowhere to go. He was delighted. He had won, and he believed that he had finally broken her!

Grandma had finished her story for today and Sarah could see that she was emotionally exhausted to have to re-live all that pain. But Sarah also knew that though Damon both thought and hoped that he had broken her, she was not broken. Sarah knew that she was to get up fighting again to make a new life for herself, a life where she could have the home she always dreamed of, where God would live, where a prayer life and a loving family life could exist. Grandma would do it and be amazed by how God would bless her in the future and how He could turn her sorrow into joy.

Chapter Six

MISTAKES AND QUICK FIXES

"**H**oney, today I thought I'd change course a bit to explain how attractive something can appear if it claims to be a solution to one's problems. When I recognized the danger in some of the advice these provided, I began to understand how incredibly subtle Satan is and how he uses our need to draw us away from God. So let me tell you what happened. I'd like to go back into the same type of narration I've been using because it helps me remain separate from the experience to a certain extent. Is that okay?"

"Of course, Grandma. The narration you have devised also helps me because I too can, to a certain degree separate the consequences of your story from you . . . from the person I love so much that I feel anger when I know someone hurt you."

"Oh Sarah, that is what I wanted to avoid. I wanted to tell the story impersonally, but just don't know how. Although what occurred may seem harsh and though I did feel its difficulties at the time, God performed incredible miracles in my heart and life . . . and it was all turned into a blessing. Really it was."

"Okay Grandma, I believe you . . . in fact just by thinking back on the life you had once I was around, and seeing who and what you have become . . . I can see that . . . that . . . well . . . that God must have . . . well . . . healed you somehow . . . and . . . well . . . done something!"

"He did a lot! He allowed me to learn, to see where I wanted my life to go, what kind of a person I wanted to be, and brought me into my faith and the incredible offer He provides to every person who ever lived or died. So, how could I not appreciate what occurred?"

"I guess you're right Grandma . . . but it is becoming quite an eye-opener for me. I've never in my life heard anyone who was thankful for their troubles. But again, you have me curious so please continue your story."

"Okay . . . here we go."

"Carey had been a close friend of Victoria's neighbor for many years. They met at one of the gatherings which her neighbor regularly held on the Fourth of July and on Memorial Day and Labor Day. Carey was a lovely person, beautiful, well groomed, a good homemaker and mother, and considerate. She had a strong belief in God, and was raising three beautiful and well-behaved children. Victoria and Carey would talk together when they'd see one another at Victoria's neighbors' house and learned that they shared many interests and had similar views on life. Over time, the two women developed a close relationship even though Carey was ten years older than Victoria.

"Carey was a wonderful friend. She'd telephone regularly, she'd visit often, and she'd invite just as often. She was quick to prepare a cup of tea and serve something special to go with it. Though her children were older than Victoria's, she didn't mind when Victoria brought her children and would make a special treat for them to enjoy as well. Carey had an empathetic nature and was a good listener.

"With her very fair and beautiful complexion and her blond hair styled in a pageboy cut which fell softly to her shoulders, Carey was very pretty. She had large sad, thoughtful, intelligent, light blue eyes with long dark lashes, which gave her an ethereal look of fragility. She was about five feet five inches tall, and though considered slender by others, she worried that her hip measurement was a little larger than she wanted. She always wore black because she felt it was slenderizing to her figure. To everyone else, she was close to perfect.

"Carey's dad was a builder, so he had built her a home, paying for most of the materials himself. It was a large ranch-style house with a well thought-out floor plan and a wonderfully large bright and airy kitchen. Carey loved to cook and made healthy well-balanced meals for her family. She also made terrific (and healthy) blueberry muffins, which everyone loved and which Victoria looked forward to enjoying whenever she visited. Carey kept her home neat and was an all-around excellent homemaker.

"But, she was unhappy in her marriage because her husband chose to spend his time at the local bar and in the company of other women. Carey didn't know how to cope with this and at first tried to fix her marriage, but later just accepted that it would never be right. Both husband and wife fell into an atmosphere of being room-mates rather than husband and wife. Carey looked for solace through her church, friends, and self-help books; but she wasn't able to find the answers which could help her find any real joy in life. After years of searching, she began to meet with a priest in her church for counseling who understood how she felt and who became a friend in whom she could confide.

"In Carey, Victoria found a friend to talk to about her own marriage, and together they shared their heartaches, usually over a cup of tea. They talked about what they hoped for in life, about their faith in God, their love for their children, the negative impact their husbands had on their children, and about what they could do about their situations. Neither woman felt they had a marketable skill which would allow them to earn enough money to leave their husbands and support their children. They'd both tried counseling, but after a while, even the counselors could do nothing if the husbands weren't willing to talk about why they did the things they did. Carey's husband, however, was not violent and had never struck Carey. Carey feared for Victoria's life when she heard and saw what Damon did to her.

"When the last of Carey's children was close to completing high school, Carey met a woman who suggested she'd find the help she sought through the use of astrology. Carey began to attend classes in astrology, and with the help of her instructor, she developed her astrological chart and one for her husband. These charts indicated that a divorce would take place the following year, and after that, Carey would enter into a period of great happiness; further, she would become the loving person and great teacher which she was destined to become.

"Hand in hand with this experience, Carey began having tarot card readings. The cards confirmed what her astrological charts told her; that she would be divorced. The cards told her that once she was free of her marriage, she would meet someone special, someone younger than she was. She looked forward to this day and now had something to hope for. Shortly thereafter and amazing to Victoria, Carey and her husband obtained an annulment of their marriage even though they had three grown children and had been married for well over thirty years. With this annulment, they could each re-marry someone else and do so in their church.

"But as events unfolded, Carey went from one relationship to another, always being told by the cards or the charts that this would be the love of her life, always having these divination tools tell her what to do and when to do it. Carey always followed the advice which the astrological charts and tarot cards offered and Victoria began to worry about her friend.

"As Carey studied astrology and tarot and began to understand these mechanisms, she created charts and did readings about her family members and her friends. Carey telephoned Victoria one day, quite upset by indications in her charts that Victoria would be terribly concerned by an accident which was soon to befall Victoria's daughter. Carey explained that she had drawn up Victoria's astrological chart as an exercise in her classes and discovered that Victoria's daughter would soon have a boating accident and sustain an injury to her rib cage. She'd also done follow-up inquiries through the tarot cards and these had confirmed what the charts had determined.

"This was incredible to Victoria because of how specific the message was. Up to this point, she'd thought that tarot and astrology were "just for fun." Frighteningly, ten days later, the accident occurred exactly as predicted. When this happened, Victoria felt bewildered and wondered what all this meant. At that moment, she became a believer in everything that Carey could tell her and wanted to know about her life and her future, wanted a personal astrological chart, wanted to study astrology, wanted to have a chart done for every member of her family. Victoria bought books from the bookstore and haunted the library for more books; she poured over the information and began to understand how to make sense out of the words and the charts and even how to draw up a chart.

"She learned how to use an ephemeris which listed the positions of the planets at varying times and how to use this to create an astrological chart. She purchased her own ephemeris so she could create charts for her family members. Meanwhile, Carey also studied astrology and tarot and became proficient in them and began to offer these services to others. She would phone Victoria every day with the advice which came from the cards.

"Victoria began to hunger for the information Carey obtained from the cards and the charts. Not yet divorced herself, Victoria asked for information about her husband, about other women, about the future, about divorce. She thought that if she could just know what to do, she could fix everything. Victoria, like Carey, was hooked.

"But after a few months of seeking advice from Carey through the cards and charts, Victoria began to notice that the advice she was given was not really "right" somehow; that it seemed destructive and contrary to biblical principles. So Victoria stepped back and looked carefully at what years of this type of advice had brought to Carey's life.

"Victoria became wary of this practice and noticed that the choices which Carey made for her life and which had been suggested by the tarot cards or through the astrological charts were becoming devastating to her life. As Carey's life unfolded day by day, Victoria noted the situations and choices which she knew deep in her heart could not possibly be pleasing to God.

"Carey was allowing her astrological chart and tarot card readings to direct her every move, every relationship, every choice. She allowed the cards to describe the "rightness" of entering into a number of love affairs often with people Carey would never have chosen on her own. The "cards" told her she was a bearer of love and instruction to these men and that she was "meant" to help them through the circumstances which they were experiencing. Carey believed this with all her heart. No matter what Victoria said or did, Carey continued along this path believing it to be God's will for her and therefore her destiny.

"Victoria could plainly see that the choices Carey made were ungodly and she became afraid for Carey's soul salvation. In time, Carey's financial state became dire. She tried to earn money by developing a clientele for tarot readings and astrological charts, but she could never make enough money to sustain her. She went deeper into debt while the cards told her all would be okay and that she must be patient and continue building her clientele. It broke Victoria's heart to see Carey slip into a life of solitude and hardship. Victoria saw this destruction and didn't know how to help her friend.

"Victoria turned to the Bible and began to study everything she could find in scripture about astrology and fortune telling. She wanted to learn what God said on this subject and purchased a concordance so she could look for words relating to astrology, soothsaying, and fortune-telling and through its cross reference, locate those verses in the Bible. Victoria found an incredible number of warnings about these subjects and diligently researched everything she could find. Victoria also found words describing God's direction for their lives and the need to depend only on Him, not something else. She saw how astrology and tarot had become what scripture called "other gods" to Carey. And then understood how scripture was God's gifts of safety and redemption for His children . . . if only they would listen.

"After learning what the Bible said, Victoria burned the astrology and tarot books she had purchased because she did not want anyone else to have access to them. As she watched them burn in the fireplace she was sure that her imagination was working overtime because the books appeared to curl into the most horrible and agonized faces as they burned. When she mentioned this to her minister he told her that those faces were of the spirits attached to those books.

"Victoria compiled information for Carey and made copies of the scriptures which addressed astrology and all related topics. She made up a little journal for Carey, which contained all the information she had acquired, and she asked her minister to visit Carey and talk to her about what she was doing. Carey welcomed his visit and though they discussed the words in scripture, Carey would not listen. She did ask her own minister if she could continue in her astrology studies with the approval of her church, and he told her that he would consult with someone in a higher office and get back to her. Within a few weeks sadly, Carey was informed that it was acceptable in her church to pursue her studies in astrology and Tarot and to give these readings to others.

"Victoria was worried for Carey and could do nothing but pray for her, and from that day on, Victoria carried a fear of all occult practices in her heart. She now understood the power behind them and knew that such power came from Satan. This experience became Victoria's first recognition of the powerful and cunning force of Satan and the beginning of a deep perusal of scripture. It broke her heart to see Carey remain on such a dangerous path. She felt that anything that proclaimed astrology and fortune-telling as a harbinger of light and goodness for others could only be out-and-out lies and could only be satanic . . . and never come from God.

"Victoria also recognized the desire in mankind to know the future, and also began to see that these practices temporarily imbued man with a power which they could use to their advantage . . . or so they thought. They were drawn to it for selfish purposes and when they were hooked, Satan could do with them as he pleased. Victoria didn't like to acknowledge that there was indeed a desire for one-upmanship which initially drew people . . . and Victoria . . . to these practices.

"Victoria tried again and again to dissuade Carey from using tarot cards and astrology to guide her every step. Carey would phone her every time she saw something worrisome in Victoria's life through her cards or charts. But Victoria did not want to listen; she was afraid because she knew the source of this information.

"Sadly, in time, Victoria was forced to run away from their friendship because she could not prevent Carey from trying to tell her what was to come into Victoria's future. Victoria was frightened and horrified to see evil work so subtly and so surely. She was astounded that some of the actions suggested by the cards could be viewed as being God's will when they were so obviously ungodly. She wondered what had happened to Carey's good sense.

"This was Victoria's first realization that advice for situations such as these could be found in the Bible and compiled from many different areas in the Bible and put together to form a complete overview for tackling her concerns. She was amazed by how clearly the verses from scripture provided warnings and direction. She compiled a list of the verses which she had shown Carey, and kept them in a little box on her desk. She wanted to remember them and to have them on hand should she meet someone to whom she could also warn about the power behind these practices. On occasion she would re-read them so they would stay in her memory and specifically remembered three of them.

Take ye therefore good heed . . .
lest thou lift up thine eyes unto heaven, and . . .
seest the sun, and the moon, and the stars, even all the host of heaven, shouldest
be driven to worship them, and serve them.
—*Deuteronomy 4:15, 19*

Therefore shall evil come upon thee;
thou shalt not know from whence it riseth . . .
Stand now with thine enchantments,
and with the multitude of thy sorceries . . .

Let now the astrologers, the stargazers,
the monthly prognosticators, stand up, and save thee.

—*Isaiah 47:11-13*

For he built up again the high places . . .
and worshipped all the host of heaven, and served them.
And he built altars for all the host of heaven
in the two courts of the house of the LORD.
And he made his son pass through the fire,
and observed times, and used enchantments,
and dealt with familiar spirits and wizards:
he wrought much wickedness in the sight of the LORD,
to provoke him to anger.

—*2 Kings 21:3-6*

"Once Victoria knew that she could no longer turn to Carey, she longed for another woman with whom she could discuss her concerns; and though she had many friends, they were happily married, and she did not feel that she should burden them with her troubles. They all thought she was happily married. Divorce was unusual in those days and a stigma.

"A few years before she was divorced, Victoria, in desperation turned to her sister for help. It was when she'd decided to try one more time to save her marriage. Surprisingly Victoria met with an empathetic ear and Victoria was reminded that a while back her sister had given her a necklace, and perhaps this meant that Francesca wanted them to become closer. So Victoria told her sister about Damon's abuse, and Francesca gave her advice. Nothing that Victoria had done had worked, so perhaps following her sister's advice would work.

Francesca told her that with some men, a woman needed to prove she was desirable to other men and could thus be independent. She told her that men hated a subservient woman and admired an independent woman. She suggested that Victoria go out at night to show Damon that she was *not* the "wimp" he thought she was and show him that she too could have a good time. Francesca told her that by making him jealous, she'd make him see how lucky he was and he would want to stay at home at night.

"Francesca offered to take Victoria to the place where she spent time, and guaranteed that they would have a good time together. Victoria's children were old enough to stay by themselves, so she decided to join her sister one evening . . . but it was, for her . . . a horrible evening. Victoria pretended to enjoy the evening and, being a natural people pleaser, did not want her sister to be disappointed in her, so she did not complain. But it was an atmosphere which Victoria hated.

"They had gone to a bar. There was a dance floor toward the back. Men and women were there by the droves, and many people wore wedding rings, yet to Victoria anyone could see that they weren't with their spouse. Francesca had left her wedding ring at home. Music blared loudly, drinks flowed, people mixed, and many would dance to the roaring noise of the rock music. Francesca steered them to the bar to sit, and many men eyed them from across the room, later walking over to them to initiate a conversation.

"Victoria was introduced to a psychologist, an airline pilot, a physician, and an engineer all in one evening. They were all interested in her, and she was impressed by the stories they told her about their careers. She was amazed by the educational background everyone in the bar seemed to have. But she was nervous and uncomfortable and excused herself to go to the ladies' room, asking her sister to accompany her.

"In the ladies' room, Francesca burst out laughing as Victoria told how surprised she was by the number of men with such a great education and interesting vocation. Francesca explained that this was part of the game, that none of them were who they said they were, that everyone lied, that it was expected and was part of the game everyone played to escape the realities of their dull lives. Francesca sardonically commented that the psychologist was probably a part time stock boy in the local Wal-Mart. Victoria had never heard of this "game" before and was appalled by it. How sad, she thought. Why lie, why pretend, why do these things? Francesca told her to watch and listen carefully when they went back, and she would recognize that what Francesca told her was true.

"So back they went, and Francesca began telling the men hovering near them at the bar that Victoria was an airline stewardess based out of California and here on a two-day layover. She made up incredible stories about the celebrities Victoria knew and the exotic places she had visited. Everyone seemed to believe Francesca and even asked Victoria questions. But Victoria was embarrassed and frightened, not wanting to respond with a lie. It was something that she had never done and something she didn't want to do. It was difficult to weasel out of giving anyone her phone number so Francesca gave it for her, but gave them a fake number.

"On the way home, Victoria told her sister that she wasn't cut out for a place like that, and Francesca told her that she needed to give it a fair chance and go at least three times before she gave up. She told Victoria that she would see a change in Damon in a few short weeks. Victoria trusted her sister's advice and agreed to try again because she was so desperate to find something which would work.

"The next time was much the same. Victoria was not used to drinking, and after two drinks, she asked for a glass of Perrier with lemon, hoping no one would know it wasn't liquor. She danced this time, hoping it would eliminate talking and lying. But even on the dance floor, the game was played, and the lies flowed. She kept her word and went for the third and last time. Francesca told her she needed to choose one man to have a conversation with so she could receive the flattery necessary for her to re-gain her confidence which would make her feel like a whole person again and teach her to stand up to Damon. Victoria thought that her sister must believe that this advice would help her find a way to be happy and to change Damon's behavior.

"But Victoria hated it and never returned to that scene, not even when she was single again. She felt that following her sister's advice had been another mistake made and regretted. Sadly, Francesca was furious with her refusal to continue going to the bar, demanding that she go, and their relationship again dwindled; her sister telling her she was a "Holy Roller," a "goody two-shoes," and a "lost cause." Francesca felt that Victoria was judging her because she did like the bars, the men, and the flirtations. Victoria knew that those places were not for her and felt badly that her sister was so angry, but the bar scene was not one she could deal with, so she never went again. It had been a big mistake on her part and had only fueled Francesca's anger with her.

"Before Victoria finally went to see a lawyer, she made another mistake, but one which gave her the courage and self-esteem to get through the divorce proceedings. In fact, she knew that despite knowing it was wrong, she'd do it again in a heartbeat because it had changed her life for the better, helped her to see herself as someone who could be loved by someone else. Despite knowing it was wrong and wondering if God forgave sins one would again repeat, Victoria made her decision.

"Damon had repeatedly told her that she was worthless. He said that she'd never be able to "make it" out in the world, and if she ever left him, she would end up in the "gutter." He'd also said, time and time again, that no one liked her, that people felt sorry for her, and that she was the "least desirable woman in the world," and the biggest "wimp."

"Victoria had taken a part-time job and met someone at work who shared her views and with whom she could talk openly. In time, she told him of the troubles in her marriage. He liked Victoria and considered her a wonderful woman, friendly, talented, and intelligent. He admired her work ethic and her honesty. He admired how kind she was to everyone, even those who didn't deserve her kindness. As he listened to her story, he'd encourage her efforts to make her marriage better. But over time, with the physical abuse she told him about, and from which Victoria's black and blue marks came, he felt that she should divorce Damon, sure that she would find someone worthy of her in no time. He always had a positive attitude which Victoria admired and he was wise and kind. He was ten years younger than Victoria.

"Victoria knew that he liked her as a friend and as a team player at work. She'd seen firsthand how good his communication skills were and had watched how he handled discord at work. She admired his win-win philosophy of never putting anyone down, never losing his temper, and always being willing to talk things out to a resolution. She grew to respect him and used him as a role model.

"She felt, over time, that he would ask her for a date if she were single. She'd daydream about him and sometimes imagine a life with him when things were especially bad at home. She knew he'd never actually date her until she was divorced because he was such an honorable person and also felt strongly that their age difference would be a problem in her mind because he had a whole life ahead of him. With a woman his age or younger, he would have children and share so much more than he could with her.

"Both of them always seemed to place the feelings and the well-being of others above their own. Recognizing the kindness in one another drew them together in trust. They both felt blessed to have such a nice friendship.

"All this occurred near the end of the year when Victoria had been trying to be perfect at home and before she filed for divorce. She did not seem to be making headway with Damon and wished there was some magic solution to make their marriage work.

"One night, Damon came home with bright red lipstick all over one side of his shirt collar. Seeing this was like putting a knife into Victoria's heart. But it made her see her marriage as it really was and not how she imagined or hoped it was. It made her understand . . . finally . . . that her marriage was and had been for a very long time simply a convenience for Damon. But because she had vowed to be the perfect wife for the rest of this year, she gritted her teeth, smiled up at him, and said she'd wash the lipstick off his collar in the morning. She said this quickly, and with the same breath told him lightly that she'd done his wash that day and ironed his shirts. She wanted him to realize she had glossed over the lipstick part and would show no anger, ask no questions, and wasn't upset. She could tell he was surprised and suddenly felt free of the pain for the first time in over twenty years.

"The next day, she thought about the lipstick, the first tangible evidence of her husband's close proximity to another woman. She thought about how she had been fooling herself all these years. She wondered about what he always said about her being unattractive, about her lack of sexual appeal, lack of warmth, whether or not she was considered cold. She wondered whether or not Damon was right about her. She had nothing to compare herself to. She'd heard from Damon for years that no one else would want her. Yet, she also knew that many people considered her pretty and some thought her beautiful. Nevertheless, it was Damon's opinion which had mattered.

"Thinking about this, she went to the library the next day and brought home books about intimacy, and pleasing a man and read them from cover to cover. She didn't find much in these books that she hadn't known. In fact, the books proved that she was fairly well informed. She had from time to time purchased beautiful lingerie and had tried to be enticing, but there was doubt in her mind; and she wondered if maybe this was, after all, the crux of the problem.

"Victoria decided to discuss this with her friend at work. He was the perfect candidate for this conversation because he was honest and open . . . and a man who would probably know what men looked for. When he heard Victoria's concerns, he burst out laughing. Victoria was dismayed, hurt and embarrassed. But then he told her that he had laughed because she was so incredibly off base. He told her that she was lusciously appealing not only in how she looked, but also in the way she talked and smiled and walked. He told her that unless she felt that there was a physical problem, any man would be happy with her. He went on to explain that intimacy was important but worked only if both partners shared that intimacy . . . and felt loved and could be tender and communicative with one another . . . and trusted one another.

"He explained that loving someone came from the heart first and then from the mind. When true love could express itself emotionally or from the heart, and spiritually from a mind desirous of its righteousness, before expressing itself physically, it would produce an unsurpassed intimacy. Lust however, was different and needed very little to express itself but it was not something of lasting value.

"Victoria listened carefully to his words and thought about what he'd said and suddenly realized that intimacy and heart was lacking in her relationship with Damon. In fact, she'd never witnessed any intimacy between Damon and *anyone* else . . . not his mother, his siblings, his friends, children, or even with her. That it had always been missing.

"Listening to her friend, Victoria longed to know what it would be like to experience closeness and tenderness and communication with someone. She'd begun noticing husbands who touched their wives when walking or sitting together. She watched them lightly touch their wife's waist or stroke their arm or lay a hand on their leg in a way that said "I love you," or they might kiss their head or hand, or rub their neck. And Victoria realized that she had never experienced these moments with Damon and, in fact, would be rebuffed if she had tried to touch her husband. *He'd never even hugged his children or his mother. It was Damon who was flawed . . . him, not her!*

"In that moment, Victoria decided that if her friend would be willing, she wanted to be closer to him. She wanted to learn, once and for all, that there was nothing wrong with her. In the back of her mind she knew what she wanted was wrong, but suddenly, she didn't care. Suddenly she wanted this with all her heart. The lipstick on the Damon's collar had been the final straw. She wanted to know what it was like to experience tenderness and touch and communication . . . and trust with someone.

"Victoria's friend laughed when she excitedly asked him for a date . . . a real date. To him she was adorable and he'd been in love with her for quite a while. He understood her need and he also understood that she would surely gain confidence from having someone openly adore her as he did. "Okay" he'd said, "Tomorrow we are going to go out to dinner together and just talk and communicate and . . . I might even reach over and touch your hand or put my arm across your shoulder and you can sigh and tell me how wonderful I am".

"Victoria laughed then too and though he spoke of just a date, Victoria hoped it would become more than that. And it did and it was. In fact, it was wonderful! The tenderness of it touched her heart; it was an incredible experience. For the first time in her life, she felt truly attractive, loved, whole, and confident. She learned for the first time that tenderness was a key factor in loving someone because it made everything so much better and gentler and somehow . . . good. She felt as if she were flying and would find herself singing for no reason. Her face glowed with happiness, and she no longer worried that she was unworthy of being loved.

"They'd spend hours talking and talking, walking, and walking. She was happy with him. And she was grateful for his friendship. They shared something special, and she never wanted to hurt him in anyway. She wanted him to be happy. He'd taught her what a real relationship was like. It wasn't just being intimate, it was respect and admiration, it was trust and courtesy, it was consideration and thoughtfulness. It was expressing love in words or gestures or actions and smiling into someone's eyes. It was to trust one another with everything. It was gentle. It was a communication and intimacy which she'd never had before.

"She also loved and admired the way he argued. He never raised his voice, never name-called, never seemed to show anger. He was, she thought, like a lawyer arguing a case before a jury, trying to sway with profound reason to his way of thinking. He was reasonable; he listened, and . . . he could be swayed if the facts of the discussion proved him wrong. She wanted to learn to argue the way he did if she ever had to argue! She wanted to learn from him.

"Victoria considered a future with him. He was her best friend. He'd given her a gift that no other person had . . . the gift of herself . . . of who and what she was . . . and of what she wanted in life . . . and of how to truly love someone. But she knew that a future with him would be unfair to him. He had never been married, had never had children, and had told her many times in the past when they were just office buddies that he wanted children someday. She had two grown children and would not have more. He was ten years younger and had not suffered the ravages of emotional pain as had she. How could she love him and saddle him with her past, her baggage? How could she deny him the youth, children, strength, and innocence of a wife closer to his age?

"The wife that Victoria envisioned for him would be fifteen years younger than she was! And she would also be of the same faith which he and his family practiced. She would give him children and she'd adore him just as much as Victoria adored him. If someone really loved someone else, wouldn't they want the best for them, wouldn't they bury their own selfish desire for the needs of the one they loved?

"She talked to him about her concerns, about her faith, the guilt she felt about their relationship, her difficulty in continuing something she felt was wrong, the children he deserved to have someday, her moral system, and his future. He told her he loved her, but he also understood her and understood that what she said was true. But he also told her that he believed that they could overcome the obstacles and that he was willing to give up some of those things for her. He told her that life did not always give you everything . . . and that what they had was so special that he would never miss whatever she felt she could not give him. But she did not agree with him. She knew that she had to walk away for now to satisfy her need to be right with God . . . and fair to him. He hoped that she would come back. Somehow he understood that she would not.

"They talked for hours, and together they decided not to continue their relationship at this time, but to revisit their relationship after she was divorced. Maybe then they would decide to move forward together. She told him that she asked God to intervene and bring about what was best for them. That last night that they were together was one of the most beautiful and heartwarming nights Victoria ever experienced . . . and it was to set the standard for both of them for the future . . . whatever that might be. Both cried because of the tenderness they felt for one another and the heartache they feared from their pending separation, but both understood that their conversations carried some merit and that Victoria was adamant that he have everything he deserved in life.

"It was hard to walk away; there were many a day when temptation came again for both of them. But Victoria remained firm in wanting to do what she felt in her heart was "right," and he was willing to support her decision because he loved her. Victoria loved him for this and knew he was one of the most upright, empathetic and loving people she had ever met. She considered him a role model, someone she could trust and admire, and she was grateful for what he had brought into her life.

"Victoria, even to this day, felt that he had given her the gift of confidence in herself as a woman. He'd also given her the gift of understanding that there were many facets to loving someone, and the first was the honor and respect between them. He had also given her a role model upon which she would base her future friendships. He taught her what communication meant, that there was a higher standard in how to disagree, and how important she deemed these attributes for her future . . . both in a husband and in her own communication skills with others.

"Though they planned to see one another again when the divorce was final, it never happened. The divorce took all Victoria's strength and two years to resolve; she'd had to find a new place to live and a full-time job. During this time, she and her friend kept in contact through a weekly phone call, and his strong values, kindness and sage advice were a source of strength and comfort to her. Then, unexpectedly a wonderful career opportunity opened for him, and Victoria could tell that he wanted to accept the offer. He asked her to go with him, but she couldn't because of the pending divorce. Victoria encouraged him to accept the offer and he moved to a different area, a new company, and a few years later . . . he married that young, lovely, wonderful wife Victoria wanted for him. Victoria was happy for him even though she sometimes wished she had never let him go.

"And so, Victoria was grateful that she'd learned there were good men in the world, men with values and integrity, with self-control and dignity; and she determined to make the right choice in the future and look for these qualities in a future husband. For now, she wanted to work on developing these standards in herself and in her family and other interactions. She drew closer to God and tried to develop her faith and had thanked God for allowing her that wonderful experience. She wished that she could know what God thought about her thanking Him for something that the Bible said was wrong. Yet she somehow felt that it hadn't been wrong and that God had given her that experience. Later, years later, one of her ministers told Victoria that Damon had "divorced" her in God's eyes probably in those first few years of her marriage and that when Victoria met her young man she was, in essence, in old biblical terms . . . single. Victoria then realized that God was a circumstantial God who looked upon the heart more than the deed and for this she was doubly thankful and humbled . . . and amazed and thought of the words: *"I will be gracious to whom I will be gracious."*

When Grandma ended her narration and quiet suddenly enveloped them, Sarah left her chair to walk over to her Grandma to hug her and tell her that she loved her. Tears continued to slide down Sarah's cheeks and the lump in her throat hurt terribly. "Grandma, I love you more than words can say and I have always loved and admired who you *are* . . . but now I can honestly say that I love and admire who you *were*, too! Your heart was so incredibly loving . . . and you tried so hard . . . and you had so much strength! Grandma . . . I would have punched someone!"

And the two laughed together at the image of Sarah punching someone, and the sadness passed.

Chapter Seven

ON HER OWN

"It was difficult for Victoria to be completely on her own after twenty-seven years of marriage. She had always worked toward the well-being of her home and family and had never had a full-time job or been solely responsible financially. Her children had married and were busy developing their own lives and could not appreciate what Victoria was experiencing. They hadn't yet met these challenges in their own lives and couldn't understand the panic she'd feel or the fear-driven high standards of self-set goals.

"Neither friends nor family members could understand what Victoria meant when she told them that she was experiencing panic attacks. They saw her as beautiful, accomplished, successful, and finally about to seize the opportunities of a new and wonderful life. Victoria understood and even believed their response on an intellectual level but it was the emotional level which caused the pain and which she couldn't seem to master. It was the abused wife syndrome she'd read about which caused her panic and which she knew she had to somehow overcome. It might take a long time, but she was determined to succeed.

"Now, however, it was panic she surely felt and, on many occasions, she gave in to tears and fears and immobility. No one knew what she suffered. She knew that even if she tried to explain its horrors, no one would understand and so she suffered privately. Yet sometimes she felt resentful because the people who claimed to love her didn't see her agony nor appear to want to help her. She knew however that it was simply because they did not understand how severe her panic was. Victoria remembered an anecdote one of the older members of her congregation told her. She said that if one was standing in the ocean when the tide was coming in, the water would slowly climb a little higher on the body. When the water reached the neck, one could stretch their neck a little bit to prevent the water from reaching the mouth. If the water reached one's mouth, they might tilt their head back and tightly close their lips. And if the water reached their nostrils, they would surely not only tilt their head but would also stand on their toes. This sweet, wise little lady would stand on her toes and look adorable as she clamped her lips closed, tilted her head back, and stuck her nose in the air!

"Victoria's friend likened this story to the trials and tribulations of life saying that when bad times came, we may have to stand on our toes with our head tilted up and back, but we will *never* have to fear that the water will reach our nostrils because God will *always* intervene at just that moment, and cause the water to recede.

"So, when the fear came, Victoria would think: *The waters are high; they may close over my mouth, but they will not reach my nostrils, and I will not drown.* This story sustained her. She wrote it on a piece of paper and taped it to her mirror and would read it and repeat it out loud when she felt the panic begin.

"Little by little, Victoria began to assert herself and use her creativity to build her new life. She made a list of what she wanted to accomplish and prioritized it carefully so she could set reasonable attainable goals. She thought if she focused on one thing at a time, she'd make it. But she was still determined to create the type of home and family life she so loved.

"Victoria had rushed to finish her college courses while the divorce was dragging on. She'd found a way to accelerate graduation by taking courses at two colleges so they would not know how many credits she carried. She did nothing but study while she was enrolled in the two separate programs simultaneously. At the end of two years, she transferred the credits from the two-year program to the four-year program, finishing in less than three years. When the transcripts were put together and someone caught the number of credits she'd carried, they weren't sure it was "legal" but had to accept them because Victoria had earned them . . . and had obtained such good grades in them. To do this, however, her life revolved around study; and she used her incredible willpower to finish and focus intently on her goal.

"But that accomplishment still didn't provide her with the résumé she required; she needed some "hands-on" experience to convince someone to give her a good job. After some thought and lots of discarded résumés, she developed a résumé which cited her years of community service without explaining these were not paid positions until the very end of the résumé. This and her academic record gave her what she needed to get the job she wanted. Victoria knew that God had His hand in every one of her prior accomplishments, and had even arranged that community service so many years ago in anticipation of this moment. She was humbled by that thought. Her winning, loving personality and attitude gave her the edge in an interview as well, and the interview also allowed her to demonstrate her new found confidence and communication skills.

"A year after her divorce, Victoria purchased a house. Knowing she wanted a lot of house with little money, she bought an old Victorian home in dire need of renovation. Standing in the downstairs dining room, she could see the sky shining in above the second floor bedrooms. But she was undaunted, thinking a new roof would be a good thing! She brought this house back to life and filled it with friends and family and holiday fellowships . . . and love . . . and also laid down two strict rules. The first rule was that in her home, a table would never be laid without grace being said; and the second rule was that when someone stayed overnight, no one would go to sleep without those in the house praying together.

"By now Victoria had a grandchild and began to create wonderful memories of her home by making it warm and inviting. Victoria loved clocks, especially the ones which ticked loudly and chimed every quarter hour. She had floor clocks and wall clocks, mantel clocks and table clocks. She'd set them to chime a minute apart so every quarter hour the clocks would chime consecutively. All over the house, the clocks would chime even through the night. They never kept her awake. She loved the sound of them.

"She'd stripped, stained, and varnished the exquisite chestnut moldings throughout the house; and they were beautiful, matching the hardwood floors throughout . . . even into the kitchen. Traditional furniture, Oriental carpets, and antiques completed the warm, homey atmosphere she created for herself. Everyone enjoyed visiting and roaming the old house with its many tiny rooms where over the years her grandchildren would search for the packages they knew she had for them. They'd invariably find the wrapped packages hidden under a bed or behind a pillow on one of her benches or on the bottom shelf of a table.

"They weren't allowed to open the packages until they found them all. Victoria, would tell them how many there were, and they'd race through the house looking for them, bringing them to the sitting room, piling them on the floor, yelling to one another about how many were found, and then run off in search of the next one. Naturally they found them all and then they would be told to divide them by color into separate piles. Then they would learn which color belonged to which child. They loved this game and the adults who were present also loved it. It wasn't until her grandchildren were older that they realized how much time and effort Victoria put into doing this for them.

"Victoria enjoyed finding ways to keep her grandchildren busy for a while so she would have a little time with her daughter without them clamoring for her attention, and the little packages gave them that time. When her grandchildren later reminisced about this memory, they realized how clever their grandmother's ideas were, and wanted to remember them so that they could use these little tricks with their children and grandchildren someday. It was killing two birds with one stone . . . lovingly!

"In Victoria's quest to insure that her home was a godly home (something she did not have in her marriage with Damon), she began an exploration of the Bible to help her achieve her goals. As she read about prayer and gathered the verses from all parts of the Bible which spoke of prayer, she came up with a catchphrase to remind her of what she wanted to cover in prayer every day.

"Sometimes her grandchildren would groan at the length of her prayers if they were staying overnight because they weren't used to this at home and would much rather have Victoria tell them one of her wonderful stories. But she'd bargain with them, telling them that they'd only get a story if they were willing to pray. But she'd speak fast when she prayed, and she'd get it all in even as concise as it was, and every member of her family would be mentioned by name! They might have groaned sometimes, but they did learn.

"Victoria studied the Bible to understand what prayer should consist of and came up with the acronym PAPPIT for remembering what prayer should include. She developed the acronym by using the first letters of the words praise, accountability, petition, protection, intercession, and thanksgiving. When she'd talk about prayer, she'd whip out her list and ask one of those with her to read what PAPPIT meant:

1) Praise: praise God for His goodness and power
2) Accountability: admit sins, ask for forgiveness and mercy
3) Petition: petition for help in those matters that concern us

4) Protection: ask for and acknowledge God's protection
5) Intercession: pray for others both on earth and in eternity
6) Thanksgiving: thank God for all He has done and will do for us

"She knew that her grandchildren didn't participate in formal prayer at home aloud with one another, but that they did pray individually. She also knew that when they were having troubles, they'd remember what she told them, and would pray about those troubles. Sometimes she was amazed that so much of what she told them actually stuck in their mind. "Your morning prayer", she'd say, "should include our thankfulness for what God has done for us and should contain a humble request for His guidance and protection throughout the day. Evening prayer should conclude the day, again with thankfulness for His guidance and protection throughout the day, with acknowledgment of His amazing love, grace, and power; with an intercession for others in need; and finally, again with a humble request for His continued guidance, love, and protection."

"Victoria also knew that not everyone takes the time to do this because sometimes they would get up late and have to rush to get ready for school; and at night, everyone would go to bed at a different time, and then just forget or were too tired. But she felt that it was important to teach children that with and through prayer, they need not worry about their life, for God is always with them.

Sarah remembered Grandma telling her these things and praying with her, but too often, she just seemed to forget to pray. She did pray occasionally, however, and tried to do a good job of it, though it was invariably a short prayer. But when Grandma visited and because they all had different schedules, she'd have to corral everyone separately to pray with them . . . when she could.

"Prayer", she'd said, "in the morning, at night, before each meal, and whenever need, concern or thankfulness fills our heart, moves God's heart to look after everything we need." Grandma would invariably tell them the story about God looking after the birds and how God said that if He looked after them, surely He would look after His children. Grandma would look for the verses to which she referred and read it to them. Sarah was surprised that she remembered those verses from her childhood.

Behold the fowls of the air: for they sow not,
neither do they reap, nor gather into barns;
yet your heavenly Father feedeth them.
Look at the birds of the air, for they neither sow
nor reap nor gather into barns; yet your heavenly Father
feedeth them.

—Matthew 6:26

and

Are not two sparrows sold for a farthing?
and one of them shall not fall on the ground without your Father.
Fear ye not therefore.

—Matthew 10:29, 31

Sarah recalled that Grandma had said that God never wants His children to pray the same repetitious prayer over and over again because when they rush through repetitious prayers, they don't hear or listen to their meaning. Grandma said that God wants His children to have an intimate relationship with Him by really talking to Him as they would someone else. Grandma always said that prayers that are short but from the heart are better than long memorized prayers. She said that God is truly our Father in heaven, and He loves us like a father loves his children. Grandma found the verses where God tells His children how to pray and handed the battered old list to Sarah:

And when thou prayest,
thou shalt not be as the hypocrites are:
for they love to pray . . . that they may be seen.

—Matthew 6:5

But thou, when thou prayest, enter into thy closet,
and when thou hast shut thy door,
pray to thy Father which is in secret;
and thy Father which seeth in secret shall reward thee openly.

—*Matthew 6:6*

But when ye pray, use not vain repetitions, as the heathen do:
for they think that they shall be heard for their much speaking.

—*Matthew 6:7*

Sarah knew that Grandma never stopped studying scripture. She believed in the power of prayer. She said there were no greater guarantees on the face of the earth than the guarantees God gives if we listen to Him. Grandma would tell the whole family about these guarantees, but when Sarah was younger she never thought about them, especially as they might apply to her life.

But now, hearing Grandma talk about her past and learning about Grandma as the courageous Victoria battling for her independence and a special way of life, Sarah thought, *Now that I'm older, and especially now that I've seen the heartache of my students and their families, and of course, Grandma's story, I can see how these guarantees could mean the difference between life and death, between hope and hopelessness.* Sarah began to recognize that what Grandma had uncovered was what kept her going despite what she lived through. She had gone through so much tragedy and it seemed to Sarah that she hadn't yet scratched the surface of all that Grandma had to tell her!

Grandma also taught them about God's promises and now handed Sarah yet another list to include in her journal.

If any of you lack wisdom, let him ask
of God, that giveth to all men liberally, and upbraideth not;
and it shall be given him.

—*James 1:5*

If ye then, being evil, know how to give
good gifts unto your children, how much more shall
your Father which is in heaven give good things
to them that ask him?

—*Matthew 7:11*

And it shall come to pass, if ye shall hearken diligently unto my commandments
which I command you this day, to love the LORD your God, and to serve
him with all your heart and with all your soul,
that I will give you the rain of your land in his due season, the first rain
and the latter rain, that thou mayest gather in thy corn, and thy wine, and thine oil.

—*Deuteronomy 11:13-14*

Sarah knew that Grandma prayed. She knew that she always asked for wisdom in God's ways and asked that she be given the ability to understand and to recognize where she was wrong and what she was to learn from scripture. She asked God to set in place every step she took so it would be pleasing in His sight. She told Sarah that little by little, her understanding increased, and she began to understand what God wanted and how she could conduct her thoughts and actions accordingly. It hadn't come overnight, she'd admitted, but it had been a gradual change, bringing a slow but welcome and joyous peace to her heart. She could trust again, and she was happy and this helped her when even more terrible circumstances entered her life.

Grandma explained that she wanted to pass along to Sarah what she had learned and told her that as she studied the Bible; she began to understand that she had not been equally yoked in her marriage to Damon. Sarah remembered that phrase . . . equally yoked . . . clearly from earlier conversations and remembered that when she was a teenager, Grandma and she had talked a great deal about choosing a mate. Grandma stressed the importance of learning how one can make that choice the right choice. Grandma had never spoken in fairy-tale terms that a prince in shining white armor would arrive one day to carry Sarah to a palace where she would live happily ever after. She said that those were the stories she read as a child, and she had believed them, expecting all things to end as the fairy tales did and that she had been sorely disappointed when they didn't!

Instead, Grandma spoke about how bad times were a part of life and a part of our growth process. She spoke about how people needed to be prepared to tough out the bad times and carefully learn how to communicate well and listen with their heart when someone brought their concerns to them. And she would tell Sarah and her brothers that they needed to remember that Satan could overpower any couple's love for one another and destroy it. She'd say that while we could not win against satanic power on our own, we could call on a greater power which could win that battle for us.

When Grandma spoke about being unequally yoked, she'd said that the Bible described this phenomenon and related it to a marriage. She explained that on a farm or in the olden days, two oxen would be joined together with a type of wooden necklace around both their necks, which was joined in the middle. This would hold the two in a side-by-side position, enabling them to work together to pull a heavy cart or plow. The yoke helped them maintain an even gait. She explained that if their gait was evenly matched assuring that the placement of their feet would combine the power of their weight and muscles it would help them pull the heavy load and equally share the burden. If their gait were not synchronized, the weight would be too much for them and would cause the load to tilt to one side, making them stumble. This was true in a marriage. If one is pulling properly and the other is not, both can fall as a result.

Grandma would often talk about the importance of marrying someone with whom we would be "equally yoked." *If a couple is equally yoked, spiritually as well, they will have greater strength to fight Satan and maintain their happiness over the long term.* The short term is easy, Grandma said; it's the long term, when the going gets tough, when Satan attacks, which is the hard part and is when having an equal and proper yoke is most effective. *Weakness doesn't show itself when everything is going well, just when things get tough. Our character is proven during the bad times.*

Sarah understood that Grandma's devastating marriage had been the impetus for the urgency she felt to teach them how to work under the blessing of God so they would marry someone with whom they would be equally yoked. She explained that if they were unequally yoked, scripture wanted them to "come out from among them and be separated." Grandma had originally believed she was required to stay with her husband, and she had never found the verses in scripture which said otherwise during her search earlier in her pain. But later, she found the following scripture, which helped her understand the circumstances which encouraged and supported her decision to leave. She wanted to share these words with every woman who had ever been continuously harmed by someone they loved:

Be ye not unequally yoked together with unbelievers:
for what fellowship hath righteousness with unrighteousness?
And what communion hath light with darkness?
And what concord hath Christ with Belial?
or what part hath he that believeth with an infidel?
And what agreement hath the temple of God with idols?
for ye are the temple of the living God;
as God hath said, I will dwell in them, and walk in them;
and I will be their God, and they shall be my people.
Wherefore come out from among them, and be ye separate, saith the Lord,
and touch not the unclean thing; and I will receive you.
And will be a Father unto you, and ye shall be my sons and daughters,
saith the Lord Almighty

—2 Corinthians 6:14

Chapter Eight

THE WHOLE TRUTH

With each part of the narration, Sarah thought that surely Grandma's heartaches ended with that part of her story and she'd think, *"How much more could anyone be required to endure?"* When they sat together once again, and Sarah mentioned this to Grandma, she admitted that when she'd finally reached a point of relative peace in her life she too had thought that all would be well from that point on. She said that when she'd found a job, completed the renovation of her home, and settled in, she did think that she'd already seen so much heartache in her life that the rest of her life would surely be smooth sailing, but she'd been wrong.

She went on to describe a series of events which brought the whole truth . . . all the missing parts of her story, home to her. When everything fell into place, she could hardly believe that she hadn't seen the handwriting on the wall sooner than she had. She explained that she'd not thought herself naïve or stupid, but that was what she felt as the truth emerged.

"The discovery of the truth Sarah, left me so shaken and unwilling to believe that anyone could have plotted so well or for so long to hurt another. When the truth hit, it was devastating because I had simply never suspected, never thought that anyone was capable of planning and plotting for so long and with such vehemence to cause harm to someone else. I had been blindsided. It had hurt so badly, that the pain came to mind as the mouth of a dinosaur gripping me around the midsection, lifting me skyward, and biting into my ribs to ensure his grip. It was a frightening picture and a palpable agony. I had panic attacks thinking about it and took medication for a while to ease the agony of such cruelty. The realization that anyone could have so much malice toward someone was not reasonable to me. Especially when I'd placed my trust in those people . . . and in my world, they were supposed to behave under a distinct set of rules and responsibilities.

"Learning the whole truth made me realize that I would have to climb out of this pit of shock by myself. I would have to make myself whole again. Then, recognizing that I had nothing to do with what they had done, I realized that now I was free to direct my life in any fashion I desired. I understood that the past had to be put into perspective as something which could no longer hurt me. I knew that the future was in my hands, and I could accomplish this job of living and loving and do it well"

And so she did . . . eventually. But it was easier said than done.

"Victoria hated the fact that she could still feel sorrow and love for the people who could perpetrate such cruelty toward her, but she did. And she could not purge the past until she understood it fully. She needed closure. She needed to put the blame where it should be, which was not at her feet. When she could do this, she could allow herself to look at what had been done with empathy and be able to forgive. But knowing it and doing it were two different things. She believed that God wanted her to forgive, but that he'd provided mankind with memories so they could use those experiences to protect them from the same harm again. Therefore, Victoria decided that she did not have to forget and to pretend that all was well. It was not. But . . . she had to forgive.

"The first inkling of truth came one evening when her parents were to visit and mentioned to her that Francesca had asked to come along. A visit from her sister was unusual. During the evening, Francesca kept everyone laughing and was telling one of her jokes when something she said made Victoria feel the old fear again. Caught up in the joke and the punch line and with everyone laughing, Francesca embellished her joke by referencing her experiences in a place called "The Bicycle Club." She often told drawn-out jokes but when she began to relate her experiences when going to this club twice a week to socialize and to dance, she spoke about the friend who accompanied her and how long it took them to get to this club from where they lived. Victoria could sense that Francesca was watching her carefully as she told her story.

"When Francesca finished her story, Victoria had clearly understood all she had said, but she did not demonstrate her understanding, choosing to ignore the hurt her sister once again sought to deliver. Victoria did have excruciating pain in the pit of her stomach from her sister's cruelty and her newly revealed past actions, however, she kept her emotions hidden and would not give her sister the satisfaction of knowing she had hurt her again. Victoria played dumb!

"This Bicycle Club of which her sister spoke was the bar which Damon visited at least twice a week. Victoria had discovered the name of this hangout from one of his friends. Now, through her sisters story, learning that Francesca went there regularly and had never told her was a blow to Victoria. This club was at least a forty-five-minute drive from where her sister resided, so it was not a place that she would inadvertently and unknowingly simply drop in to experience.

"Dissatisfied with Victoria's lack of response, Francesca went on to describe the club, the dancing, the people who went there, and the name of the town where the club was located. She also mentioned that their cousin went there on occasion after work. When she finally finished, Victoria, knowing that until she acknowledged this new attack, Francesca would keep talking. Victoria asked her sister in a calm voice if she had gone to that club when Damon was there; and her sister said, "Yes, of course, I'd meet him there after work, and we'd spend the evening together . . . quite often actually." Victoria then asked Francesca why she had never told her, and she said coolly, "You never asked . . . you were too stupid," and got up to leave. Her parents followed meekly behind her to be taken home. They had heard the exchange.

"Victoria cried when they left. Not because of what her sister had done years ago, but by her blatant cruelty even today. She also cried because again her parents, afraid of confrontation, stuck their head in the sand simply because it was easier for them that way. Her father, she knew, would be upset by what her sister had done and, though afraid to confront her, would, through the loyalty of his heart, try to console Victoria in the days to come. But her mother was unconcerned by the betrayal Victoria felt. For some reason which Victoria could not fathom, Her mother saw no harm in Francesca's long term relationship with Damon at the bar and without Victoria's knowledge. Her mother seemed unable to understand why it was wrong and Victoria did not have the strength to explain that for Francesca to spend two evenings a week dancing and drinking with Damon and not tell Victoria was . . . wrong. Her mother later simply kept stating that Victoria needed to get over it and forgive her sister. Her mother felt that what her sister had done wasn't important and should not be painful.

"A few years before Victoria's divorce, her cousin left his job at the company where Damon worked. He'd spoken about the bowling team and mentioned that Francesca was always there hanging around and, in fact had later joined the team and played with them. She would then go to the Bicycle Club with them after bowling. This was the same team which Damon played on, but Victoria at the time thought that her cousin must be mistaken and for some reason had never pursued his comments. She'd thought that he had mixed-up events and now, wondered why she had let the matter go. It was a very long drive from her sister's house to that bowling alley and then to that bar. Victoria wondered if it was because her heart and mind couldn't compute the disloyalty of her sister's actions. Perhaps subconsciously she had simply not wanted to know the truth. Now, she did know the truth.

"This was when Victoria decided that she wanted closure. She decided to find the whole truth so that she could obtain that closure once and for all. She thought of the many occurrences which now fit together. She located people who might have some of the pieces which would fit into her puzzle. She telephoned, told them what she knew, and asked them if they would be willing to tell her what they knew. She explained that she wanted closure, that it was long over, but she needed them to talk with her so she could protect herself in the future and could put the heartache to rest.

Everyone willingly spoke with Victoria and told her what they knew. What they said fit the puzzle perfectly. One person was aware of the necklace her sister had given her because they'd overheard Francesca telling Damon that it had been a gift to Victoria from her lover. Another told her that Francesca told Damon that she had been asked to accompany Victoria to one of the bars Victoria went to whenever Damon did not come home, another spoke of Francesca and Damon dancing together at the Bicycle club.

"Suddenly Victoria remembered the night that her husband came home and held a rifle to her head, and it all began to come together. It was then that she understood that she was looking into the eyes of pure unadulterated hatred, pure jealousy, pure evil, and a plot which her sister spent years putting into practice. It wasn't an impulsive act by Francesca, born of a moment of poor judgment, but a plot which had been planned and executed over the course of many years.

"It was at that moment that Victoria understood Damon's hatred and realized why Damon had used her to better the properties he kept buying; having her renovate them and then selling them at a profit to accumulate the monies he wanted. She saw the weakness of him as a man. She was forced to face his incredible lack of character. He too hadn't acted impulsively, but with great foresight to harm her. She knew that God would deal with it and suddenly no longer felt pain. It was done. She had closure.

"All the separate stories merged, and Victoria saw clearly and for the first time the extent of what Francesca had done. Suddenly, she understood everything that had occurred. Her sister had given her the necklace, but she told Damon that Victoria told her she'd received it from her lover. The night Damon had held his rifle to her head telling her he was going to kill her could possibly be connected to him spending time with Francesca and her telling him that Victoria asked her to go to the bars with her to pick up some men. That's why Francesca had wanted her to go to the bar with her. Francesca's activities on his bowling team may have been how she initiated contact, established a friendship so she could put her plan into action. Her trips to the Bicycle Club were so they could become more intimate, possibly have an affair. And Victoria wondered what else she might have done and remembered the letters and the break-in. Now she believed that Francesca was the author of the anonymous letters and had been responsible for the break-in of her home.

"When her son married after Victoria's divorce, the family attended the wedding with Grandma's family on one side of the banquet hall and her ex-husband on the other. During the festivities, Francesca crossed the room to ask Damon to dance; and Victoria noticed that they danced together as if they had danced often. While it registered in her mind, it was again a thought that she simply put away, not connecting it to anything her sister had said or done.

"She remembered another incident too. Rarely had her sister visited her, but on this occasion, she had dropped in with her four children. The youngest child was a baby a few months old. Victoria's son was about six years old and when they changed the baby's diaper he asked why the baby didn't "look like a boy." They'd remarked about the curiosity stage of children. Francesca related this incident to the family but what Victoria did not know was that Francesca told everyone that Victoria's son had molested her youngest child. Victoria hadn't known what she'd said until years later. Shortly thereafter, her father had begun treating Victoria's son with a coldness which was unusual for him, and when she asked him about it, he did not respond. Victoria did not connect the two incidents although she now remembered she'd seen her father in his stocking feet kick her son as he stepped past him one day and had been shocked. Perhaps her sister's story had been what had turned her father against her son. *Didn't anyone realize that her son had been six years old?*

"She also remembered that about nine years after her divorce, her insurance company called to tell her that, because Damon had left his job under a disability claim, she would no longer be required to make premium payments on a policy she carried on Damon. However, to qualify for this waiver, she was required to obtain his signature and the signature of one of his physician's. Victoria sent the papers to Damon to sign and forward to his doctors so the premiums would be waived. She'd told Francesca about it, happy with this news. A week later, Damon told the insurance company that he would not sign the premium waiver papers unless Victoria changed the beneficiary from herself to her children. She had wondered at the continued cruelty of her husband's nature in that incident even nine years after their divorce. He refused his help and wanted to take that paltry sum from her!

"Victoria decided to pay the premium as she usually did. However, when she told this to the insurance company, the representative was furious about such an act of cruelty on the part of Damon and forwarded the papers directly to the physician's and worked it out for Victoria's benefit. The agent was not supposed to do that, but speaking with Damon and listening to how vindictive he was in his refusal to sign the papers, and finding Victoria so willing to let Damon's cruelty go unchallenged by paying the premium made the insurance representative decide to help Victoria.

"And then she remembered a party she had attended at her sister's mother-in-law's house. Victoria had walked into the kitchen for a glass of water where Francesca's two oldest daughters were gathered. When Victoria took some water they congratulated her on her choice saying that they knew it was difficult to be a recovering alcoholic and were proud of her. Victoria laughed, thinking it a joke about the water, and said something inane like "there's nothing like a cold glass of water." They replied seriously that Victoria shouldn't worry about her addiction if she had beaten it and reiterated that they really were proud of her. Victoria hadn't understood what they meant at the time but now cringed remembering this incident and wished she had asked questions that day. She felt so naive and wondered how she could have misunderstood their meaning. Had Francesca told yet another story to keep her children from a closer relationship with their aunt? Had her sister's jealousy been so great that she'd deny her children a relationship with their aunt and cousins? In her heart, Victoria knew this was true. She felt very sorry for her sister and, at the same time, shocked by her behavior.

"Victoria also recalled the words of the psychologists at the school where Francesca had been diagnosed as a sociopath and looked up the definition of a sociopath, and as she read, she felt she was reading a description of her sister. The gist of what the dictionary said was that a sociopath evolves from an emotional and behavioral disorder. It said that a sociopath had a clear perception of reality except for social and moral obligations and pursued immediate personal gratification. It also said that sociopaths had no compunction about committing criminal acts to satisfy their desires. Other references described an incredible capacity for lying, no remorse for what they did or caused, a need for control, and that they often have a winning personality belying their actions. It was frightening to read because these definitions fit Francesca so well.

"And at that moment, many small things came together in a pattern which supported the larger things. These demonstrated that Francesca had indeed plotted and planned to systematically hurt her. She saw what her sister had done and sorrowfully knew it was too late to make corrections. The damage had been done. She recalled her sister coming to say good-bye to her when the divorce was final. Victoria had packed her car and was leaving for her new home in another state to be near her daughter. Her sister had remained at the rental property when Victoria left. Victoria had carefully left the premises neat and the rental leases and bill files and keys for Damon, doing her part despite the fact that he had, in essence, stolen the property from her. Now Victoria wondered what damage her sister may have caused there.

"There were probably dozens of incidents which Victoria did not know of. She now saw her sister as a very sick woman, ruled and owned by her jealousy and hatred and her inability to see herself as she was. It was then that Victoria made the decision to stay away from Francesca from that day forward if she could.

"She also thought of the lack of character Damon had displayed before they were married in running from his responsibilities in the armed services and at college. She remembered his unrelenting hatred toward his father despite his father's overtures for peace. She remembered his continual hatred and intolerance toward his mentally challenged brother. And she knew that Francesca's plan would not have worked if Damon had had a good and moral character. He had been a weakling, and he had never even tried to improve his moral character.

"He had been a willing partner to Francesca because he was also driven by his need for control and the jealousy which had allowed and fed his fears and prompted his cruelty. She felt sorry for him, for his terrible weakness and the cruelty which he'd applied, not only to her, but also to his father and brother, his children and his grandchildren. She wondered what he would find when he died and what price he would have to pay. She had closure now. She finally understood.

"Victoria knew the truth; she had the closure she sought for so long and was free to move on to a new life. She may have been damaged emotionally and weakened physically, but she would deal with these truths, put them behind her, and face the beauty of what she knew God could now place in her life. Closure had been the first step. Until she could understand clearly what had occurred and why, and let it go, and forgive . . . she could not regain her strength, and fully understand how to approach her new life. She would have been bound to the past. But like all the challenges, most of which she'd already faced, she would overcome this too!

"Whenever she had been at a loss, she'd turned to the Bible for answers and always found them. She knew she could do this again. Perhaps now was the time to act, and now was the time for healing. The Bible was the place that she would look for why people did bad things and what she could do to protect herself in the future. The Bible was where she learned how to deal with life and work toward a future with her Heavenly Father.

Chapter Nine

LAYING THE PAST TO REST

"Victoria had to deal with what she learned, with the cruelties and betrayals she had experienced. She could have been bitter, and she admitted to feeling bitter at first and even wanting to hate them, but she didn't know how to hate. She'd joined a spousal abuse group to understand what others felt and how they coped, but she was surprised to find people who did not heal and, even after many years of counseling, were still angry and bitter and unable to trust. The counselors in that group had encouraged their anger and didn't seem to notice the fine line between anger and hate which Victoria could see as detrimental to the soul.

"She wondered what good it would do to be angry. She recalled the man haters she'd met who were in that group and she felt that they could never remarry successfully if they could not trust and still carried their hatred. She somehow understood that one needed to heal before they could trust and truly love again. How could anyone accomplish this if they continued to hate and carry their anger into their future? So she left that group and embarked on her own quest to understand, to learn, and to move on. While it was sometimes a struggle, she knew that she would do it.

"Slowly, Victoria picked up the pieces of her life and, though despondent at times, tackled the challenges ahead of her. She'd gone back to school, bought a house, and gotten a good job. She'd included her community and charity work in her résumé to fill in the years that she had not worked, and this was enough to provide her with the job she wanted. She credited getting this great job to the power of prayer and God's gift to her.

"As she healed, made new friends, completed the renovating and decorating of her house, and gained success in her job, she'd often reflect on the past because she was curious about why certain things happen and why people behave badly to one another. Her new project was to study the Bible to find out how Satan worked. She felt that rather than blame Francesca or Damon for what they had done, she would try to discover what role, if any, Satan might have played and be playing in their lives.

"She wanted to learn about Satan; his power, how cunning he is and so deceptive that one hardly knew it was him knocking on the door of their heart and mind. What she found in the Bible about Satan taught her the five basic characteristics of Satan and many of the things he can cause mankind to do.

"Victoria learned from Scripture that:

SATAN is a

1) Liar: "When he speaketh a lie, he speaketh of his own: for he is a liar and the father of it." (John 8:44)

2) Sly, cunning: "Now the serpent was more subtil than any beast of the field which the LORD God had made." (Genesis 3:1)

3) Murderer: "He was a murderer from the beginning, and abode not in the truth, because there is no truth in him." (John 8:44)

4) Deceiver: "The serpent beguiled me, and I did eat." (Genesis 3:13) Also, "Satan, which deceiveth the whole world." (Revelation 12:9)

5) Tempter: "Then was Jesus led up of the Spirit into the wilderness to be tempted of the devil. And when the tempter came to him, he said, . . . " (Matthew 4:1, 3)

Additionally, Satan can

Move men to do his bidding (1 Chronicles 21:1),

Walk back and forth on the earth (Job 1:7),

Cause illness (Job 2:7),

Take God's word from men's hearts (Mark 4:15),

Enter man (Luke 22:3), (John 13:27),

Blind the minds of them which believe not (2 Corinthians 4:4),

Transform himself (2 Corinthians 11:14)

Send messengers to hurt man (2 Corinthians 12:7),

Hinder people (1 Thessalonians 2:18),

Produce signs and has powers (2 Thessalonians 2:9).

The previous verse (2 Thessalonians 2:9) states, "The working of Satan with all power and signs and lying wonders."

"When she learned these things about Satan, and saw them all grouped together, she wondered what chance mankind had to fight him. It appeared that he was capable of turning hearts, minds, and actions in directions one would never take otherwise. Satan could do all these things . . . unless one had the wisdom of God's direction, the power of prayer, the protection of the angels, and the armor of God. Without them, mankind was easily led and lost. And because so few have all this information, because they know no better, God wants us to feel compassion for them and forgive them. The verses which explained this concept about the entities who seek to harm mankind were implanted in Victoria's memory.

> *For we wrestle not against flesh and blood,*
> *but against principalities, against powers, against the rulers*
> *of the darkness of this world, against spiritual*
> *wickedness in high places.*
>
> *—Ephesians 6:12*

"Victoria had also read that God further instructs us by this promise and warning:

> Behold, I set before you this day a blessing and a curse;
> A blessing, if ye obey the commandments of the LORD your God,
> which I command you this day: and a curse, if ye will not
> obey the commandments of the LORD your God, but turn aside out of the way
> which I command you this day, to go after other
> gods, which ye have not known.
>
> —Deuteronomy 11:26-28

"And He softens His words by reminding us:

> Now therefore hearken unto me, O my children:
> for blessed are they that keep my ways.
>
> —Proverbs 8:32

> For every one that asketh receiveth; and he that seeketh findeth;
> and to him that knocketh it shall be opened.
> Or what man is there of you, whom if his son ask bread,
> will he give him a stone? Or if he asks a fish, will give him a serpent?
> If ye then, being evil, know how to give good gifts unto your
> children, how much more shall your Father which is in heaven
> give good things to them that ask him?
>
> —Matthew 7:8-11

"Victoria wanted to know what the armor of God is and realized that by knowing who and what Satan is, by knowing the difference between what God wants and what Satan wants, and through the power of God's protection, we can avoid what otherwise would happen. God always shows us what to expect and what to do and gave us scripture to help us understand:

> Put on the whole armour of God, that ye may be able
> to stand against the wiles of the devil.
>
> —Ephesians 6:11

Wherefore take unto you the whole armour of God,
that ye may be able to withstand in the evil day,
and having done all, to stand.

—Ephesians 6:13

The night is far spent, the day is at hand:
let us therefore cast off the works of darkness,
and let us put on the armour of light.

—Romans 13:12

"Victoria also learned that the armor of God is the protection we gain through our prayer life, our tithing, our overcoming thoughts which aren't godly, and through our fellowship with one another, especially by going to church.

Suddenly Grandma's voice faltered. She'd worked so hard to talk about Victoria's life . . . her own . . . in a dispassionate tone, but now, remembering the pain and the struggle, she faltered.

Sarah's heart went out to her and she realized how difficult it must be for her to dredge up memories which she'd struggled so hard to forget. Sarah reminded Grandma that she'd always been so thankful that they could talk about everything and that there was no subject which was taboo.

But Grandma began to cry, because she was remembering the cruelty and to this day could not fathom such heartlessness. She found it so hard to separate the people she loved from the spirits of evil who'd owned them and directed their ways. She wanted to leave the room rather than distress Sarah, but Sarah would not let her leave and held her and told her to go ahead and cry and let it out. She tried to speak but stammered . . . then tried to re-assure Sarah by telling her that regardless of the pain, these times were the best times of her life because they were the times of her greatest growth. She said that even her marriage of twenty-seven years which was when she felt her greatest sorrow, had taught her about the illness of the soul so similar to any illness of the body. She now felt her that

Damon and Francesca were ill spiritually so had had no defense against Satan; thus he could rule their lives and decisions. She spoke about Satan bringing one-third of all the angels in heaven with him when he came to Earth and how they all provoked mankind and could enter and govern people who did not put God in their life. She felt this had happened to those who treated her so badly, and to understand this made it easier for her to forgive them and pray for them. But sometimes she felt so bad for them and who they'd become that she couldn't help but cry. She was glad though that she'd seen the gleam of these spirits in Damon's eyes so she could believe that it was the spirits to which he'd succumbed and not his soul which had perpetrated so much cruelty.

> *Then goeth he and taketh with himself seven*
> *other spirits more wicked than himself, and they*
> *enter in and dwell there: and the last state*
> *of that man is worse than the first.*
>
> —*Matthew 12:45*

Then she spoke about how God wanted our homes to reflect His will and that God is always willing to give us time to grow, but at some point, He will say, "That's enough". God wants to bring changes to our lives which will lead us to a better place in our lives despite the pain of change and our fear of change, even when we kick and scream against that change . . . but it can only happen if we open our hearts to Him and *want* to live as better people.

She opened the little box on her desk which contained the verses which explained how God wanted us to live and what rewards He provides if we follow Him and follow His way of life. Grandma handed Sarah the list she had made of God's promises so Sarah could read them:

1) We will be forgiven our sins. (Ephesians 4:32)
2) We will not have to worry. (Matthew 6:34)
3) We will have strength against the devil's wiles. (Ephesians 6:11)
4) We will be granted wisdom. (James 1:5)
5) We will not be condemned. (Luke 6:37)
6) God will make an everlasting covenant with us. (Isaiah 55:3)
7) The Lord will recompense and reward our work. (Ruth 2:12)
8) We will be safe and secure. (Proverbs 1:33)

In return, God asks us to do the following:

1) Teach our children in the ways of God. (Ephesians 6:4)
2) Pray in the morning and at night. (Deuteronomy 11:19)
3) Keep the Sabbath holy. (Exodus 20:8)
4) Cover the transgressions of others. (Proverbs 17:9)
5) Not to provoke one another. (Colossians 3:21)
6) Be kind and tenderhearted. (Ephesians 4:32)
7) Be overcomers. (Revelation 2:7,11, 26)
8) Care for widows and orphans and revere the elderly. (Proverbs 16:31)
9) Have fellowship with one another, speaking of our faith. (Acts 2:42)
10) To do good and to share. (Hebrews 13:16)
11) Pray without repetition. (Matthew 6:7)
12) Set the right example and not be hypocrites. (Matthew 7:15)

And so Grandma learned to deal with what had occurred, to move on, to forgive, to do better in her own life, and to use the Bible to find the answers and the direction for her life which she sought.

Chapter Ten

A NEW LIFE

Sarah loved the story about how her grandmother met her second husband, how Grandma felt when they married, and what happened in the ensuing years. Grandma told her that she was so frightened when she walked down the aisle that her knees were knocking. But despite Grandma's fears, they were happy together and shared their faith in God. They stayed married through good times and bad, sickness and health, until Grandpa died. Grandma's second husband was a gift from God for the entire family. He became their handyman, counselor, mediator, and a role model. He loved them first, and thus their love followed easily.

Now that Grandma was a new person and no longer even known as Victoria, Sarah decided to ask Grandma if she thought that she could complete her narration identifying the heroine as "Grandma" rather than as "Victoria". Grandma laughed with Sarah's use of the word heroine, and was secretly pleased because perhaps this indicated that Sarah understood the story as a lesson rather than as a criticism. She thought that it might be appropriate to switch from Victoria to Grandma because at this point in her story, it was "Grandma" who lived in such joy and understanding, not the "Victoria" who'd suffered at the hands of others. She realized that she no longer wanted to be the young naïve Victoria, nor think of her troubles, but remember instead who Victoria was now and how thankful she was now for those troubles. So Grandma turned to Sarah with a smile and said, "Okay Sarah, let me give it a try!"

"Grandma had been "single" for five years before she met Grandpa. The story of how they met, why they married, when they did, and their first few years together was a remarkable story about faith and the joy which comes from being obedient to God. Grandma felt inadequate to choose a husband once she understood the importance of this choice, so she "hired" someone to choose him. Through prayer, she commissioned God Himself to choose who she would marry. And it seems that He did!

"Once Grandma's new job was in place and secure, and the house she was renovating was completed, she began thinking about finding a husband. She'd always thought of herself as "the marrying kind." "This time," she thought, "I'll be equally yoked!" She prayed diligently that God would provide her with the right husband, hand chosen by Him, definitely not by her! She wanted someone who would share her faith in God, love her family, communicate well and often, and be kind to everyone.

"Grandma had always loved to dance and wondered if this might be a way to meet someone with whom she could share a similar interest. She wasn't going to go into a bar because she didn't want a husband who enjoyed bars, and so she'd thought about a dance venue in a wholesome atmosphere. She shared her thoughts with a friend at work, and they looked in the newspaper to see if dances were listed.

"They found a number of different events from which they could choose and decided to try each one until they found what was right for them. There were square dances, round dances, contra dances, and ballroom dances and each was listed in the paper; and they all said, "Singles invited." Many said, "People of all ages invited," and many offered free lessons before the start of the dance. One was held in a huge recreation hall in a park, another in a ballroom in a hotel, another in a Knights of Columbus hall, and one in a building in an industrial park. They decided to try each dance and set out on their adventure, agreeing to leave if the building was not well lit, didn't look safe, or didn't seem "right" for them once they entered.

"The first dance they chose was the square dance, which offered a lesson in the beginning and soda, juice, chips, and cake for refreshments. Some people danced beautifully, others were just learning, and everyone was willing to teach newcomers. The square dance was an incredible workout; they loved it, but it was a lot of work because they were literally skipping and swinging every minute. They were wet with perspiration before the evening was over. Even the "regulars" had come with neck bandanas with which to wipe the sweat from their faces.

"On the way home, they decided that a slower type of dancing would work better for them. With each decision, Grandma again checked with her minister to be sure that she had his blessing . . . and his prayers . . . to ensure God's blessing on what she was about to do. The next dance they tried was one that advertised "round dancing", which was similar to square dancing, but practiced in a line instead of a square, and provided a constant change of partners. This too was a workout, but at least when they reached the end of the line, they would wait out a set of steps and rest until the next set began, and then be brought back into the line again. This was less strenuous than the square dancing but still hard work and lots of exercise. But they did meet quite a few new people because they changed partners after every set of steps.

"Grandma felt however that it was difficult to feel ladylike when profusely perspiring from the exercise, so they decided to try all the ballroom dancing events next. There were many ballroom dances' from which to choose, but eventually, they found one in a lovely large well-lit hall specializing in ballroom dancing for singles and offering a free lesson preceding the dance. They enjoyed this dance; its location, its music, its ambience, and met a nice group of people who were also making friends and honing their dance skills. From samba to tango and from cha-cha to swing, they enlarged their repertoire of dance steps at each dance they attended, laughing at mistakes, taking pride in mastering some of the more intricate steps.

"A year or two went by and Grandma continued to ask God to find her a husband. She felt she was not astute enough to choose the right person and could easily make a mistake. But, she reasoned that if God picked him, she would know that he would be the perfect choice for her. She'd asked her ministers to pray for a husband for her, and they did . . . and smiled at her determination. They laughed at all the prerequisites she'd jokingly list for this perfect man! Her silly list of prerequisites made her friends tease her with the words, "Lots of luck!"

"He was to have blue eyes, a nice smile, be tenderhearted, smart, educated, financially independent, and know how to pray, and . . . go to church regularly. He also had to get along well with his family and friends! Grandma joked about her list, thinking that while these were attributes she thought admirable, she might get and even love something quite different. The truth was she wanted what God wanted for her. But she had fun making her list and making everyone laugh from the absurdity of how long the list grew and how inconsequential many of her prerequisites really were.

"One evening, Grandma met someone she thought very special. They danced together, and she was impressed by what a good dancer he was . . . far better than she. After another few dances together, he walked over to her table and asked if he could sit with her and her friends. They talked for a while, and he proved himself a good conversationalist and very kind and cordial to the others at her table. She'd already noticed that he had blue eyes and a nice smile! One evening as the dance was about to end, the group at Grandma's table all decided to go to a nearby diner for "breakfast." When they finished eating, four of them stayed and talked for hours, feeling comfortable with one another and talking about all kinds of subjects from politics to religion.

"Grandma noticed that when her new friend Peter disagreed with something someone said, he didn't get angry, but would talk even more about the subject in an effort to persuade others to his way of thinking. She saw that he was a good listener and that he not only listened carefully to her way of thinking but also agreed with many points she'd make. She liked that his mind was not a closed mind, but open to the thoughts of others.

"Everyone liked him. He wasn't disparaging toward others, he appeared very sociable and seemed to like everyone . . . and thus he fit another few of the many prerequisites she had jokingly placed on her list. They began to date and Peter would gladly help her with any repairs around the house. When one of her friends would phone when he was visiting her, he'd always ask her to tell them hello from him. When they joined other friends for an evening out, he'd remember when someone had been sick and ask if they were feeling better. If he received a call from his sisters or brother or mom, he'd put Grandma on the phone for a while so they'd get to know one another. And to Grandma's delight, they were all so nice to her and very anxious to meet her. Grandma loved the way they interacted with one another and how they spoke about them both visiting his family after Christmas.

"Often, they would go out for dinner to an area filled with a variety of restaurants, some offering quaint eating areas outside the main restaurant right near the street where they could enjoy the hustle and bustle of the people passing by. They would enjoy an appetizer at one restaurant, an entrée at another, dessert at yet another, and they loved walking from place to place together while they talked. One evening, Grandma needed to end their evening early so she could attend a Bible study group. Peter insisted on coming with her. Grandma was pleased that a Bible study did not seem to intimidate him, and that he appeared to genuinely want to come with her. In a short while, this prince charming asked Grandma to marry him.

"But Grandma was afraid to make a commitment. She asked her minister to meet with them, hoping he would talk to him about their faith and how it was a way of life, and not just something they did for an hour on Sundays. So, her minister arranged to visit and spent an hour in another room talking to Peter, but who, unbeknownst to Grandma was to soon become Grandpa to Grandma's family. When Peter and Grandma's minister walked out the room where they'd been talking and joined Grandma and the minister's wife, he told Grandma that he really liked Peter very much and suggested that she should marry him because he was sure that their union would have God's blessing. He told all of them that he'd been impressed when Peter told him that he believed that he could make Grandma happy and not that Grandma could make him happy. He also told them that Peter, while not making any commitment to join Grandma's church, did make the commitment to accompany her whenever she went. That had been the clincher for the minister!

"And so Grandma did marry Peter. With knees knocking and heart pounding and feeling an incredible panic, Grandma married again. All of Peter's relatives attended the wedding. Grandma had instantly loved each of them when they met for the first time a month prior to the wedding. They welcomed her and made her feel like a sister. All of them loved one another from that very first day and tried to get together often, and always phoned and sent a card for a birthday, an anniversary, Christmas, even for Valentine's Day!

"Grandma's friends and relatives came too, some from other states, to share this special day with her. Her aunt, uncle and cousin, and two of her friends came from hundreds of miles away. The group totaled over two hundred people. Her children were there; her four-year-old grandson, her new granddaughter of less than two months, and another grandchild who was still "in the oven" also attended their wedding.

"Friends decorated the church with flowers, and others prepared the sumptuous dinner held after the wedding. Another friend sang a beautiful heartrending song for them during the ceremony. Grandma wore a pale peach lace jacket with a long skirt of peach-colored chiffon. She wore shoes which had been dyed to match her dress and a peach hat and veil. She had sewn a headpiece of seed pearls which her mother wore at her own wedding onto the hat. It was beautiful. She wore her hair in an elegant French twist. Her daughter was her maid of honor, and her son gave her away. It was a happy day.

"As time went on, Grandma recognized the magnitude of God's blessing. She grew to love Grandpa more and more everyday and to respect him more than she'd thought possible. His honesty and kindness and upright heart were a joy to her. He never missed coming to church with Grandma and won the family over with his willingness to visit, have them visit, and help the family whether it was to give advice, listen, or make repairs at their homes. God had truly stepped in and equally yoked Grandma.

"They sold both their homes and bought one which was theirs together. They took a month long honeymoon and traveled to some of Grandpa's favorite places in Europe; places which he wanted to show Grandma. When they returned, they had fun hunting for and adding the extra furniture and decorations which would make their house a home. Grandma found Grandpa to be handy around the house, easygoing, amazingly helpful with "women's work," and willing to live in a manner which was pleasing to God. They were happy together. And soon Grandpa did join the church, impressed by the love the congregation showed one another and by the faith and dedication of the ministers.

> *Honour the LORD with thy substance, and with the*
> *firstfruits of all thine increase: So shall thy barns*
> *be filled with plenty, and thy presses*
> *shall burst out with new wine.*
>
> *—Proverbs 3:9-10*

"Grandpa had also shown Grandma one of her greatest errors in life. He told her that she had painted pictures in her mind of what life *should* be and that this had brought her disappointment. The first picture that she'd imagined was one of doting parents who were perfect role models, parents who shared their wisdom about how to deal with life's problems, were faithful children of God, and were best friends for life. The second picture was of their child, grown up, getting married, looking like a princess, and always smiling. The third was a picture of her home, all white, with a picket fence, roses on the front porch trellis, and a lush green lawn surrounding the house. The fourth was of her children, a boy and a girl, dressed in their Sunday best, well behaved, looking content and smiling their perfect white smile.

"Grandpa asked Grandma how anyone could be happy if they kept trying to make those pictures become reality. He pointed out that the reality which was missing in the first picture was that parents made mistakes, sometimes didn't have all the answers to life, and were often too busy to be doting parents. The second picture implied a fairy-tale life and overlooked the fact that people had flaws and problems. The third picture didn't show the bees on the porch, or the Japanese beetles in the roses, or the brown spots on the lawn, or the spiders on the trellis. And the fourth picture did not indicate that sometimes children present with crooked teeth, runny noses, and grass stains on their clothing.

"Grandma realized that she had always been striving for perfection so she could please everyone and ward off criticism or punishment. She acknowledged that this had exhausted her. She was grateful that Grandpa was a realist and loved her in spite of her imperfections. This made Grandma want to do even more for him and inspired her to become a better person. In time, she learned to relax and didn't work to the point of exhaustion to please everyone else. Little by little, she learned and she relaxed.

"She also found some verses in scripture which were to help husbands and wives understand how to make a marriage work.

Husbands, love your wives,
even as Christ also loved the church,
and gave himself for it.

—Ephesians 5:25

So ought men to love their wives as their own bodies.
He that loveth his wife loveth himself.

—Ephesians 5:28

Nevertheless let every one of you in particular
so love his wife even as himself;
and the wife see that she reverence her husband.

—Ephesians 5:33

Wives, submit yourselves unto your own husbands,
as unto the Lord.

—Ephesians 5:22

Pleasant words are as an honeycomb,
sweet to the soul, and health to the bones.

—*Proverbs 16:24*

Strength and honour are her clothing;
and she shall rejoice in time to come.
She openeth her mouth with wisdom;
and in her tongue is the law of kindness.

—*Proverbs 31:25-2*

Chapter Eleven

THE ARMOUR OF GOD

"Grandma finally found happiness and love with a partner in life with whom she could create a godly home. She knew the power of Satan and worried about his coming to wreak havoc again. She remembered that God had spoken of the "armor" he offered as a protection for His children and she wanted to understand this gift and how to use it.

> *Put on the whole armour of God, that ye may be able*
> *to stand against the wiles of the devil.*
>
> —*Ephesians 6:*

"She made a list of what she knew and from that point tried to discern what else she might need to do.

1) She knew about the power of prayer, an important piece of armor, which had gotten her through the changes in her life and had brought Grandpa into her life.
2) She'd learned how to recognize Satan when Carey went through her difficult times and learned about the spirits (fallen angels) who worked for Satan here on earth.
3) She'd learned what God asks of us by reading His words in scripture.
4) She'd learned not to let the birds which fly overhead (bad thoughts) land on her roof (in her mind) and that saying no loudly worked well for her.
5) She learned that God blesses those who seek Him.

"But she had also learned that there were three additional ways to gain protection, and these were the following:

1) Find the means to learn the words of God and believe and apply them.

This is my beloved Son,
in whom I am well pleased;
hear ye him.

—*Matthew 17:5*

Now therefore are we all here present before God,
to hear all things that are commanded thee of God.

—*Acts 10:33*

They went both together . . . and so spake,
that a great multitude . . . believed.

—*Acts 14:1*

When they heard this, they were baptized
in the name of the Lord Jesus.

—*Acts 19:5*

The word is nigh thee, even in thy mouth,
and in thy heart: that is, the word of faith,
which we preach.

—*Romans 10:8*

2) Give to God a tithe of 10 percent and use your God given talents in the vineyard.

And of all that thou shalt give me
I will surely give the tenth unto thee.

—*Genesis 28:22*

And concerning the tithe of the herd,
or of the flock, even of whatsoever passeth under the rod,
the tenth shall be holy unto the LORD.

—Leviticus 27:32

3)   Have fellowship with one another, praying for one another.

And they continued stedfastly
in the apostles' doctrine and fellowship,
and in breaking of bread, and in prayers.

—Acts 2:42

"Grandma realized that by going to church regularly, she'd learned so much about her faith. God's words were clearly explained. Sometimes she hadn't thought that she had retained everything she heard and had not understood all that had been said, but over time, these words penetrated her heart, and God opened her understanding. She was continually surprised that she could bring God's word to mind when she needed to make a decision or faced a danger.

"She remembered rebelling against going to church when she was a child because it was hard to sit still, and remembered that in those days what she heard from the altar seemed incomprehensible. She regretted that now, for perhaps the horrors of what she had experienced could have been avoided if she had listened and learned. She knew that children *needed* to learn about God at a very young age to be equipped to fight Satan when he came to them.

"Grandma watched families bring tiny babies to church and teach them to be quiet during the service, and she'd seen mothers place a nickel or a quarter in the baby's fist and teach them to drop it in the offering box, training them in the ways which pleased God. She wished with all her heart she had known then what she knew now and could have done the same with her children at an earlier point in their lives. She wished she could undo that failure on her part, wished she'd found the right church, the right ministers, the right teachers to help her learn what to do.

Teach me thy way, O LORD;
I will walk in thy truth:
unite my heart to fear thy name.

—*Psalms 86:11*

He layeth up sound wisdom for the righteous:
he is a buckler to them that walk uprightly.

—*Proverbs 2:7*

Hear, ye children, the instruction of a father,
and attend to know understanding.

—*Proverbs 4:1*

The thoughts of the righteous are right:
but the counsels of the wicked are deceit.

—*Proverbs 12:5*

"Grandma wanted her family to understand the importance of learning God's words. She felt that all of us learn from a variety of venues such as talking with a good minister, listening regularly to sermons, and reading the Bible. She wanted her family to avail themselves of every advantage God offers and every protection possible for their walk through life. She wanted them to embrace every action which would be pleasing to God. She wanted them to tithe and to understand that God always returns in one way or another, everything we give Him, sometimes "a thousandfold." And she wanted them to know that the earlier someone attaches their heart to God, the better equipped they will be for life's hard times.

"She understood that some people never really thought about these things and perhaps didn't think they were important. Sometimes younger people felt that they were invincible, and only needed to go to church when they could. She also knew that her family thought her "very" religious and knew that she would talk about God in some way when they were together. She realized that because her daughter had married someone with whom she was not equally yoked in faith, her daughter had to care for her children's spiritual education herself. What Grandma wanted for them was becoming a reality because of her daughter's strength and determination. Grandma was so thankful.

"Grandma did her best to help her daughter and to pass along to them what she had learned. She understood that few people really tithed, not because they didn't want to, but because no matter how much someone earned, they'd spend even more and not have anything left over with which to tithe. She'd learned however that one's tithe should be the first thing that comes out of one's income, not the last . . . that was where the blessings lay.

"Grandma had also learned that the fellowship which scripture spoke of was to have family and friends of faith gather together, usually for a meal, and should include praying together (and for one another) and sharing experiences of faith. This helped each person go through their difficulties, reminded them of God's help, and . . . when prayers were answered, produced experiences of faith. Fellowship also allows us to know when we must "bear ye one another's burdens," which means we should listen to the troubles others have and offer help. This builds the trust and intimacy which families and friends should share with one another.

"Grandma had also learned that many people cut and run when problems arise, others bury their head in the sand, but when a family can stand together to solve those problems and when they can apologize to one another and demonstrate their desire for a loving relationship no matter what, trust and respect can grow . . . and trust is the key to having a good relationship.

Bear ye one another's burdens,
and so fulfil the law of Christ.

—Galatians 6:2

And let us not be weary in well doing:
for in due season we shall reap, if we faint not.
As we have therefore opportunity, let us do good unto all men,
especially unto them who are of the household of faith.

—Galatians 6:9-10

Sarah remembered the visits her family had had from ministers and youth leaders from time to time, and understood that Grandma was right when she said she could sit and listen to them all night long. Her ministers were filled with good advice, godly direction, care and love for them, and analogies from the Bible which fit the circumstances they were experiencing. Sometimes they'd sit, awestruck, as the ministers would speak of the end-times and what was to come. It was interesting and fit in perfectly with what was currently happening in the world. But somehow, Sarah had never been impelled to act on what she had learned because their life had been so hectic and busy. But now she began to think about her faith and what she wanted to do in response.

Grandma told her that every time we hear an explanation of the words of God, it makes an impression on our soul and feeds the Holy Spirit within us, giving us more with which to fight evil when it visits. She said that not one of us is immune to a visit from Satan unless we are already in his pocket. He doesn't look to destroy those he already owns. *Why would Satan waste his time trying to bring down people who had no faith, did not care one way or another about God?*

Grandma explained that only those who seek God and try to live in a manner which is pleasing to him are worthwhile targets to Satan. Grandma said that we can ask for God's protection and that we benefit and are strengthened from hearing God's words, from prayer, from tithing, and from helping others by touching the heart of God by these activities.

She said that having these protections in place allows us to sidestep the efforts of Satan against us. She explained that this was how the temptation of Christ was thwarted; Christ had God's help and He knew how to say no. Not only are *we* tempted, Jesus Himself was tempted by Satan, and He resisted.

> *Then was Jesus led up of the Spirit into the wilderness*
> *to be tempted of the devil.*
>
> *—Matthew 4:1*

> *And when the tempter came to him, . . .*
>
> *—Matthew 4:3*

Then saith Jesus unto him, Get thee hence, Satan.

—Matthew 4:10

Then the devil leaveth him, and, behold,
angels came and ministered unto him.

—Matthew 4:11

From these verses, Grandma had explained, we can begin to understand that Christ simply said no to the devil and reminded Sarah that it was quite similar to how Grandma yelled out the word "no" when thoughts came to her which weren't kind or loving or forgiving. It had worked for her. But first, she'd had to develop a watchfulness which would warn her early on when the thoughts had come; this took a little practice. She said that sometimes she'd realize the thoughts had been in her mind for quite a while before she realized what they were. She'd learned now to watch for them more carefully and catch them before they could "roost."

"Sarah", she would say, "if life is always good, we should take a better look at our life, check that we are on the right track, because Satan doesn't bother to harm those he already has in his pocket, only those who belong to God. Satan can also reward those who are his as is proven by what he promised to give Christ. This again is where our free will should be exercised. We cannot serve two masters."

No servant can serve two masters:
for either he will hate the one, and love the other;
or else he will hold to the one, and despise the other.
Ye cannot serve God and mammon.

—Luke 16:13

Grandma had explained that when we consciously choose to follow God and begin adjusting our lives to His standards, Satan will attack. To some, that's a great reason not to choose God, but those who choose Satan will have a disastrous end. Those who are complacent about God, unwilling to make a commitment, they too may have a disastrous end. Those God loves because they have chosen to follow Him will be attacked, but God turns the attack around and uses it to chasten those He loves and to bring about a refining process in their hearts. The miracle is that He always creates a miracle from our sorrows. Just as gold is refined to become pure, so must our hearts be refined to become pure.

As many as I love, I rebuke and chasten.

—*Revelation 3:19*

And I will bring the third part through the fire,
and will refine them as silver is refined,
and will try them as gold is tried:
they shall call on my name, and I will hear them:
I will say, it is my people:
and they shall say, The LORD is my God.

—*Zechariah 13:9*

Grandma explained that gold had to be heated to a very high temperature to remove the impurities from the nugget taken from the ground. God uses the refining process as an analogy so we can see how it relates to us. We are born in original sin, and we continue to sin throughout our lives. When we make a commitment to God and want to spend eternity with Him, we have to be tested and refined until we are pure and ready to become the Bride of Christ.

Sarah also recalled that Grandma had asked if they thought that they'd be okay with God if they died today. They'd stumble over the answer because suddenly they weren't sure. After all she had learned in the past month from Grandma, Sarah knew that she would have to answer with a "no" today and that she needed to put more into her faith to please God.

Grandma went on to tell a story about death—the story of the rich man and Lazarus, about them dying on the same day, and finding themselves in two different places after death.

There was a certain rich man, which was clothed in purple
and fine linen, and fared sumptuously every day:
And there was a certain beggar
named Lazarus, which was laid at his gate, full of sores,
And it came to pass, that the beggar died,

and was carried by the angels into Abraham's

bosom: the rich man also died, and was buried;

And in hell he lift up his eyes, being in torments, and seeth

Abraham afar off, and Lazarus in his bosom.

—Luke 16:19-23

This passage in scripture tells the story of two men who died. One man, the rich man, had everything he could want—wonderful clothing, an abundance of good food, a brother whom he loved, and a great deal of money. The other man was a beggar, with sores on his body, lying outside the gates of the rich man's house asking for food. Both these men died on the same day. The rich man awakens in hell where he is tormented and thirsts. The beggar, Lazarus, awakens in the bosom of Abraham, across a chasm which separated him from the hell where he saw the rich man.

Abraham was beloved of God, and because he was obedient to God's word, God accounted righteousness to him, giving him access to heaven. Thus the description of Lazarus finding himself carried to Abrahams bosom was an indication that he was in a place of comfort and protection, and rest. While the rich man found himself in hell, in torment.

And beside all this, between us and you there is a great gulf fixed:

so that they which would pass from hence to you cannot;

neither can they pass to us, that would come from thence.

—Luke 16:26

Here, scripture tells us that there was a great gulf between hell and heaven and that they could not pass from one place to another. This indicates that once you die, you are assigned one of these two places and cannot cross the gulf to the other side.

And many of them that sleep in the dust of the earth

shall awake, some to everlasting life, and some to shame

and everlasting contempt.

—Daniel 12:2

This passage in the book of Daniel speaks of those who die who will awaken either to everlasting life or shame and contempt forever. These verses agree in their message that upon death we will be assigned to one of two places and that our actions while we are alive will determine to which place we go.

> *To him that overcometh will I grant to sit*
> *with me in my throne, even as I also overcame,*
> *and am set down with my Father in his throne.*
>
> —*Revelation 3:21*

> *And it shall come to pass, if ye shall hearken diligently*
> *unto my commandments which I command you this day,*
> *to love the LORD your God, and to serve him*
> *with all your heart and with all your soul. That I will give you the rain*
> *of your land in his due season, the first rain and the latter rain,*
> *that thou mayest gather in thy corn, and thy wine, and thine oil.*
> *And I will send grass in thy fields for thy cattle,*
> *that thou mayest eat and be full.*
>
> —*Deuteronomy 11:13-15*

Chapter Twelve

FORGIVENESS

Sarah now realized the extent of the many difficult circumstances Grandma had faced. She was glad that the phase of life after Grandma's divorce had been a good one and that her second marriage, new home, and newly found strength had finally brought her joy and peace. Grandma told her that when her husband became active in church and willingly prayed with her, she felt as if God had given her everything she could possibly want. They had created a lovely home together, developed new friendships and kept the old, established themselves in a loving congregation, and they shared their faith. They delighted in their vacations, and in having and attending fellowships together, and in going out for a candlelight dinner on occasion. Life was good, and Grandma was very grateful that God had blessed her so abundantly. But there was to be another test, and it would be her most difficult and so Grandma began her narration once again.

"When Grandma was raising her children, she brought her family together for Christmas, Thanksgiving, birthdays, anniversaries, and other holidays by inviting everyone to dinner. Her sister never came, but the other relatives would come and always had a good time. Grandma often met her mother and her aunt at one of the shopping malls where they would spend a day together. They would shop and then have lunch, and enjoyed this chance to talk and to enjoy looking at all the beautiful home accessories they loved to see in the stores.

"As her parents aged, Grandma cared for them. When they retired, her dad was concerned about her mother's long-distance phone charges, so

Grandma arranged to have their bill sent to her every month. She bought household items for them whenever needed, bought clothing for her mother, treated them to special gifts on their special occasions, took care of repairs in their home, and placed their medications in a weekly organizer whenever she ordered and picked up their prescriptions. She also helped them with their food shopping and took them for their physician visits and sometimes took them on vacation with them. She was always happy to do things for her parents.

"When they stopped driving, Grandma did all their grocery shopping, took them to the mall and out to eat, to the dry cleaner and hairdresser, and phoned or visited them every day. When they entered their mid-eighties, they drew up a trust which provided an equal share of their estate to her and Francesca upon their death. Grandma thought this an excellent idea, and despite her sister not "being there" for her parents as she and Grandpa had been, she thought it only right that they should share whatever might be left of their parents' estate. Her parents' best friends witnessed the signing of these documents along with the lawyer and notary. They appointed Grandma the executor of the estate because she was the oldest child and because she was so close to her parents.

"Her father developed cancer, and Grandma nursed him, taking him for a series of daily chemotherapy treatments, waiting hours for him, packing a picnic lunch for him, and caring for him if he felt sick when they arrived home. She also administered a series of daily injections to enhance his platelet count and, with her husband, spent sixteen hours a day at the hospital to give him nursing care when he broke his hip.

"Grandma also cared for her mother who had macular degeneration, congestive heart failure, and the onset of Alzheimer's disease. She took her to her doctors and helped her in her quest to find devices which would help her read and watch television as her eyesight waned. Her Alzheimer's was a fearful disease. Only those close to her saw the change in her personality. She could be demanding, and Grandma did everything she could to help her.

"Throughout these hardships, Grandpa was everyone's rock, especially Grandma's, helping with the groceries for her parents, making repairs around her parents' home, taking Grandma out to dinner when she'd spent the day at doctors' offices or washing her dad when he was so sick with the effects of his cancer or any other chores which were required. Grandpa never flinched when Grandma's mother complained and demanded more and more of them. For nine years, Grandma and Grandpa spent much of their time caring for Grandma's parents.

"Four months before her father's death, just after he broke his hip, Grandma's sister moved into her parents' home . . . keeping her own home . . . but taking control of her parent's home as well. Grandma was happy to have some help as it had taken quite a toll on Grandma and Grandpa to care for her parents during the previous nine years. At first, Grandma thought that Francesca might be desirous of making amends for all the hurt she had caused her parents over the years. But that was not her sister's real motive.

"Grandma took a long-awaited vacation with Grandpa when her sister moved into her parents' home. Grandpa was grateful that finally they had a chance to get away, and they took three weeks for this special long-awaited vacation, believing with relief that Francesca had finally come through to do something good.

"When they returned from their vacation and offered to pick up their share of the work of caring for her parents, Grandma discovered that Francesca had sold their parents' home and moved them into her own house. It was later discovered that her sister had pre-arranged much of this before Grandma and Grandpa left for their vacation. It seemed wrong to Grandma that her sister would do this while they were gone, and hadn't said anything about this to them, but Grandma accepted her sister's decision, thinking it would be easier on Francesca to have them at her own home rather than travel so far to care for them as Grandma and Grandpa had to do.

"What Grandma didn't know was that Francesca had moved her parent's savings accounts, checking accounts, and all proceeds from the sale of their home into a bank account in her name and had also discontinued all medical care for her father. Grandma never learned of this until after her father died, and the doctor phoned her to ask why her father had never been brought back for the treatments he required. Grandma was appalled by this news. She wondered if Francesca had done all this to gain control of the money, knowing that her father would never have approved of what she had done.

"Less than a year after being moved into Francesca's house and having his medications and treatments discontinued without Grandma's knowledge, their father died; and the entire family attended the funeral. Years later Grandma realized that if her sister had indeed discontinued his care to gain control of the money, her sister's sin would actually be the murder of her father in cold blood.

"The next year, her mother died; and Francesca never informed Grandma of her mother's death until the day after her funeral, a cruelty which had truly blindsided Grandma. While her mother lay dying, Francesca took, dispersed or hid all the money, policies, IRAs, jewelry, silver, porcelains, paintings, antiques, and furnishings which had belonged to her parents. The trust which had been established by her parents now held no assets. The retirement fund which her parents had so scrupulously saved to help their children in their later years was now in the pocket of only one child—the child who only came to help them during the last years of their life and had given them so much heartache in earlier years.

"Grandma wondered what her parents thought from their grave and how sad they would be to know that Francesca had done such a thing. It was amazing that her sister felt no remorse. So, Grandma and Grandma's children would receive nothing from her parent's estate despite the fact that their parents wish was to have everything shared between the two sisters. Everything Grandma's parents had in terms of money, antiques, furniture, paintings, dishes, porcelains, silver, and jewelry, had been stolen by her sister.

"Because Grandma would never consider such an act, she was shocked by the blatant theft plotted and performed by her sister. But she was even more surprised by Francesca's lack of remorse and the planning which had gone into her "operation." It had been pure evil. Grandma knew that to accomplish such a deed, planning, perfect timing, and systematic work had taken place; so it wasn't a deed of passion, a deed resulting from an immediate or impulsive response to anger, but a deed of malice and aforethought . . . again. Francesca had even encouraged Grandma to take a vacation just to clear the way for her to execute the sale of the house she'd already positioned for a quick disposal.

"Grandma went to the bank to inquire when the money had been moved hoping that Francesca had not done what Grandma thought she had and not planned her actions so far in advance. Since Grandma's name was on the original accounts, Grandma was entitled to know when the accounts were closed and how much was in them at the time. The bank agent was sympathetic. She understood the situation and allowed Grandma access to the information she sought about when the money had been removed, how much was taken, and where it went. They were only allowed by law to provide Grandma with the zip code of where the money had been placed. And indeed, Francesca had first moved the money, putting it all into her name, when she sold her parents' home just after her father had become immobilized by his broken hip. Grandma also learned from the attorney who had drawn up her parents' trust, that her father had desperately tried to protect Grandma by asking the lawyer to draw up a second trust so their monies could be separated. He had also tried to warn Grandma about Francesca's plans a week before his death, but her sister had drained the batteries to the only phone to which he had private access from his wheelchair, and their connection was too weak for them to continue their conversation.

"When Grandma learned that three days before her father died he telephoned the lawyer who had drawn up their trust begging her to set up a second trust for Grandma so she would be protected, Grandma felt so sorry for what her father must have been experiencing. He was in a wheelchair, at the mercy of Francesca and so concerned knowing what Francesca was planning to do. The lawyer could not complete the procedure in time as her father died a few days after phoning the lawyer.

"Grandma worried that even from eternity her parents would feel betrayed, and she felt a terrible remorse for what happened, what her sister had done to them. Grandma was at first very upset by what had happened because it was a large amount of money and would have assured her of comfort in her older years. But this time, Grandma's response to what Francesca had done was different. There was very little pain.

"Grandma wanted to do everything, feel everything, think everything by the book . . . God's book; and she was determined to do it right. She would trust in God and not be concerned about her loss.

She remembered the scripture which assured her that not a single hair would fall from her head without God knowing and approving.

Grandma had learned the lessons of the past well, knew what the Bible said, and knew that while Satan instigates attacks through people to harm a child of God, he can do nothing unless God allows it. She knew beyond a shadow of doubt that when God allows bad things to happen, some wonderful good will come of it. So she went to her minister, and together they prayed and asked God to help her respond correctly . . . in a manner which was pleasing to Him.

"Grandma could not sleep at first and felt deep sadness about her sister and a deeper sadness and fear that her parents would be suffering, knowing from eternity what Francesca had done. She remembered the story of Lazarus and the rich man and how the rich man worried about his brothers who were still alive.

> *Then he said, I pray thee therefore, father,*
> *that thou wouldest send him to my father's house:*
> *For I have five brethren; that he may testify unto them,*
> *lest they also come into this place of torment.*
>
> *—Luke 16:27-28*

"Grandma knew that her parents had placed their trust in Francesca, and her sister had broken that trust. Grandma knew that her mother had Alzheimer's disease and she understood that Francesca would have manipulated her mother to achieve her end. If so, this would grieve her mother greatly when she learned the truth in eternity. And Grandma knew that her mother did know; that after death, her mind would be clear and her sisters' actions and motives easily apparent.

"Her minister told her to pray diligently not only for her parents, but also for her sister and to ask God to provide Grandma with the peace over the matter that she needed. She followed this advice. But it wasn't easy for Grandma. In the beginning, she found it so difficult to pray for her sister; the words seemed false in her mouth, stuck in her throat, and she felt like a hypocrite. But Grandma persevered and kept on praying. And slowly it became easy, and with those prayers, her peace was restored. Her heart was finally at ease because she also knew that she had conducted herself in a manner which was pleasing to God instead of railing against His will. This time she had done it right!

Grandma also said that she understood that everything anyone had in life was a gift from God. That He had the power to give and the power to take away. She also knew that He allowed loss to attend the children of God because it measured their character and proved their trust and loyalty. It was these who God wanted as a bride for His Son.

"Grandma used her free will to apply herself to the task of praying for Francesca. She used her free will to say no to those thoughts which again flew as birds over her head and desired to land in her mind. She used her free will to be thankful for what God had allowed, whether she'd liked what occurred or not. And she used her free will to welcome the experience because she loved God and trusted Him. She'd get it right this time if it killed her!

"Grandma felt an excitement to see how it would all pan out, for she knew, beyond a shadow of a doubt, that God loved her and would care for her in this matter in some way, even if it meant not here on earth but when she died. She remembered that God had told Abraham that his obedience would be counted to him as righteousness, and she thought that such an accolade would be wonderful to receive.

And I will be with thee, and will bless thee;
for unto thee, and unto thy seed, I will give all . . .
Because that Abraham obeyed my voice,
and kept my charge, my commandments,
my statutes, and my laws.

—*Genesis 26:3-5*

By faith Abraham, when he was tried . . .

—*Hebrews 11:17*

And he believed in the LORD;
and he counted it to him for righteousness.

—*Genesis 15:6*

"Grandma also remembered the story of Joseph and his brothers and realized how that paralleled what had happened to her and understood that perhaps during the thousand-year kingdom of peace, Francesca would come to understand and have remorse as did Joseph's brothers.

"The story of Joseph and his brothers had also made an impact on Grandma's heart. Joseph had been the favorite of his parents and this had caused his older brothers to be jealous of Joseph. When his parents gave Joseph a new coat and had no coat for the others, they plotted together to kill Joseph. One day when the three brothers went hunting, they threw the seventeen-year-old Joseph into a dry well, and as a caravan of merchants passed, they sold him into slavery. Then they killed a goat and placed the blood from the goat onto Joseph's new coat and brought the coat to their parents, claiming that an evil beast had killed Joseph.

"The merchants brought Joseph to Egypt where, over the years, he worked his way from a lowly slave to becoming a favorite of the king. The king admired Joseph because of his wise advice and honest nature. A famine came to the land because of a great drought, but Joseph through God's help had predicted that this would occur and had advised the king to store enough grain for two years so the famine would not affect them.

"Hungry people came from far away searching for food. And one day, when Joseph was thirty years old, his brothers entered the great hall of the palace from where Joseph governed and they begged for grain. They did not recognize Joseph because he had been a child when they sold him and was a man now. But Joseph recognized his brothers right away, yet did not tell them who he was. Joseph realized what a great blessing had come to him from the harm which his brothers tried to do, so he forgave his brothers and readily gave them the grain they needed; still without telling them who he was. Later, when the brothers realized that the governor was their brother Joseph, they fell at his feet, surprised by his act of mercy toward them.

> *They . . . lifted up Joseph out of the pit, and sold Joseph*
> *to the Ishmeelites for twenty pieces of silver:*
> *and they brought Joseph into Egypt.*
> —*Genesis 37:28*

> *Joseph was a goodly person.*
> —*Genesis 39:6*

> *And Joseph saw his brethren, and he knew them,*
> *but made himself strange unto them, . . .*
> *and he said unto them, Whence come ye?*
> *And they said, From the land of Canaan to buy food.*
> —*Genesis 42:7*

Then Joseph commanded to fill their sacks
with corn . . . money . . . provisions.

—*Genesis 42:25*

And Joseph . . . entered into his chamber, and wept there.

—*Genesis 43:30*

"Grandma was happy and her heart was at peace because she understood the great blessings God creates out of tragedy. She now saw difficulties as something which measured faith and commitment to God . . . and character. And she was joyful because she knew that what she had accomplished spiritually was worth far more than anything else. Grandma was content. But God had more in mind for Grandma; an even greater blessing was to come.

"Fifteen years before Francesca's theft, Grandma had given her mother the gift of a beautiful chiming mantel clock. It worked beautifully and sounded the Westminster chimes. She'd chosen the chiming clock for two reasons. One was because her mother had admired one that Grandma had and two because her mother was terribly disappointed in her own clock because it never worked properly despite calling many experts in to repair it.

"Grandma explained that her mother's original clock, which had never worked properly, had been purchased at a furniture store about thirty years earlier and was a Daneker eight-day windup clock of solid rock maple which came from Germany. It had never worked. Her mother had tried everything to fix the clock. She brought it to a number of different clock smiths and still, the clock would never work. Her mother had asked Grandpa to fix it, and though Grandpa worked for hours with it, he could not get it to work either. Finally her mother contacted a company representative, who came to look at the clock, and amazingly he was able to start the clock, but the moment he left, it stopped and would not run again.

"When Grandma gave her mother the new clock, her mother was delighted. The new clock chimed every quarter hour and bonged the hour and worked beautifully. It was also beautiful to look at, though not as big as her other clock. Grandma's mother told her to take the clock which had never worked, explaining that she was disgusted with it because of all the trouble it caused and that while she had kept it for decorative purposes only, she did not want it anymore.

"Grandma took the clock home and over the years Grandpa tried to get the clock to work, but never could. They too took the clock to a clock smith, who was able to start the clock for a while, but it would stop after a few minutes, and he eventually gave up. Grandma kept the nonworking clock because it was so beautiful, despite the fact that it served no real purpose. Grandpa continued to work on the clock on occasion, but without success, and eventually gave up once again. The clock sat on the fireplace mantel, without working, but they were happy with it. They had plenty of other chiming clocks in the house.

"Sixteen months after her mother died, Grandma and Grandpa moved and were engaged in the process of unpacking their moving boxes. One day, while Grandpa was at the super market, Grandma decided to unpack more of her knickknacks so they could be washed and placed on the end tables. She had just unpacked a small Hummel statuette. They had placed her mother's Daneker clock on the mantel of the fireplace near a hallway which led from the living room to a bedroom in their new home. Grandma could see the clock from where she was standing in the living room while she was unpacking the box of knickknacks.

"Grandma was the only one in the house, yet suddenly, Grandma thought someone said something to her. She looked up from the wrappings startled, to see who had spoken. She looked around, but no one was there. Puzzled, she resumed what she was doing, thinking that perhaps she heard a car going by with its radio blaring. A minute or so passed when Grandma felt herself shiver with a sudden chill and thought again that she heard a voice from somewhere. More intent on listening that time, Grandma thought that the voice didn't seem to enter her ears, but her heart; and it was a strange and unusual sensation. She stopped what she was doing and listened carefully.

"With her heart pounding, Grandma realized that it was her mother speaking to her. Her mother instructed Grandma to look at the clock, and Grandma did. Then her mother told her to walk to the clock and start the pendulum swinging. Grandma was terribly frightened. Her mother had died over a year ago, so what could be happening? Grandma didn't move. Again, her mother's voice instructed her to walk to the clock and start the pendulum. Grandma did what her mother asked and gave the clock's pendulum a push to start it swinging fully expecting it to stop in a few seconds.

"At first, Grandma, watching the pendulum swing, believed that it would stop in a minute or less as it always did. But as Grandma watched the pendulum, it kept going; and the clock chimed. Five minutes passed with Grandma riveted in front of the clock, not moving a muscle. She became aware that the muscles of her calves were sore from how rigidly she stood before the clock. She hadn't been aware that she still held in her left hand the Hummel she had so recently unwrapped and was surprised that it hadn't broken under the pressure of her closed fist as the tension rose in her body.

"Grandma heard her mother speak again, telling her that the clock would continue to work. Grandma stood, still looking at the clock, and shook her head up and down in agreement to her mother's words and in awe of what was happening. Then she heard her mother's voice again. And she heard an incredible anguish in her mother's voice. A terrible sorrow emanated from her mother and Grandma could feel the horror of an excruciating pain moving in her own heart. Grandma understood that this was the pain her mother was feeling and it was immense. And then her mother said, "Please forgive me, Victoria, I'm so, so sorry." And Grandma knew beyond any doubt that her mother referred to what Francesca had done; how Francesca had manipulated her to accomplish her goal.

"Grandma broke into tears. She felt joy, she felt awe, she felt happy, and she felt such a deep heart rending sorrow for her mother all at once. Her throat hurt from the anguish that she sensed and she gently told her mother that there was nothing to forgive, that she loved her very much, and that everything was okay. And the heavy sensation of incredible agony which Grandma had felt in her heart from her mother's terrible sorrow lifted; and Grandma sensed that her mother was relieved, that she had been unburdened, that she knew her daughter would be okay, and that now she was free to leave. And then Grandma could feel that her mother had left.

"Grandma knew that her mother had said what she had come to say and heard what she needed to hear. She also felt the extent of will power that had emanated from her mother in order to prove what she did through the clock. Somehow she understood that for her mother to come to her had taken an incredible effort on her mother's part. Grandma didn't know how she knew this; just that she did. Grandma knew that Francesca's terrible behavior and vicious actions had been heavy on her mother's heart and had prevented her from obtaining the peace and resolution she sought after her death when learning what Francesca had done. Grandma knew it must have required an effort far beyond her comprehension for her mother to have come to her and to cause the clock to start . . . and then continue to work. But for Grandma, the experience was such an incredible gift; it was such an immeasurable treasure; it was an experience of faith which would live in her heart forever. She rejoiced and thanked God. She knew that God had allowed her mother to do this to give her closure and to assure her that her mother loved her and that the harm that Francesca had done did not and could not surpass eternity and what God could do with it. She knew in her heart she would see her mother again someday and that all was well between them. The pendulum continued to swing, and the clock continued to work. Grandma also realized that if she'd had every penny that had belonged to her parents and could exchange it for what this single experience had meant to her today, she would gladly give it for this gift.

"Grandma immediately went onto her knees and prayed when she realized her mother had left. She thanked God for such a wonderful experience of faith and for allowing her to be touched by her mother's heart, to experience her mother's love for her. She prayed that her mother and father would receive grace and would not be hampered by what her sister had done.

"When Grandpa arrived at home, and Grandma told him what happened, he listened carefully to her tale and was amazed by it. He walked to the clock and watched it, baffled by its continued ticking and chiming. He watched the clock intermittently the rest of the day. He was awed by the fact that the clock continued working for he knew the years and effort that had been placed into trying to get the clock to work. He was humbled by God's love for Grandma, which was manifest by His allowing such an experience to take place. The evidence of the clock bolstered his faith as well. They both thanked God every day for the gift of that experience. Sarah then looked over to the clock watched it tick and marveled. It was still working.

"But God wasn't finished. There were more great gifts He wanted to give Grandma.

"About a year after the clock miracle, friends who were seeking advice for their estate planning asked Grandma and Grandpa to accompany them to a seminar about aging and assets. They accepted the invitation to attend the seminar with their friends, and during the course of the evening, all four learned a great deal about the intricacies of proper planning. Grandpa was intrigued by a part of the seminar which addressed how one could obtain a life insurance policy which would provide for Grandma's financial needs in the event of his death. Grandpa hadn't realized that he could still obtain a policy at his age. He had an excellent retirement income, but it would be reduced upon his death, and he'd always worried about that, wanting Grandma to have everything she would need when he was no longer here.

"He'd been even more concerned when Francesca had stolen the money from her parents' estate which they had planned would become a part of Grandma's inheritance and used for her old age. Grandma's parents had explained to their children that they wished the proceeds from their estate to fill whatever gaps inflation might create in their retirement income. Grandpa had worried about Grandma's future, but after Francesca's theft, he worried even more. He wanted to care for her in every way. He was truly a good man, always putting others ahead of himself

"As the seminar speaker addressed the benefits of a life insurance policy, he was asked a question about the age and health restrictions and the speaker replied by telling the audience that even older and ill people can be granted a policy. He said that because their company purchased so many policies, sometimes those with borderline health issues were approved, and a policy granted when other companies denied the application. Grandpa did have some health concerns, but the speaker said their company was willing to submit any application; so Grandpa decided to make the purchase, submit his health records, have the required physical examination, and see what happened. He applied for a policy which would enable Grandma to purchase an annuity at least equal to the income which would be lost at Grandpa's death. He did not believe that the policy would be granted because of his health record, but amazingly, the policy was granted. He was surprised and felt relieved not to have to worry about Grandma's future should something happen to him.

"One night, a few days after the policy went into effect, Grandma and Grandpa talked about the wonderful experiences which had transpired over the past few years. As they listed their blessings, they would think they completed the list, and there would be yet another wonderful blessing to recall.

"Not only had God gifted them with an incredible gift of love by bringing them together, and another act of love in allowing Grandma's mother to speak to her, but He also provided the opportunity to learn so much about forgiveness and attaining a peaceful heart and developing such a close relationship to their Heavenly Father. They marveled at the opportunity they had been given to become a child of God and to learn about God's plan of salvation. They also marveled at the fact that the insurance policy which God had sent their way would give Grandma far more comfort and return than what Francesca had stolen. Whenever they looked at the clock, they were reminded of God's love and grace, of the wonder of life after death, and of the special gift of their relationship with one another. They appreciated the fellowship of their friends and family, which was grounded in honor and integrity and the loyalty which Grandma had always longed for. They were so pleased by the faith of their children and grandchildren, which they also recognized as a gift from God.

"With the opportunity which God gave Grandma to learn from her sorrow and to finally understand where the treasures in life could really be found, the realization also came that this time, they had "gotten it right" . . . and God had blessed them for it. God had replaced far more than what had been lost. And they were grateful. And they prayed together to thank God for what He had done and what He had taught them.

"It was so like the story of Job, how he remained faithful to God despite Satan's vicious attacks. God had allowed Satan to attack Job but stopped Satan short of taking Job's life. Job remained faithful to God, never blaming him, and always willing to accept what God allowed even when it seemed so unrelenting and difficult. Job was refined from a nugget of gold into the purest, most beautiful gold possible. And in the end, God not only restored everything Job had lost, but doubled it.

> *And Satan answered . . . put forth thine hand now,*
> *and touch his bone and his flesh,*
> *and he will curse thee to thy face.*
>
> *—Job 2:4-5*

> *So went Satan went forth from the presence of the LORD,*
> *and smote Job with sore boils*
> *from the sole of his foot unto his crown.*
>
> *—Job 2:7*

> *But put forth thine hand now,*
> *and touch all that he hath,*
> *and he will curse thee to thy face.*
>
> *—Job 1:11*

There came a great wind . . . and smote . . . the house . . .
it fell . . . and they are dead.

—Job 1:19

Though after my skin worms destroy this body,
yet in my flesh shall I see God.

—Job 19:26

The LORD gave, and the LORD hath taken away;
blessed be the name of the LORD.

—Job 1:21

In all this Job sinned not.

—Job 1:22

For I know that my redeemer liveth,
and that he shall stand at the latter day upon the earth.

—Job 19:25

And the LORD turned the captivity of Job, . . .
also the LORD gave Job twice as much as he had before.

—Job 42:10

When Grandma finished her narration she told Sarah that she remembered the verse in the Lord's Prayer where it clearly says that we will not be forgiven our debts unless we forgive others for theirs. She said that if we can master those ten special words from the Lord's Prayer, God will love us for it and will reward us.

And forgive us our debts, as we forgive our debtors.

—Matthew 6:12

Epilogue

TRIUMPH

Grandma's story had been told. Sarah had all the information she required and finally understood the incredible teaching experience which Grandma's story represented. As she read over her notes she could recognize God's hand in Grandma's life and His determination to draw her out of a life that perhaps she'd been destined to live. God had indeed protected Grandma. Every psychology book that Sarah had ever read taught the trauma which could have resulted from what Grandma experienced. Yet Grandma came away better, not worse from her experiences.

Sarah marveled that Grandma never forgot her lessons of life. She'd firmly exercised her free will to trust God and to forgive. She had learned over the years what to do, how to feel, and how to pray, and had put these lessons into action. She had forgiven Francesca and Damon, still prayed for them, and no longer looked back. She'd never forgotten them in prayer.

Certainly Grandma had not been perfect. She'd slipped many times, had let the bad birds of thought land from time to time, felt anger and disappointment, had not shooed the bad thoughts away. But in the end, she always came back to God, to the altar of grace asking forgiveness for her lapse and trying her best to get back on track.

Sarah had learned from Grandma that King David had made mistakes and sinned many times in the eyes of God. She knew that God punished David for what he had done. But she also knew that God loved David because of his unerring faith and because of the deep love that David had for God.

The story of David gave Grandma the courage to pick herself up, dust herself off, and try again to do what was right.

The story of Grandma's life isn't what Grandma wanted her journal to be about, or what she wanted her legacy to be; rather, it was what came out of the disappointment and hurt in that life. The treasure wasn't her story at all, but the path which God showed her and the fact of His protecting presence . . . that was the treasure! She had said that the only thing special about her . . . in God's eyes . . . was that she said yes to God; she let Him guide her and teach her and in and through that she was blessed. She longed to share with others how that decision brought the greatest of all gifts to her; those which would last for all eternity. *Just say yes to God!*

Sarah now knew that not everyone is willing to listen or to learn, but perhaps a story about a woman with whom others could relate may make an impression, if not now, maybe at a later date. Grandma hoped that by hearing her story, seeing the process by which she learned and the path which led her from one truth to the next, someone like her whose heart is hurting may begin to heal and they may begin to understand how God works. Perhaps it could bring others the closure that could help them lay aside the past.

Grandma knew that if we learned about the mistakes she'd made, the emotions she'd felt, the anger and sense of betrayal she'd suffered, and the times she questioned God, we'd see the tiny baby steps she'd had to make to finally understand what was asked of her, what God really wanted from her. She knew that trusting God, really trusting him, was not just lip service but a real willingness to give up our home, our money, our spouse, or our children to Him. She knew that our pride and our ego had to bend to His will, bend through a testing process each of us would have to endure . . . and she knew that we had to find the key to making us better people, making us fit for God to use.

Life is a classroom, not meant to be easy but to challenge us to learn. The good times are our respite from the difficult times. But if we learn, if we grow, if we love, if we forgive, we will graduate to the most glorious future we could ever imagine. We will be with God for all eternity.

As Grandma's story came to an end, Grandma told me that the final test in her life was the one which taught her the value of forgiveness. Now in her old age, another test loomed, her truly final test. She was to face death. Her faith and acceptance were to be tested through that process as well. She wanted to die with complete trust in God, total acceptance in her heart, and be willing and able to express her thankfulness to God for all He had done and was doing for her and those she loved. She said that everything which comes to us in life has God's approval. She said that when life is difficult, God teaches us something special for our future with Him. But the prerequisite is to be *willing* to listen, learn, and follow. She said that God suffers when we suffer and rejoices when we come through these times successfully. She told me to think about how much God suffered when His Son suffered, and how God and all the angels in heaven rejoiced when Christ's suffering was finished and He had achieved such an incredible feat for every one of us.

Grandma did die with her faith intact and with thankfulness in her heart. I was there. She opened her eyes, looked at me, and said, "I'm going home now, Sarah, God be with you always" and then closed her eyes for the last time. I cried because I knew I would miss her so very much. I didn't think I would ever again have such a teacher in my life. I'd finished writing her story. She'd told me everything she wanted to tell me, and I reacted to her story just as she hoped I would.

As Grandma's story unfolded, I'd done much research into the Bible myself and was surprised to find so many directives and so much help and understanding throughout those pages. The Bible wasn't the book of rules I'd thought it to be, but rather it was a book of hope and of incredible gentle warnings which help us find the right path and help us avoid the traps of Satan. It was, it is, truly, in essence, a book of love.

Grandma made a believer of me, and she knew this before she died. She was so happy when she saw my awe and my interest and the growth of my belief and understanding as her story unfolded. She said that reaching me was fulfilling the goal she spoke of early in the project. "If my story could help just one soul, I'll be happy," she'd said. And she'd done that with me.

I have taken Grandma's quest as my own. I want with all my heart to help "just one soul" through her story. I too will come across situations in life which I won't like, situations which will make me, for a minute anyway, angry with God and probably questioning His will. Like Grandma and like my own parents, I too will make mistakes and hope to be forgiven for them. I know that perhaps some of those I love will break my heart, will misunderstand me, but I can understand why these things happen now and can trust the One who will never disappoint me by following Grandma's lead. I will trust God and do what He asks and accept what He allows. Even when it hurts!

Grandma had always tried her best. She wanted to do what God asked of her, and I saw the resultant goodness in her heart. I was almost blinded by happy thankful tears when I realized the beauty of what lived in her heart for everyone she loved and prayed for . . . despite the heartache they caused her. The explanation of why bad things happen to good people satisfied me and made it all worthwhile. God's love empowered me and showed itself perfect. I want all that for myself and for those I love. I will carry Grandma's legacy into my life and I'd like it for you too.

Hear counsel, and receive instruction,
that thou mayest be wise in thy latter end.

—*Proverbs 19:20*

Scriptural Index

What we fight

When we are tested

Bibliography

The Holy Bible, King James Version, published by The New Apostolic Church, Canada, Thomas Nelson, Inc., Camden, NJ, 1972

James Strong, LLD, STD, *Strong's Exhaustive Concordance of the Bible*, Abington, Nashville, thirty fourth printing 1996, copyright 1890

Henry H. Halley, *Halley's Bible Handbook*, Zondervan Publishing House, Grand Rapids, Michigan, 24th edition, Copyright 1965

Henry M. Morris, *Many Infallible Proofs*, Moody Press, Chicago, 3rd printing 1977

Henry M. Morris, *The Bible and Modern Science*, Moody Press, Chicago, 1951, 1968

Donald Grey Barnhouse, *The Invisible War*, Zondervan Publishing House, Grand Rapids, Michigan, 12th printing 1976 copyright 1965

Robert Boyd, *Boyd's Bible Handbook*, Eugene, Oregon: Harvest House, 1983, pgs 122-124.

Helen Gumienny Glowacki, *When God Took Grandma Home*, 2007, Xlibris Publishing Company.

When God Took Grandma Home

AN EXCERPT

Sarah had been trying, without much success, to develop her to-do lists. She'd been so lethargic lately that she put off the chores she knew were her responsibility to complete. She also knew that Grandma would be upset with her if she saw that Sarah was shirking those responsibilities. She was, after all, usually a neatnik, compulsive in getting everything done and cheerfully worked to the point of exhaustion.

Sarah always felt that she was like Grandma in that respect and usually she did get things done. But lately, she'd been so tired, and sad, which was unusual for her. In fact, she felt as though there was a lead weight in her heart and didn't know why.

After her grandmother died, she brought many wonderful pieces of furniture and accessories from Grandma's home to her apartment. Her brothers told her to take everything she wanted even if she planned to save it or store it for the new home she and Matt planned to purchase. Most however she put temporarily into storage, but some she brought right to her apartment. She loved every one of Grandma's things, and their sentimental value was an extra bonus. Josh too took a few things, but his taste ran to more modern architecture. Caleb and Ann also took some of the furnishings but they'd already filled their home with those things which Ann loved, so most was left for Sarah.

Grandma's clocks were especially precious to her. Each one tick tocked loudly, and amazingly, the ticktocking sound from each clock was very different. All chimed every quarter hour, some softly, some loudly—each with a distinctly different type of sound—some with a different melody as well. Grandma loved clocks and had one in every room. She too had a clock in every room in her apartment, and having kept most of the clocks from Grandma's collection, now, every room in her and Matt's new home will have its own ticktocking chiming clock! Maybe two!

She remembered the silly words and sounds Grandma used when Sarah was just a baby and Grandma wanted to describe the sounds her clocks made. She'd make a deep sound, like a man's voice . . . saying, "Bong, bong, bong," and ask Sarah which clock she was imitating. She wanted her to point to the grandfather's clock when she said that. Then she'd speak in a little girl's voice, high and sweet, saying, "Ticktock, ticktock," when she wanted Sarah to point to the table clock on her nightstand. Her kitchen clock went ticky, ticky, and the wall clock in the bedroom hall went ti-ck, to-ck. Every clock had its own unique sound.

She'd imitate the different sounds each clock made, ticking and chiming. And through them she taught Sarah how to listen. She'd say, "Listen to the quiet of the house," so Sarah would learn to hear the ticking of the clocks. She said the more Sarah listened to the quiet of the house, the louder the ticking would seem. At first, she couldn't hear anything; but as she learned to concentrate, she could hear the ticktocks. Grandma said that loving God correctly was like that . . . we first had to quiet our mind and listen to our heart . . . then we'd hear Him.

Sarah could remember Grandma pursing her lips, holding finger to her lips, and quietly saying, "Shhhhhh," and Sarah would be quiet; and Grandma would cock her head from side to side as if hearing something, and Sarah would listen, and she'd smile still with her finger to her lips.

And so Sarah learned to listen, anticipating the beginning of the chimes and following the sounds from one clock to another. Sometimes Grandma would carry Sarah in her arms and run from room to room as one clock finished and another began its ritual. Grandma set her clocks a few minutes apart, so when they'd chime, the chiming would fill her house for a long time.

When Sarah was a little bit older, they would run from room to room together, being careful not to slip on an area rug they might cross as they hurried to arrive in the room before the chimes ended, their shoes clacking on the old hardwood floors. They'd laugh and shout to one another. Sometimes Grandma would try to fool Sarah and change the location of some of the clocks. Then Sarah would have to change direction and run to another room. They both thought it great fun.

Because of the wonderful memories of chasing the sounds of the clocks with Grandma, Sarah too wanted to have clocks all over the house, one in every room. Even to this day, she especially loved to come home after work, open the front door, and listen for and hear the quiet of the house. Then, once she heard the quiet, she would listen for the ticking of the clocks. For Sarah it was a wonderfully welcoming and comforting sound. And it was an exercise in relaxation to make one self listen! Neither Grandma nor Sarah had ever been bothered by the chiming while they slept. Sarah missed her grandmother terribly.

Sarah had been so sad lately, and the emotion made her tired. She put off doing the things she needed to do and felt guilty about it. She was not much fun to be around. She knew that she should be making many lists: lists of what she and Matt would need for their wedding, of where Matt and she might want their new house to be located, of qualities the house should have, of what she needed to accomplish for her thesis, of what her students needed. But she couldn't. She was just too tired.

Yet Sarah had the energy to move furniture and find just the right places for the treasures she had brought to her apartment from Grandma's house. She didn't seem to be sad during these times, perhaps because there was a satisfaction at the end when everything looked so nice. Her apartment was perfect for Grandma's furnishings and accessories. It's as if Grandma always knew that someday they would end up here, with Sarah. Even Matt said that they really look great.

Sarah's apartment building was located on a quiet street lined with large old trees, their trunks gnarled and thick, with branches that reached high toward the sky. The trees formed a canopy over the roadway, meeting in the middle, and they filtered the sunlight even on the brightest days. The filtered light created an ethereal world of lush green leaves which appeared to forbid loud sounds and made her feel as if she should whisper. Deep green hedges of ixora with their profusion of orange-red blossoms spilled over the curb toward the road and reached onto the cement sidewalk waiting to be pruned, the thickness of their foliage further supporting the incredible beauty of this different world.

The building had wonderful architectural detail. It was built of natural stone which also formed the openings for its large arched windows, some with diamond-shaped mullions which provided a European flavor to the building. The double front doors were large and stained a dark rich color, preserved by a varnish which enhanced the grain of the wood. The doors were deeply carved to form squares and rosettes, and its flat edges sported huge hinges and locksets which appeared medieval in style. The curve of the arched transom over the door provided the required architectural balance to the windows.

Leading up to the doors were four wide stone steps, rising from an uneven walk made of slate and edged with thick plantings of pachysandra. There was an ornately fashioned black wrought-iron fence along the perimeter of the property which provided a sense of orderliness and privacy. Huge lanterns flanked the entry, matching the iron fence in size and in the ornate curve of its thick iron support.

Inside the apartment were spacious rooms with high ceilings and many tall narrow windows edged with thick chestnut moldings stained with a wonderful chocolate color which matched the darkly stained hardwood floors. Even with the dark woods of the room and the lush outside plantings, there was an abundance of light because of the height of the windows. Sarah loved the style and feel of her apartment building because she loved its aura of antiquity and strength and elegance. So did her fiancé Matt.

Sarah decorated these rooms over the years with hand-me-downs from the family, mostly Grandma's stuff, and everything was made of the rich dark woods. Their age, colors, and quality blended well with the feeling of the building and the grounds, and along with the architecture of the apartment, they gave the rooms an old-world eclectic look. This was a look Sarah loved and would choose even if she had much more to spend on furniture.

Matt helped her paint the walls a deep camel color, which they planned to use throughout the new house they intended to purchase before their wedding. Because they both loved Sarah's apartment, they decided to buy an older home which would obtain its character from the richness of its architectural elements. She was glad she and Matt shared the same feelings about houses.

They both liked how the walls looked with the dark hardwood floors and wanted this look in the new house they planned to purchase. The color combination would provide them with a neutral base from which to choose their other colors. It was amazing that Grandma had used these same colors for her walls and floors.

Sarah and Matt also loved the ambience of Oriental carpets over dark wood floors and would probably use the ones they placed into storage from Grandma's house. Most of Grandma's rugs had a touch of that camel color in them, either along the border or interspersed throughout the pattern of the rug; so naturally they would go well with the camel-colored walls they planned to have. Sarah was so glad that she and Matt both loved Grandma's furnishings and agreed on how they would decorate their home. It would probably be a source of contention if they'd each liked a different style!

As Sarah walked around her apartment and saw her grandmother's things, she would often touch them, feeling the smoothness of the wood or the filigree of a frame, and she would remember her grandmother. She might remember when she'd purchased one of these items or what she felt about it or what she'd say about it. They all brought Sarah joy and comfort, good memories, and a sense of home and safety. She would never give these things up. Never.

Sarah felt blessed as she thought about the various areas of her life and the plans she had for the future. So she asked herself, why she cried. She didn't know the answer yet, but did know that she must find a way to stop. She did know that when she was sad, and would walk from room to room, touching these pieces which were once her grandmother's; she thought of her and missed her all over again.

In the past, whenever she worried over something, she could go to her grandmother for advice; and Grandma would say something special, something she'd learned from the Bible which would comfort Sarah. She'd reassure her of the power of her prayers. They'd pray together, and she'd say to Sarah, "My dearest, darling sweetheart, love . . . you are ever in my heart and in my prayers." She always said that to Sarah. But lately, Sarah hadn't been praying as much; first she'd been so busy, and now, this lethargy had engulfed her.

Is my grandmother's death still affecting me? Even after all this time? I do cry from missing her, feeling a pain in my heart. But why would I begin grieving now, months after she died? Could my problem be a kind of delayed grief?

It was difficult for Sarah to understand this on an intellectual level because she considered herself a realist. She was a psychologist. She studied mental health. She studied how people deal with death and the stages that many must go through to go on with their life. She was aware that some people move quickly through some stages of healing and get stuck in other stages. She believed in the old axiom that time heals all wounds and that though it might take some time, it will happen.

Maybe understanding what God says about this will help me. Maybe that's what I need to do. That's how Grandma always tackled problems. Maybe I'll review the stages of grief and compare these with what I can find in the Bible. I've got to get to the bottom of this. Could grief be my problem? Am I stuck somewhere?

About The Author

Helen Glowacki is an interior designer, writer, teacher, and motivational speaker. She was the host, writer, and producer of the television series *The Contemporary Woman*, broadcast by UA-Columbia Cablevision, which addressed interior design and the health, relationship, parenting, and life issues of interest to women.

Helen has also co-hosted a number of twenty-four-hour telethons featuring celebrity guests to help raise funds for various community projects and she has appeared as a guest co-host for a cable television game show.

Her writing credentials include an extensive background as a freelance feature writer and a staff writer for four newspapers; author of many newsletter articles; and developed hospital services marketing manuals for the INOVA Hospital System. She was also the designer and editor of a newsletter for the Martin/St. Lucie Chapter of the United States Amateur Ballroom Dancers Association.

A graduate of William Paterson University, Helen received her Bachelor of Arts degree in communications, magna cum laude. Helen also has earned an Associate in Science degree with honors and is a registered nurse. She has served on the boards of directors for two associations and taught interior design for adult school programs. Some of her larger design projects include Avon Headquarters in Morton Grove, Illinois, and Chilton Hospital in Pequannock, New Jersey.

Helen has received a number of community service awards and has been listed in *Who's Who of American Women* and *Who's Who of Women Executives*. As a popular speaker at ease with an audience, Helen has enthralled audiences with her use of Divine Proportion in all aspects of design. Her topics also include how God brings a blessing from heartache and what God's plan is for mankind. Her venues have included women's groups, church groups, community service and religious organizations, high schools and colleges, libraries, cruise ships, and large adult and assisted-living condominium complexes. She has also appeared as a guest on a radio show and has performed dance routines for theater groups, television, army camps, and veteran's hospitals.

Helen has donated her *"Grandmother Series"* of novels, her *"Why God Why Series"* of non-fiction books and her popular books about political correctness, depression, and substance abuse to cancer centers, drug and alcohol rehabilitation centers, prisons and mission schools, most notably to *The Henwood Foundation* in Zambia, Africa to provide testimony of the help and direction God provides for His children. She also posts articles on her Facebook wall which address man's relationship with God,

Helens greatest joys are her husband, two children, and four grandchildren, and singing in the choir of the New Apostolic Church. She and her husband enjoy ballroom dancing and have performed for various charitable functions. Her heart's desire is that through her writing she might help others find the love and comforting presence of God.

To learn more about Helen's novels and her non-fiction books, visit her website @ www.helenglowacki.com.

To become a distributor or to purchase in quantity for fund raising projects or simply to help in her work to provide testimony, please send an email to helen@helenglowacki.com.

Helen's readers can also visit the author on Face Book at http://www.facebook.com/pages/The-Grandmother-Series/155300907853909?ref=ts.

By Helen Glowacki

Novels

(Book Size 6 x 9)

__When God Broke Grandma's Heart__: (208 pages) Rising from sorrow to become a beacon of faith Grandma struggles in an abusive marriage until God moves her from being unequally yoked and broken to the healing of His love and forgiveness. She teaches her granddaughter Sarah where to find the answers to how God will help them in the hope that Sarah will carry that legacy to those she loves.   **Paperback: ISBN 978-1-9847-2110-8**

__When God Took Grandma Home__: (272 pages) About the heartache of drug addiction and the enemy who destroys children through addiction, this is an excellent read which explains why God allows righteous anger, why we should pray for those in eternity and offers an incredible experience of faith for Matt and Sarah about why God even allows such heartache to occur. **Paperback: ISBN 978-1-9847-2111-5**

__When Grandma Chased the Spirits__: (222 Pages) The magnetism of idolatry, it's invisible power, and the heartache of bearing a child out of wedlock brings debilitating panic attacks to Mary and affects her husband Kevin. When Matt and Sarah tell them about their faith, God engineers a miracle to correct what that they thought impossible to resolve. **Paperback: ISBN 978-1-0847-2112-2**

The Granddaughter and the Monkey Swing: (298 pages) A wedding, a broken engagement, renovating and decorating a home through Divine Proportion, the truth about Halloween, and the gift of role models create a tender story of friendship. Helping with the planning and through the problems of a wedding culminates in the unveiling of a secret which Matt kept from Sarah. **Paperback: ISBN 978-1-9847-211309**

*Grandma's Little Book of Poetry: **The Story of God's Plan of Salvation***: (276 pages) This is a beautiful and whimsical story for all ages which begins when Sarah finds a manuscript in Grandma's desk and recognizes the story Grandma read to her and to Josh and Caleb when they were children. It is a story of the angels as they watch the inhabitants below them struggle to find God. **Paperback: ISBN 978-1-9847-2114-6**

Abiding Faith, Hidden Treasure: (262 pages) Serving in Iraq, Jim loses his faith to see a loving God allow so much heartache. Barbara invites him to dinner where Grandma shows him why creation and evolution co-exist and why God's enemy creates the injustices Jim blames on God. Letters from the grave bring them all an incredible experience of faith. **Paperback: ISBN 978-1-9847-2115-3**

And Then They Asked God: (296 Pages) When Rebecca and Jayden arrive at their college campus they are overwhelmed by betrayal. Losing the values Rebecca once cherished fills her with guilt so monumental that she cannot forgive herself. Chaldeth the evil angel is defeated when God's grace frees Jayden and brings Rebecca's recovery. **Paperback: ISBN 978-1-9847-2116-0**

Non-Fiction Books   (Book Size 5 ½ x 8)

Politically Incorrect: The Get Some Gumption Handbook when Enough is Enough: (408 pages) Fifty timely and controversial issues are examined under the politically correct approach along with a description of what scripture tells us is the approach that God wants His children to take. **Paperback: ISBN 978-1-4507-9074-1**

Overcoming Depression: How To Be Happy: (258 pages) While we all face heartache, and all feel sad from time to time, true depression comes from a satanic attack which robs us of hope and destroys our trust in God. Thus our Heavenly Father tells us through scripture how we can tap into His blessing and find joy even in tribulation. **Paperback: ISBN 978-1-4507-9077-2**

What No One Tells You About Addictions: (222 Pages) Discussing the merits of tough love, the selfish co-dependency of the enabler, what scripture tells us about spiritual warfare and invasion, and generational sin, make this book a must read. **Paperback: ISBN 978-1- 4507--9075-8**

The Why God Why Series   (Book size: 5 ½ x 8 ½)

To What Purpose?: (126 pages) The first book of the *Why God Why* series is written to provide answers to questions about why we are here and what we need to learn. It is written in an easy to read and easy to understand manner and a book you will want to share with others. **Paperback: ISBN 978-1-4507-7580-9**

Why God, Why?: (126 pages) This second book in the *Why God Why* Series describes why we experience heartache, its purpose, and how to face it. It answers questions about God's plan for us and what we need to do to be found worthy. **Paperback: ISBN 978-1-4507-7581-6**

Why Trust Scripture?: (126 pages) This third book in the *Why God, Why* Series addresses the challenges made against scripture, who wrote the Bible, the importance of the sacraments, what role Satan plays, and how health and the Bible are related. **Paperback: ISBN 978-1-4507-7582-3**

What Should I Know about Life after Death and the Coming Tribulation?: (126 pages) What occurs following death, what will happen during the tribulation, and what the seven seals could mean to us are explained in this fourth book of the *Why God Why* series. **Paperback: ISBN 978-1-4507-7583-0**

What Does God Want Me to do Right Now?: (126 pages) This fifth book in the *Why God Why* series provides a concise explanation of what God asks of us, how we can live up to His expectations, what is required to become a part of the Bride of Christ, and what God plans for the future with or without us. **Paperback: ISBN 978-1 4507-9076-5**

Do Our Little Sins REALLY Count?: (126 pages) Most of us believe that the little sins we commit each day are not important on the grander scale, but what does scripture tell us? And what do the words "God's righteousness" really mean to us? An interesting and unique look at the requirements God has set forth for Himself. **Paperback: ISBN 978-9847-2117-7**

To order any of these books visit www.helenglowacki.com. To become a distributor or order in quantity, email the author at helen@helenglowacki.com

More Book Reviews

Rev. Richard C. Freund, President, New Apostolic Church USA, Sea Cliff, New York: Magnificent writer, a story that makes the reader become emotionally involved, a joy to read, strong Christian values. *"When God Broke Grandma's Heart"*, best seller quality.

Rev. Fred Krueger, (Ret.) Lutheran Minister 12 yrs and Clinical Social Worker 26 yrs, Dallas, Texas: "Inspiring, grabs the heart, author headed to the bestseller list, a pleasure to read, masterful. *"When God Took Grandma Home"* filled with insight into God's plan!

Rev. Richard C. Freund, President, New Apostolic Church USA, Sea Cliff, New York: *"When God Took Grandma Home"* "Delights, brings comfort to those who grieve. Inspires, gives insight into the after-life, masterful portrayal.

Reverend Derryck Beukes, Montana-De Aar Congregation, Northern Cape, South Africa: Dear Helen, I personally often use your articles in my soul care visits, especially where youth are involved. I can assure you that your articles made a difference to my way of thinking, and I am busy encouraging fellow priests to read your works, as they are so factual and insightful! Thank you for your hard work. II thank God for you, and the wisdom He gave you! Please continue with the excellent work.

Deacon Shadreck Wilima, Overspill Congregation, Ndola, Zambia: Your articles prompt realistic examples which New Apostolic Christians need for their everyday living.

Youth Chairperson, Sunday School teacher, Mulenga Ernest, Lusaka Central Congregation, Lusaka, Zambia: Through your writing I am constantly reminded of what to be aware of. I pray that God keeps you in the hollow of His hand, guards you and guides you to reach your brethren as you do me. Thanks for caring for the souls of many.

Reverend Aurelio Cerullo, Atripalda Congregation, Campania, Southern Italy: Your books and articles, and even your social networking are a means to bring brothers and sisters the words of our faith and to touch the hearts of those who do not know our faith. Our goal can still be found through the grace of the apostolate and in this sense, the word's from 1 Corinthians 15:58 assumes an important meaning: "*Therefore, my beloved brethren, be steadfast, immovable, always abounding in the work of the Lord, Knowing That your labor is not in vain in the Lord*". Now that I am a minister of God for about a year I too am grateful to our beloved Father in Heaven for having opened the eyes of my soul, for having removed the plugs from my ears of my heart to hear and listen to His will in connection and communion with those who precede us, guided by the light of the Holy Spirit. God's work always evolves and adapts to the times and even via computers, cell phones and smart phones. I Thank God for having been able to know you, you're a very valuable pearl. God bless you richly.

NOTE: *The articles which some of these reviewers refer to were posted on the author's Facebook wall and are excerpts from Helen Glowacki's non-fiction books. Not included in this list are reviews by the ministers who oversee The Henwood Foundation's New Apostolic Mission Schools in Zambia and clear all reading materials prior to distribution.*

Reverend Andrew Muliokela, Alexandria Virginia Congregation: *The Granddaughter and the Monkey Swing* and this series of books is awesome! A journey unlike another, read a great novel, learn about confidence, love and support but also learning Bible verses at the same time! Helen Glowacki teaches through her books and I recommend them 100%. You'll enjoy the journey!

Reverend Kevin Speranza, Palm Beach Gardens Congregation, Florida: *And Then They Asked God* so happy I read this, weaves and documents biblical precepts, addresses political correctness, moral & political corruption, biased teaching, the insidious growth of socialism renamed progressivism, self-importance, guilt and its debilitating power. WELL DONE! Identifies danger, artfully shows Biblically how to address them.

Frederick Rothe, Retired NAC Minister, Fort Pierce, Florida: I am a retired minister who spent 48 years serving God and another 30 in the congregation. These books contain an accurate account of what God wants of us and why we sometimes suffer. The application of scripture and the people in the stories stand for the principles God wants in all of us.

Patricia Robinson, wife of a Retired Rector, Fort Wayne, Indiana:
5 star rating: *When God Broke Grandma's Heart*: WONDERFUL INSPIRATIONAL NOVEL. I enjoyed this book. It is well written, and filled with Bible references about how to achieve peace of mind and soul.

Colette van Loggerenberg, wife of a Minister of the Scottsville Congregation of Pietermaritzberg, South Africa: *Grandma's Little Book of Poetry: The Story of God's Plan of Salvation:* This has to be one of the BEST EVER books that I have read.....If you ever get the chance to get one of Helen's novels...READ IT. It's like a fairytale but a TRUE fairytale.....Close your eyes and picture this: Grandma with her hair in a bun, glasses perched delicately on her nose, sitting in a rocking chair with her grandchildren sitting on the floor next to her with their BIG eyes hanging onto her every word.....but with a twist!!!!! If you have doubts about PRAYERS...read this book. I LOVED IT...thank you Helen Glowacki!

Debbie Espeland, wife of a Rector, Palm Beach Gardens Congregation, Florida: 5 star rating: **When God Took Grandma Home** is so HEARTWARMING! This book touched my heart. It is both heartwarming and very spiritual.

Aletta Venter, wife of a Deacon, Scottsville Congregation, Pietermaritzburg, South Africa: *"Grandma's Little Book of Poetry: The Story of God's Plan of Salvation"*. What a learning process for me. Oooh I just **love** the way the angels are telling the story, **very original!** When is mankind ever going to learn? The inhabitant's lesson was to learn of good and evil. And they failed miserably each time. The devil has his agenda, and the inhabitants are the target. They call upon God for help, the angels rejoiced. Great....!!!

Reverend Luke Jansen, Sr. V. P., Medical Connections, Boca Raton, Florida: "To Ms. Glowacki, author of **The Grandma Series**: grateful for your books, refreshing to find a Christian author who sees the *difference* between religion and spirituality AND that the two can and should be used in the same sentence."

Aletta Venter, wife of a Deacon, Pietermaritzburg, South Africa: *"Abiding Faith, Hidden Treasure"* is the deepest and most rewarding novel I have ever read, touched my soul, made me cry, author's understanding of God's work is astounding, opens the mysteries

Katharina Leipp, Schopfheim, Germany: This is the first time I have ever heard of a female New Apostolic author and I am very impressed by your articles. I have sent your link to my Shepherd and German friends and would like you to consider advertising in our German *Our Family Magazine.*

Rosemarie Schaal, wife of a retired Minister, Palm City, Florida: *Abiding Faith, Hidden Treasure:* Reader develops empathy, feels emotion, hears a battle between scientific and spiritual knowledge. Skillful, detailed, brilliant, vivid, teaches that nothing happens that is not planned by Him.

Claudine Visagie, South Africa: I'm trying to think of a way to introduce Helen's books and articles to others... especially to our youth. They are life changing!

Rabecca Mukuta Mukato, Lusaka, Zambia, Africa: Speaking on behalf of my Dad, District Elder Mulako, your articles are brilliant because they have changed me! Because of your articles my Dad has less headaches!

Edith Stier, 32 Years as the wife of a Minister, (Ret. Dist. Ev), Clifton, New Jersey: *The Grandma Series* helps those in need, inspirational, heartwarming, ends with a beautiful example of how God explains our pain, renews hope, shows us the way, creates miracles. I love this series.

Tammera Shelton, M.S. Psychology, Odenton, Maryland: I find *"When God Broke Grandma's Heart"* inspirational, beautifully portrays need to let go of negative events and that despite injustice, no pain is for naught.

Robert W. Rothe, USMC 1970-1976, Nevada: 5 star rating: *When God Broke Grandma's Heart:* Outstanding writer, kept me riveted, an angel sent to help through trying days. Thank you for helping me find peace.

Frank Geores, from Port St. Lucie, Florida: *"When Grandma Chased The Spirits:* beautiful spiritual experience, can see caring nature and loving heart of author, eloquently reveals her love for God and search for truth. Worthy of the Star of Bethlehem rating. Thank you for sharing your magnificent gift.

Ben Lodwick, Avid Reader., from Brookfield, Wisconsin: Wow! An eye opener about God's plan of salvation, and why bad things happen to good people. Reminds me of Jim LaHaye and Jerry B. Jenkins "Left Behind Series". MUST READ!"

Dr. Walter Forman, Radiologist from North Palm Beach, Florida: *Grandma's Little Book of Poetry: The Story of God's Plan of Salvation:* a "wonderful book about success and failure in life. All Helen's novels are wonderful, a balm for the soul and an education to the seeker."

Susan Day, From Jupiter, Florida: *Abiding Faith, Hidden Treasure* : I hated to put it down, couldn't wait to pick it up, I have read all Helen's books, she proves every point, shows what to do through God's words. I am 90 and Helen's books have helped me call on God.

Georgette Rothe, From Fort Piece, Florida: *Abiding Faith, Hidden Treasure* was more than I expected, like a Biblical course making you re-evaluate your beliefs, enjoyed the journey very much.

Fred D'Alauro, from Palm Beach Shores, Florida: Internet 5 star rating: **When God Took Grandma Home:** Remarkable! Inspirational and moving. A fascinating storyteller with a real message.

Debra Forman, Chester, New York. Internet 5 star rating: ***When God Broke Grandma's Heart****:* Written from the heart, shares the strong beliefs that shelters us in times of need, courage captivates the reader. Thank you.

Anonymous: Internet 5 star rating: ***When God Broke Grandma's Heart****:* WHEN LIFE GETS YOU DOWN, PICK THIS BOOK UP, it wrapped its arms around me. A wonderful read. Congratulations on an inspiring work.

A reviewer, a reader in Kentucky: Internet 5 star rating: ***When God Broke Grandma's Heart****:* Well written, heartwarming, overcoming heartbreak through God, touches your heart. A worthwhile read for all generations.

A reader: Internet 5 star rating: ***When God Broke Grandma's Heart:*** a must read for all generations. FANTASTIC!

A reviewer Internet 5 star rating: ***When God Took Grandma Home****:* Moves you, captivating.

A reviewer, a Kentucky reader: Internet 5 star rating: ***When God Took Grandma Home****:* MUST READ! Touching story of life's tragedies and how lessons learned from these heartbreaking events can turn into blessings.

Description Of Characters

Grandma: Grandma's life was filled with sibling betrayal and marital abuse. Her love of God, home remedies and famous boxing stance touches the heart.

Sarah: Sarah helps Grandma write her journal, learns about God's plan of salvation and the enemy who wants to harm her. She carries on Grandma's legacy of faith.

Matt: Matt, Sarah's husband, has a rock-like faith but when he loses a loved one, struggles with his anger with God, until he has a miraculous experience of faith.

Paul: Paul is Matt's older brother who earned a Captain's license for a seagoing tugboat. His faith sustains him despite enduring terrible circumstances.

Mary and Kevin: Mary and Kevin become Matt and Sarah's neighbors and friends. Mary's panic attacks end when God brings a miracle they never thought possible.

Elizabeth: Elizabeth adopts Rebecca, loses her husband twelve years later, is confronted with a potentially deadly illness and searches for Rebecca's birth mother.

Rebecca: Rebecca is Elizabeth daughter and Jayden's friend. Her father's death, the illness her mother faces, and a series of challenges at college almost destroy her.

John: John, a deacon, lost his wife to a debilitating disease, becomes Elizabeth's friend, and helps his daughter and grandson through a difficult divorce.

Jayden: Jayden is John's grandson and becomes Rebecca's friend. He has learned that prayer helps solve problems and he and Rebecca begin to share their faith.

Ruth: Ruth is Jayden's mother and John's daughter. Her past experiences leave her traumatized and causes a secret anger at God until she learns to let go of the past.

Joshua and Debbie: Joshua, Sarah's younger brother, was demanding and judgmental until Caleb stepped in. Debbie looks to Joshua's family to be her role models.

Caleb and Ann: Caleb is Sarah and Josh's older brother and the family looks to him as they once looked to Grandma. Ann, Caleb's wife harbors a secret sadness.

Barbara and Jim: Barbara, Matt's sister is also Sarah's close friend. Her husband Jim plays devil's advocate in family debates, and matchmaker for his friend Wade.

Wade: Wade, Jim's boss and friend, is a big bear of a man with a loving heart who lost his wife to cancer. He adopts two children from Iraq and brings them home.

Heza and Bara: Heza and Bara endured a suicide bomber attack when Bara was one and one half years old and Heza as she was born. They are adopted by Wade.

Chaldeth: Chaldeth is a fallen angel sent to destroy Grandma's family. He plots to bring great heartache to Rebecca and Jayden and their family to break their faith.

Durk: Durk, abused by a cruel father, is a sophomore at the college Rebecca and Jayden attend. He does what it takes to get what he wants until Jim enters his life.

Professsor T. Nagorra, and Emils, and Dean Peerca: These tenured professors befriend Durk and engage in activities that bring harm to the students and campus.

Professors Doog and Sendnik, and President Legna: These three share a faith in God, a love for their country, and desire to be role models. They help save the campus.

HELEN GUMIENNY GLOWACKI